MW01075966

ANNIE HAYNES
THE SECRET OF GREYLANDS

Annie Haynes was born in 1865, the daughter of an ironmonger.

By the first decade of the twentieth century she lived in London and moved in literary and early feminist circles. Her first crime novel, *The Bungalow Mystery*, appeared in 1923, and another nine mysteries were published before her untimely death in 1929.

Who Killed Charmian Karslake? appeared posthumously, and a further partially-finished work, *The Crystal Beads Murder*, was completed with the assistance of an unknown fellow writer, and published in 1930.

Also by Annie Haynes

ANNIE HAYNES

THE SECRET OF GREYLANDS

With an introduction
by Curtis Evans

DEAN STREET PRESS

Published by Dean Street Press 2016

All Rights Reserved

First published in 1924 by The Bodley Head

Cover by DSP

Introduction © Curtis Evans 2016

ISBN 978 1 911095 23 1

www.deanstreetpress.co.uk

The Mystery of The Missing Author
Annie Haynes and Her Golden Age Detective Fiction

The psychological enigma of Agatha Christie's notorious 1926 vanishing has continued to intrigue Golden Age mystery fans to the present day. The Queen of Crime's eleven-day disappearing act is nothing, however, compared to the decades-long disappearance, in terms of public awareness, of between-the-wars mystery writer Annie Haynes (1865-1929), author of a series of detective novels published between 1923 and 1930 by Agatha Christie's original English publisher, The Bodley Head. Haynes's books went out of print in the early Thirties, not long after her death in 1929, and her reputation among classic detective fiction readers, high in her lifetime, did not so much decline as dematerialize. When, in 2013, I first wrote a piece about Annie Haynes' work, I knew of only two other living persons besides myself who had read any of her books. Happily, Dean Street Press once again has come to the rescue of classic mystery fans seeking genre gems from the Golden Age, and is republishing all Haynes' mystery novels. Now that her crime fiction is coming back into print, the question naturally arises: Who Was Annie Haynes? Solving the mystery of this forgotten author's lost life has taken leg work by literary sleuths on two continents (my thanks for their assistance to Carl Woodings and Peter Harris).

Until recent research uncovered new information about Annie Haynes, almost nothing about her was publicly known besides the fact of her authorship of twelve mysteries during the Golden Age of detective fiction. Now we know that she led an altogether intriguing life, too soon cut short by disability and death, which took her from the isolation of the rural English Midlands in the nineteenth century to the cultural high life of Edwardian London. Haynes was born in 1865 in the Leicestershire town of Ashby-de-la-Zouch, the first child of ironmonger Edwin Haynes and Jane (Henderson) Haynes, daughter of Montgomery Henderson, longtime superintendent of the gardens at nearby Coleorton Hall, seat of the Beaumont baronets. After her father left his family, young Annie resided with her grandparents at the gardener's cottage at Coleorton Hall, along with her mother and younger brother. Here Annie doubtlessly obtained an acquaintance with the ways of the country gentry that would serve her well in her career as a genre fiction writer.

We currently know nothing else of Annie Haynes' life in Leicestershire, where she still resided (with her mother) in 1901, but by 1908, when Haynes was in her early forties, she was living in London with Ada Heather-Bigg (1855-1944) at the Heather-Bigg family home, located halfway between Paddington Station and Hyde Park at 14 Radnor Place, London. One of three daughters of Henry Heather-Bigg, a noted pioneer in the development of orthopedics and artificial limbs, Ada Heather-Bigg was a prominent Victorian and Edwardian era feminist and social reformer. In the 1911 British census entry for 14 Radnor Place, Heather-Bigg, a "philanthropist and journalist," is listed as the head of the household and Annie Haynes, a "novelist," as a "visitor," but in fact Haynes would remain there with Ada Heather-Bigg until Haynes' death in 1929.

Haynes' relationship with Ada Heather-Bigg introduced the aspiring author to important social sets in England's great metropolis. Though not a novelist herself, Heather-Bigg was an important figure in the city's intellectual milieu, a well-connected feminist activist of great energy and passion who believed strongly in the idea of women attaining economic independence through remunerative employment. With Ada Heather-Bigg behind her, Annie Haynes's writing career had powerful backing indeed. Although in the 1911 census Heather-Bigg listed Haynes' occupation as "novelist," it appears that Haynes did not publish any novels in book form prior to 1923, the year that saw the appearance of *The Bungalow Mystery*, which Haynes dedicated to Heather-Bigg. However, Haynes was a prolific producer of newspaper serial novels during the second decade of the twentieth century, penning such works as *Lady Carew's Secret, Footprints of Fate, A Pawn of Chance, The Manor Tragedy* and many others.

Haynes' twelve Golden Age mystery novels, which appeared in a tremendous burst of creative endeavor between 1923 and 1930, like the author's serial novels retain, in stripped-down form, the emotionally heady air of the nineteenth-century triple-decker sensation novel, with genteel settings, shocking secrets, stormy passions and eternal love all at the fore, yet they also have the fleetness of Jazz Age detective fiction. Both in their social milieu and narrative pace Annie Haynes' detective novels bear considerable resemblance to contemporary works by Agatha Christie; and it is interesting to note in this regard that Annie Haynes and Agatha Christie were the only female mystery writers published by The Bodley Head, one of the more notable English mystery imprints in the early Golden Age. "A very remarkable feature of recent detective fiction," observed the *Illustrated London News* in 1923, "is the skill displayed by women in this branch of story-telling. Isabel Ostrander, Carolyn Wells, Annie Haynes and last, but very far from least, Agatha Christie, are contesting the laurels of Sherlock Holmes' creator with a great spirit, ingenuity and success." Since Ostrander and Wells were American authors, this left Annie Haynes, in the estimation of the *Illustrated London News*, as the main British female competitor to Agatha Christie. (Dorothy L. Sayers, who, like Haynes, published her debut mystery novel in 1923, goes unmentioned.) Similarly, in 1925 *The Sketch* wryly noted that "[t]ired men, trotting home at the end of an imperfect day, have been known to pop into the library and ask for an Annie Haynes. They have not made a mistake in the street number. It is not a cocktail they are asking for..."

Twenties critical opinion adjudged that Annie Haynes' criminous concoctions held appeal not only for puzzle fiends impressed with the "considerable craftsmanship" of their plots (quoting from the *Sunday Times* review of *The Bungalow Mystery*), but also for more general readers attracted to their purely literary qualities. "Not only a crime story of merit, but also a novel which will interest readers to whom mystery for its own sake has little appeal," avowed

The Nation of Haynes' *The Secret of Greylands*, while the *New Statesman* declared of *The Witness on the Roof* that "Miss Haynes has a sense of character; her people are vivid and not the usual puppets of detective fiction." Similarly, the *Bookman* deemed the characters in Haynes' *The Abbey Court Murder* "much truer to life than is the case in many sensational stories" and *The Spectator* concluded of *The Crime at Tattenham Corner*, "Excellent as a detective tale, the book also is a charming novel."

Sadly, Haynes' triumph as a detective novelist proved short lived. Around 1914, about the time of the outbreak of the Great War, Haynes had been stricken with debilitating rheumatoid arthritis that left her in constant pain and hastened her death from heart failure in 1929, when she was only 63. Haynes wrote several of her detective novels on fine days in Kensington Gardens, where she was wheeled from 14 Radnor Place in a bath chair, but in her last years she was able only to travel from her bedroom to her study. All of this was an especially hard blow for a woman who had once been intensely energetic and quite physically active.

In a foreword to *The Crystal Beads Murder*, the second of Haynes' two posthumously published mysteries, Ada Heather-Bigg noted that Haynes' difficult daily physical struggle "was materially lightened by the warmth of friendships" with other authors and by the "sympathetic and friendly relations between her and her publishers." In this latter instance Haynes' experience rather differed from that of her sister Bodleian, Agatha Christie, who left The Bodley Head on account of what she deemed an iniquitous contract that took unjust advantage of a naive young author. Christie moved, along with her landmark detective novel *The Murder of Roger Ackroyd* (1926), to Collins and never looked back, enjoying ever greater success with the passing years.

At the time Christie crossed over to Collins, Annie Haynes had only a few years of life left. After she died at 14 Radnor Place on 30 March 1929, it was reported in the press that "many people well-known in the literary world" attended the author's funeral at St.

Michaels and All Angels Church, Paddington, where her sermon was delivered by the eloquent vicar, Paul Nichols, brother of the writer Beverley Nichols and dedicatee of Haynes' mystery novel *The Master of the Priory*; yet by the time of her companion Ada Heather-Bigg's death in 1944, Haynes and her once highly-praised mysteries were forgotten. (Contrastingly, Ada Heather-Bigg's name survives today in the University College of London's Ada Heather-Bigg Prize in Economics.) Only three of Haynes' novels were ever published in the United States, and she passed away less than a year before the formation of the Detection Club, missing any chance of being invited to join this august body of distinguished British detective novelists. Fortunately, we have today entered, when it comes to classic mystery, a period of rediscovery and revival, giving a reading audience a chance once again, after over eighty years, to savor the detective fiction fare of Annie Haynes. *Bon appétit!*

Curtis Evans

Chapter One

"Glastwick? Next stopping-place, miss! We ought to be there in twenty minutes."

Cynthia Letchingham shivered as she sat back in the corner of her third-class railway carriage. She felt a sudden shrinking from the end of this journey of hers. After all, she wondered if she had made a mistake in coming? Then, for the hundredth time, she told herself that she could have done nothing else. But, as she mechanically watched the dreary northern country through which they were passing, her eyes filled with tears—she felt so young, so friendless, so alone. At last she took a letter from her hand-bag. The envelope was soiled and creased as if with much carrying about, and was addressed to Miss Cynthia Densham, in an old woman's shaking writing.

The mist before Cynthia's eyes thickened as she looked at it. Alas, she who had been yesterday morning Cynthia Densham was now Cynthia Letchingham, a woman flying from the man she dreaded most on earth—her husband!

She drew out the letter from its envelope and glanced over it once more:

Greylands
Glastwick
Northumberland.

Dear Cynthia,

I expect you have forgotten me. It is many years since we met, but I know you have heard your father speak of his Cousin Hannah, and I could not let this momentous occasion in your life pass without a word from me. In a very few days you will receive my wedding gift. It is one that perhaps you will think little enough of now, but at any rate it will give you what I myself prize above all things, a certain independence of your husband—a refuge to which you can turn in time of trouble. I can assure you...

Here the letter broke off abruptly and began lower down the page in a strangely different strain.

Oh, Cynthia, come to me! If you can only spare a day or two from your preparations for your wedding, come. I have tried to bear it in silence to the end, but I am old and weak and frightened — so frightened! For your father's sake, come and help me, Cynthia.

Your cousin,

HANNAH GILLMAN.

Cynthia read it over again; she felt the same thrill of amazement as when she first saw this extraordinary epistle. What could be wrong with her cousin, Lady Hannah Gillman?

At any rate, Lady Hannah lived in a country-house far away from London; she had begged Cynthia to come to her, and to the best of the girl's belief her husband had never heard of the old lady. Greylands seemed to Cynthia the only refuge to which she could go in her present sore straits.

She slipped the letter back into its envelope and opened her bag to put it away. As she did so, she caught sight of another letter folded away in the corner—a letter, the very look of which drove the blood from her cheeks and moistened her forehead with sickly fear. And yet it did not look such a terrifying affair—just a very short note, undated, with no address. It began abruptly:

I have seen the announcement of your approaching marriage to Lord Letchingham; I must make one effort to save you from such certain unhappiness. Lord Letchingham is the man whose name I refused to give your mother—the man who deceived me by a false marriage and left me to a life of shame and misery. Now that you know the truth you must do as you think fit. Only for the value of the love we bore one another in the old days have I broken the silence I had hoped to maintain to the end.

Your heart-broken friend,

ALICE WINTHROP.

If it had only reached its destination two hours earlier! But already Cynthia Densham was Lady Letchingham when she received it.

And then she had not taken it on trust. She had taxed her newly-made husband with being Alice Winthrop's betrayer. The very memory of the scene that followed was terrible and, seizing her first chance of escape, she had fled from her husband and, remembering her Cousin Hannah's letter, had determined to appeal to her for refuge. But now that the actual moment was at hand she was beginning to feel nervous, and to wonder uncertainly what kind of a reception her Cousin Hannah would give her. Quite possibly she thought, she might have changed her mind about wishing to see her; in any case, she would certainly not expect to see her now, and she asked herself for the hundredth time whether she had done wisely in coming to Greylands for refuge.

She knew but little of her Cousin Hannah, as she had been taught to call her. That Lady Hannah Gillman, the daughter of an impoverished Irish peer, was her father's cousin Cynthia knew; and she had sometimes fancied that in their youth there had been some closer and warmer tie. The girl remembered still how, when she was a child, on one of her rare visits her Cousin Hannah had been left alone with her, and she had never forgotten how she had been caught up and the passionate kisses mingled with bitter tears that had been pressed upon her cheeks.

After her father's death, however, the acquaintance had ceased; without the matter being put into so many words, Cynthia had gathered that her mother did not care for Hannah Hammond, as Lady Hannah was then. For many years, on her birthday, an expensive present had come for Cynthia from her father's cousin, with a few brief lines expressing the donor's best wishes for the occasion; that and Cynthia's letter of thanks had been the only communication between them.

Through a mutual relative, however, Mrs Densham and her daughter had heard that a large fortune had been left to Lady Hannah, and that she had virtually adopted the orphan son of her only sister, who had married a Scotch baronet and died fifteen years afterwards, predeceasing her husband, and leaving this one child, in regard to whom Lady Hannah now took his mother's place.

Then, quite casually, just before Mrs Densham's death, Cynthia had heard that there had been a quarrel, that young Sir Donald Farquhar had gone to seek his fortune ranching in British Columbia, and that Lady Hannah was left alone. She would have had no difficulty in obtaining another heir among her numerous connexions; and her relatives were still speculating as to upon whom her choice would fall when they were thunderstruck to receive the announcement of her marriage with a man considerably younger than herself, whom she had met while staying in a *pension* at Brussels. She had not suffered any hint of her intention to get abroad until the wedding was an accomplished fact, and indignation and remonstrance were alike useless.

That such of her relatives as had met her husband since their marriage had disliked him intensely, and had barely troubled to conceal their opinion that he was a fortune-hunter, apparently worried Lady Hannah but little. She and her husband continued to live abroad for some time; then there had been rumours that they intended to take a country-house in England. But Cynthia, absorbed at first in grief for her mother's death, and later on in preparations for her wedding, had heard nothing more of them until the delayed letter which had reached her on her wedding morning.

She opened her little bag, and, taking out Lady Hannah's letter, perused it once more. The extraordinary way in which it stopped short in the middle and the blotted hurried appeal at the end, with the curious contrast between the two styles, struck her more than ever. That the marriage with Gillman had turned out a failure she was quite ready to believe; but there was a tone of fear, of helplessness, about the conclusion which seemed strangely at variance with what Cynthia had previously heard of her cousin's resolution and self-reliance. However, no fresh light was to be gained by re-reading the letter, and, with a puzzled sigh, she crammed it in her pocket just as the train began to slow down for Glastwick.

Cynthia opened the window and put her head out. The station was the veriest little shanty; it looked extremely dreary and desolate in the twilight. Though rain was not falling now, it had evidently been pouring quite recently—the eaves were dripping and pools of water were lying on the platform outside the scanty shelter.

Cynthia reached down her bag and got out. The porter, the only one apparently that the station boasted, was busied with the luggage at the farther end of the platform; her trunk, already out, stood in conspicuous loneliness.

Cynthia went up to it; she waited until the many milk-cans had been safely put in and a mountain of empties had been deposited on the platform, then she addressed the porter.

"I want to go to Greylands. Can you tell me how far it is and the best way to get there?"

The man turned a red, bucolic face and gaped at her without replying.

"Can't you tell me?" Cynthia repeated impatiently. "Greylands? Mr Gillman lives there."

The man scratched his head.

"Can't say as ever I heard of it, miss," he said, the broad northern burr very apparent in his speech.

Cynthia looked at him in amazement.

"This is Glastwick, is it not?"

"Ay, this is Glastwick, sure enough; but I know nowt of the other place," the man said, beginning to move off.

"What am I to do?" Cynthia questioned, following him despairingly.

The porter eyed her stolidly.

"Mr King may have heard of it maybe," he said, with a jerk of his head in the direction of the little booking-office.

With a feeling of relief Cynthia turned towards it quickly. Two men were standing just inside.

"Can you tell me the way to Greylands, please?" she began abruptly. As she spoke, the taller of the two men moved aside and apparently occupied himself in studying the outside of a large crate of crockery that stood near; the other, a dapper-looking, sandy-haired man, in the uniform of the company, came forward to meet her.

"Greylands, miss? You mean Mr Gillman's place, I suppose. It is a matter of six or seven miles off—over Grimston way."

"Six or seven miles away?" Cynthia's heart sank. "So far?" she said blankly. "I had no idea of that. How can I get there? Is there a taxi?"

"I am afraid there is nothing of that kind to be got here," the station-master said, pursing up his lips. "You would have done better to drive from the junction."

"How was I to know that?" Cynthia said helplessly. "Lady Hannah Gillman's letter was dated from 'Greylands, Glastwick.'"

"Ah, that is right enough for the post," the man agreed. "But this is only a small place—there are no conveyances to be hired here! If Mr Gillman is expecting you, though, he will, maybe, be driving in presently."

"He is not," Cynthia said hopelessly. "Do you mean that I shall have to go back to the junction?"

"No, no, you can't do that," the man said, with an apologetic laugh. "There is no train back to-night."

"Then what on earth am I to do?"

Cynthia's underlip quivered ominously; she was tired by the long railway journey, and her nerves had been sadly shaken by the events of the past few days.

The station-master pulled his small sandy moustache thoughtfully.

"I don't know what is to be done, I am sure!" he said perplexedly. "This isn't much of a place to stop at, but—"

"Oh, I can't stay here!" Cynthia broke in hurriedly. "I must get to Greylands, if I have to walk! There must, however, be some way—"

The station-master took off his cap and scratched his head, looking round as if for enlightenment.

"Mr King!" It was the voice of the man who had been looking at the crate in the booking-office, and who had now strolled to the doorway.

With a muttered word of apology the station- master joined him.

Standing alone Cynthia glanced at her trunk outside and wished despairingly that she had waited, that she had written and informed her cousin of her coming.

At length the station-master, his brief colloquy over, returned.

"There is Will Joyce outside," he said slowly. "He's driving back to Farmer Fowkes's, as lives out beyond Greylands. He might give you a lift, if you didn't mind a roughish cart. He brought in a calf to the sale to-day."

Cynthia's face lighted up.

"I don't mind what sort of a cart it is."

"Come along, then!" The station-master was evidently a man of few words. "Bring that trunk along, Jim!" he shouted to Cynthia's first friend as he led the way to the entrance. "Ay, you will be all right with Will Joyce," he went on to Cynthia. "He may be a rough one to look at, but—"

Cynthia glanced apprehensively at the man seated in a sort of market-cart as she waited while her companion went forward and explained matters. Mr Will Joyce did not appear particularly anxious to fall in with the scheme, she thought, and it seemed quite a long time before she was beckoned to unceremoniously.

"He will take you as far as Gillman's gate," the station-master explained as, with more courtesy than Cynthia had expected, he helped her in and gave a hand with the trunk, which was hoisted up behind. "I am sorry that this is the best we can do for you, but, anyway, it is better than having to walk."

"A good deal, thank you!" Cynthia said gratefully as she drew her rug around her and dropped a silver coin into the porter's hand.

Her charioteer shook the reins, and they started off in a leisurely jog-trot fashion.

"Did you hear that young lady's name? Who is she?"

As the station-master turned, he found himself confronted by the tall dark man to whom he had been talking in the booking-office.

He looked surprised.

"I don't know, I am sure, sir. Oh, stay, I did catch sight of the name on the box; I believe it was Hammond."

"Ah"—the stranger looked after the cart in a speculative fashion—"that would be one of Lady Hannah Gillman's relatives, then?"

The station-master knocked a loose stone down the step.

"I couldn't say, sir. That Gillman—do you know him, sir?"

"No," laconically.

"He is a queer sort of fellow for a gentleman," the station-master went on conversationally. "Though he talks to you as if butter wouldn't melt in his mouth, he has got a very bad temper. I saw him beating a young horse one day, and I haven't forgotten it; though I am not over squeamish, it turned me fair sick. Well, well, it takes all sorts to make up a world, they say. I'll see that your box goes up by the next passenger train, sir," as the other began to move off.

"Thank you very much. Good day." The stranger started off down the same road as that taken by Cynthia, walking with a long swinging stride.

The station-master looked after him curiously.

"I wonder what his business down here is?" he soliloquized. "Seemed wonderfully struck with the young lady, I thought. Ah, well, she is a good-looking girl too!" with a sigh as if dismissing the subject.

Cynthia, meanwhile, was looking about her with interest. Twilight though it was, she could catch a glimpse of the distant hills, and she fancied that in the daytime the moorland for which they were making would prove good ground for exploring.

Presently the road grew rough and uneven. The market-cart was of the most primitive description, and Cynthia was jolted about and shaken from side to side till she had much ado to hold herself in her place. The driver took it all phlegmatically, never even glancing at Cynthia. At length a particularly deep rut almost shook the girl from her seat, and she caught hold of the rail in front.

"Are we far from Greylands?" she gasped.

"A matter of four miles or so," Mr Joyce replied stolidly.

"Oh!" Cynthia drew a long breath. "Is it like this all the way?"

"It is a roughish bit like just here," the driver answered, without turning his head, "but it is a good road, take it altogether."

Cynthia felt inclined to dissent most emphatically from this statement as another jerk sent her up against the speaker.

"If—it is only four miles," she said breathlessly, "perhaps I could walk?"

"You'd miss your way for a surety," Mr Joyce replied without slackening. "Happen you'll get caught in the bog. It'll be pitch-dark directly. Best bide where you be."

Cynthia shivered as she resigned herself to the inevitable.

"Well, perhaps so," she said reluctantly. "I am sure it is very kind of you to drive me," she added politely.

Mr Joyce only responded by a grunt; evidently he was not inclined to carry on the conversation, and Cynthia relapsed into silence, clinging with both hands to the side of the cart, and endeavouring to steady herself to the best of her ability. In a short time, however, the road grew a trifle less rough, the worst of the jolts grew less frequent, and Cynthia was able to sit up and survey her surroundings once more, though it was little enough she could see now. The last gleams of light were fading away; the lamps at each side of the cart only served to make the darkness more visible; in the distance she could hear the wind rising and soughing among the leaves of unseen trees. To complete her discomfort a drizzling rain began to fall. She drew her rug over her shoulders and tried to forget her miserable plight, but, look where she would, no very pleasant subject for meditation presented itself, and her thoughts flew back to Lord Letchingham.

What had he said when he discovered her flight, she wondered. Was he still searching for her? She shuddered as she told herself she had undoubtedly taken the best course.

At length Mr Joyce pulled up and said:

"Yon's Greylands."

Cynthia peered forward into the darkness.

"I don't see it," she remarked helplessly.

"Noa; but you've naught to do but follow the road. I'll show you, if you'll get down." He clambered slowly and heavily out of the cart.

"You are not going to leave me here?" Cynthia cried in dismay, as, with difficulty, she managed to make her way to the ground. "You will at least drive me up to the house?"

"I can't do that," Mr Joyce said slowly. "You can't miss it, keeping to the road, I tell you. Your trunk will be all right till Gillman can send for it in the morning." He hoisted it out of the cart as he spoke, and, opening the gate, deposited it inside a kind of small barn. "There it'll be dry and under cover." He unfastened the reins and put his foot on the step.

"You are not going to leave me like this? I cannot even see Greylands!" Cynthia cried, catching at his arm in her desperation.

Mr Joyce deliberately shook himself free as he made his way to his former seat.

"I can't do no more for you, miss. I said I'd bring you as far as Gillman's gate, and at Gillman's gate you are. It is a roughish bit of road to the house, and it ud mean a difference of half an hour to drive there and back by this light, and I've got my time to account for to my master."

Cynthia looked round despairingly.

"If you will only drive me up to the house, I will pay you."

"'Tain't that, miss. It is just as I can't. As for Greylands, you can't miss it, and there's naught to be feared of. You won't meet anyone, and walking'll get you there as quick as driving a night like this. Just go through that there gate and keep straight on. It is but a step. Good night, miss."

Thus deserted Cynthia had no choice but to make the best of the situation and try to find her way to the house. She went through the gate, only to discover that merely to keep on the rough path that apparently led across a field was a matter of some difficulty in the dark. Stumbling along, however, falling occasionally over a loose stone or an unusually deep rut, she accomplished it, and found herself at another gate, which apparently opened into a wood.

Rightly concluding this to be a belt of trees surrounding the house, Cynthia kept on her way and was soon rewarded by seeing a big gloomy pile of buildings looming before her in the darkness. This, then, must be Greylands; but Cynthia's spirits were not raised by the fact that the end of her long journey was now in sight. Instead she felt a nameless depression, an unaccountable prevision of some terrible evil; and as she stood in the great dark porch a longing to get away, an almost over-mastering impulse to turn back, to spend the night in the barn with her trunk or on the moors rather than ask for shelter at this big, desolate- looking house, took possession of her.

Chiding herself, however, for her foolishness, she resolutely stood her ground and lifted the heavy knocker.

The noise it made was startling in the intense stillness around. As it died away, somewhere inside the house a dog howled loudly—a long-drawn-out wail of misery.

Standing there in the damp and the cold Cynthia felt an eerie sense of horror, against which she struggled in vain. Loud though her knock had sounded in her own ears there was no sign of response of any kind. The same stillness prevailed; even the rustling of the wind amid the trees had ceased, not a leaf seemed astir.

Cynthia stepped back and looked up at the house. It was apparently all in darkness. With the thought that possibly her cousin might be away and the place shut up or left to a caretaker, she determined to find her way to the back. Clinging to the wall she managed to turn the corner of the house. As she did so there was a loud clamorous barking inside, and she saw that a distant window was lighted up. With some difficulty she found another door. Knocker or bell there was none, but with the handle of her umbrella she thumped loudly again and again.

Meanwhile the drippings of the eaves fell upon her shoulders, with a great splash on her hat—her only hat, Cynthia reflected forlornly as she attempted to protect herself. It seemed to her that she had stood there for an eternity, feeling in her nervous terror as though the darkness around was filled with living things—things that whispered together and gibed at her. When at length she caught the sound of heavy, lagging footsteps coming down the passage the dog howled more loudly. Cynthia felt a sudden pang of swift unreasoning terror—something seemed to whisper to her to run away, to hide herself while yet there was time; but she was no coward, and in spite of her terrors she stood her ground as the door was slowly unbarred and unbolted. Then her heart beat quicker as it was opened a foot or two, and, by the light of a dim, flickering lamp suspended above, she saw a man's face—a white, scared face, with a certain defiance underlying its ghastly pallor.

"What is wanted? Who are you?" a voice inquired roughly; but in spite of the abrupt words the intonation was that of a gentleman.

Cynthia gathered up her courage.

"This is Lady Hannah Gillman's house, is it not?" she asked in her clear girlish voice. "I want to see her. She asked me to come. I am her cousin, Cynthia Densham."

"You are—what?" There was an accent of amazement, not unmixed, as Cynthia fancied, with fear.

"Cynthia Densham—Lady Hannah's cousin," she repeated impatiently. "Is she here?"

There was a pause, a long-strained silence, then the answer came in a harsh rasping tone:

"Yes, she is here, but she does not receive strangers."

"Her own cousin, though!" Cynthia began indignantly. "At least you will let me in? Don't you understand—she has asked me to stay with her."

The man made no motion to open the door wider; instead, Cynthia fancied that he moved as though about to close it.

"You are making some mistake. Lady Hannah never receives visitors; she has no wish for them. It is impossible for you to come in."

This time the desire to shut the door was unmistakable, and Cynthia put out her hands in desperation.

"You cannot mean it? I dare not stay out here in the cold. You must let me see my cousin; she asked me to come—she wrote to me!"

"She wrote to you—when?"

"A fortnight ago at least. The letter was delayed—I only had it the day before yesterday; but she said she wanted me to come to her at once."

"What—she wrote before? I cannot believe it!"

There was an indescribable change in the man's voice. He stopped short. Cynthia felt in her pocket.

"Yes, here it is!" she cried, drawing out the letter.

He glanced at the envelope in her hand; then a curious tremor shook him. The lamp above him flickered and went out.

"Wait a minute!" he said brusquely, and turned abruptly down the passage.

Chapter Two

CYNTHIA stepped inside to be out of the damp. At the end of the passage she could see the interior of a long, low-raftered room, which looked pleasant and homely, and for a moment her spirits rose. Then, as if suddenly released from some back region, with a mingled growl and whine, a wire-haired terrier sprang towards her, menacingly, as she thought. Before it reached her, however, it stopped and sprang at a closed door at the side of the passage, scratching and giving vent to long ear-piercing howls. Cynthia wondered what could cause its excitement; but the man was coming back, still without a lamp. With an angry word he kicked the dog through the outer door, and drawing Cynthia farther in, closed it behind her.

"That dog is a perfect nuisance!" he said irritably. "I would get rid of him at once if my wife were not so devoted to him. Now, you are Cynthia Densham, you say? I ought to have recognized the name. You are the daughter of Lady Hannah's—of my wife's cousin, are you not?"

"Oh, then, you are Mr Gillman?"

Cynthia's accent was one of considerable relief as she glanced at his tall figure, outlined in the darkness against the warmth and the light of the room beyond.

"I am Henry Gillman," he acquiesced. "You must excuse this unceremonious reception. If we had had any idea of your coming you should have found us prepared for you in a very different way. But, now that you are here, you must stay the night. We must manage somehow. Come in! Can you see your way?"

"Quite well, thank you," Cynthia replied as she obeyed.

"I fancy somehow that you have not heard that we are in great trouble?" he went on. "That makes your coming so difficult. I don't see what is to be done."

Cynthia felt increasingly uncomfortable.

"No, I had not heard, though I fancied that perhaps—that Cousin Hannah—You do not mean—"

Before she could finish the sentence she set her foot in something slimy near the door at which the dog had barked and came violently to the ground.

With a sharp exclamation Gillman turned and helped her to rise. "How did that happen? I hope you have not hurt yourself?"

"No, I—I think not," Cynthia said uncertainly as she stood up, too much dazed and bruised to form any very clear idea of her injuries. "I slipped on something—there. I do not know what it is."

Gillman's expression changed curiously as he looked down. He caressed his long, fair moustache with one hand and glanced furtively at Cynthia from beneath his narrowed eyelids.

"I am very sorry! I do not know what it is—something the charwoman has spilt, I suppose; she is a careless mortal. But come in. We can at least make you a little more comfortable. You look as though the elements had dealt hardly with you."

Catching sight of herself in a little old-fashioned glass to her right as she entered the room, Cynthia hardly wondered at his words. Her hair was loosened and hung about her face in untidy wisps, her hat was askew, but her cheeks were glowing from their contact with the cool fresh air, and her eyes looked big and startled.

Gillman pulled forward a chair and stroked his chin in a thoughtful fashion.

"Presently we must see what can be done about the night; but wait and rest awhile first. Let me explain matters."

Cynthia was nothing loath. The capacious armchair rested her tired young body; the very feeling of the cool fresh chintz was refreshing.

Gillman poked the already glowing fire noisily. As he stood with his back to her, she could not help noticing his stalwart proportion and length of limb, the broadness of his shoulders. He was absolutely unlike anything she had expected, and she could not help thinking what a curious contrast he must present to her Cousin Hannah as she had been described to her, and as her childish imagination pictured her—a little, prim, delicate-looking woman, yet with a will of iron beneath her quaint, old-fashioned courtesy. With that thought the remembrance of his words as she fell recurred to her.

"How is Cousin Hannah?" she asked hastily. "You were saying you were in trouble. Surely—"

Gillman did not turn round, but went on poking the fire.

"She was taken ill a fortnight ago. It was paralysis and it has affected her spine. The doctors do not give much hope that she will ever be able to walk again. Still, one never can tell, and I fancy myself we shall see a great improvement as the summer advances."

"Oh, poor Cousin Hannah!" Cynthia cried, indescribably shocked at this intelligence. "It must have been this she meant when she wrote; she seemed to hint at some impending trouble. Perhaps she had some sort of presentiment. I have heard of such things."

Gillman turned, poker in hand.

"What did she say about it?"

Something in his tone startled Cynthia.

"She spoke of feeling old and weak and wishing to see me," Cynthia said, after a moment's pause. "I wish I had been able to, but, as I said, the letter was delayed; I only had it two days ago." Gillman laid the poker in its place carefully.

"If you had written I should have been obliged to ask you to delay your visit; but it is too late for that now. My wife has been nervous lately. Her old maid, Gleeson, who had been with her for years—as I dare say you know—left her in the beginning of the winter, and we found a great difficulty in replacing her. Then to get servants at all in a place like this is no easy matter; at present we are entirely without them."

"Entirely without servants?" Cynthia echoed amazedly. "I do not understand! Do you mean that there is no one to attend to Cousin Hannah?"

Gillman took up a position before the fire and leaned against the high oaken mantelpiece, one hand pulling his moustache and partly shading his face.

"Your cousin has the bad taste to prefer my ministrations to those of anyone else," he said, with a smile which seemed to alter the whole character of his face.

Looking at his expression in repose Cynthia had decided that, notwithstanding his undeniable good looks, the straight, regular features and the large blue eyes, the whole effect was repellent in the extreme; but the smile altered everything—it was curiously bright and winning, and the rows of straight white teeth gave an expression of superb health and strength.

He went on in a moment.

"We have a charwoman who comes up from the village to do the rough work, and in an emergency I am a capital hand at cooking. I have roughed it on a ranch in Texas as well as in New Zealand. Oh, I assure you, we do very well!"

"I dare say," said Cynthia uncertainly. "I am sure you do your best," she added politely, "but it seems such an unaccountable thing for a woman in Cousin Hannah's position."

"Needs must when—" with another smile.

"You will think I am making your cousin as unconventional as myself, Miss Densham. You will find her a good deal altered. When did you see her last?"

"Not since I was a child," Cynthia answered.

"Indeed, I really cannot remember her at all— properly, that is to say."

"Ah!" He opened the sideboard door. "I am forgetting! Here are our provisions. You see there are eggs, cakes, and I believe there is some cold beef in the larder. What will you have?"

"I should like a cup of tea better than anything," Cynthia said hesitatingly.

He laughed and said:

"The woman's panacea! I should recommend a glass of your cousin's old port myself; but, as you please," shrugging his shoulders as Cynthia shook her head. "Tea is, at any rate, easily obtainable," placing a little kettle on the spirit- lamp. "But now, if you will excuse me, I will tell my wife that you are here, and take counsel with her as to what is best to be done."

"Oh, please ask her to let me come up; I am so anxious to see her!"

"I expect she will be only too delighted to see you," Gillman replied politely. His eyes as he left the room were fixed hungrily on a corner of the white envelope which he could see sticking out of the pocket in the girl's coat.

Left alone, Cynthia rose and, crossing over to the mirror hanging on the wall, took off her hat and coiled up her disordered hair. Her thoughts were busy, meanwhile, with her curious reception and with the extraordinary *ménage* in which she found herself. That her presence there was unwelcome to her cousin's husband she saw plainly enough, but, remembering the letter she had received, she could not divest herself of the belief that in some way Lady Hannah needed her, that she would be glad to hear that she had responded to her summons.

Standing there she took the letter out once more.

"'Old and weak and frightened,'" she read. "It—there must be something she does not want her husband to know; but I cannot imagine that. If there should be ill-treatment—" Her cheeks flamed.

Gillman's step sounded on the stairs—he was coming back; and, moved by some sudden impulse, she stooped and poked the paper through the bars of the fire-place.

Gillman opened the door, glanced quickly at her flushed cheeks, and noted the sound of her quickened breathing.

"My wife seems tired and feverish to-night," he began. "I dare not take the responsibility of admitting you now; in fact, she herself says she does not feel equal to it; but she sees no difficulty in your remaining here for the night. As a matter of fact"—with that same illuminating smile—"you are not the only relative she has summoned."

"You do not mean that she has sent for Sir Donald Farquhar?" Cynthia interrupted eagerly. "I am glad to hear of it! She was so devoted to him for so many years!"

"Certainly it is not Sir Donald Farquhar! Your cousin feels his ingratitude as keenly as ever; but she has written to a young lady, standing, I believe in the same relationship as yourself—Sybil Hammond. She is coming to stay with us here either to-morrow or the day after."

"Sybil Hammond!" Cynthia repeated thoughtfully. "I have not heard of her; but I suppose she belongs to the other side of the family. She is coming to be with Cousin Hannah, you say?"

She was at no loss to understand how the matter stood. Quite evidently, she thought, Lady Hannah, thought it hopeless to expect her so soon after her marriage; and since her curiously worded letter had met with no response she determined to appeal to her other relatives.

"My wife seems to have no clear remembrance of what she said in her letter to you," Gillman went on. "She must have written it when her illness was approaching, and she found it difficult to express herself with clearness. You have the letter with you; would you mind letting me show it to her? She wants to see it."

Cynthia's eyes travelled to the little puff of blue smoke in the fire-place, to the fragment of charred ash clinging to the bar.

"Oh, I am so sorry! I never thought of her wanting to see it. I have burnt it."

Gillman laughed.

"Oh, it is only a trifle. She thought she would like to see it. I was about to say that a room has been got ready for Miss Hammond. It is at your service now, and my wife thinks you might like to take off the dust of your journey while your meal is preparing."

"Thank you," said Cynthia gratefully. "I shall be very glad!"

He opened the door.

"It is the first room at the top of the stairs. Perhaps you will kindly go up as quietly as possible. I will carry up your bag."

"Oh, that is nothing! I will take it; there is not much in it," Cynthia said with a rueful laugh. "The rest of my luggage is deposited in your barn by the gates. The man who drove me said it would be safe enough there."

In spite of her remonstrances Gillman took the bag from her.

"Perhaps I shall walk down for it to-night; but we are honest folk in these parts, if a trifle unceremonious, and it will be safe enough."

"I hope it will, for it contains almost all my worldly possessions," Cynthia said lightly as she crossed the gloomy-looking unlighted entrance-hall, which apparently opened on to the porch, through which she had first tried to gain admittance.

The stairs were of solid black oak, with a fine balustrade, but the need for silence was evident, for they were uncarpeted, and notwithstanding Cynthia's best efforts her small high-heeled shoes clicked irritatingly as she mounted the wide, low steps.

At the door she paused, and Gillman handed her the bag.

"As soon as you have finished, your tea will be ready."

"I shall not be long," Cynthia promised as she opened the door.

The bedroom was better furnished than she had expected, judging from the rest of the house. A large, elaborately-carved wardrobe took up most of one of the walls, and the middle of the room was occupied by an old-fashioned four-poster, but there was a couple of cosy-looking wicker-chairs, and a pretty writing-table stood by the window.

Cynthia threw off her hat and coat and did her best to restore something like order to her appearance; but as she bathed her glowing face in the cool soft water and twisted up her refractory locks she could not help marvelling anew at the extraordinary fashion in which a woman as wealthy as her Cousin Hannah had apparently elected to live.

Her toilet was necessarily a brief one, and she was soon ready to descend. She paused a moment on the landing outside her room and glanced round, wondering which was Lady Hannah's room. So far as she could see by the flickering light of the small lamp standing on a bracket near there were five doors beside her own, and there was evidently another floor. Not a sound was to be heard, however, and she tiptoed downstairs as quickly as possible.

Short as had been the time she had spent on her toilet, already a comfortable meal was spread upon the table. The tea-tray stood at one end, flanked by a round of cold beef, a great glass dish of junket and another of stewed fruit, while Gillman was standing by the fire-place manipulating a small iron saucepan, whence there proceeded a most appetizing smell.

As Cynthia entered he turned the contents into a dish.

"Buttered eggs," he said without looking round. "Your cousin likes them better than anything and I hope you will share her taste."

"I am sure I shall," Cynthia said as she seated herself.

In truth, the keen fresh air had given her an appetite to which she had long been a stranger, and while Gillman waited on her assiduously she made a hearty meal.

At its conclusion she sat back in her chair with a comfortable sense of well-being. Gillman, after asking her permission, lighted a cigar.

"I do hope you will be able to make yourself comfortable for the night," he began. "My wife—"

"Where's Hannah?" a harsh, croaking voice interrupted him. "Hannah wants Polly—poor Hannah! Stop your snivelling now!" with a startling change of tone.

Cynthia started to her feet. With something like an imprecation Gillman faced round. Following the direction of his eyes, the girl burst out laughing. A large grey parrot, sitting on his perch, was regarding them with its head on one side.

"Poor Hannah!" it repeated in a tone of melancholy.

"That confounded bird!" Gillman said and threw a cloth over the cage. "I beg your pardon," he went on, turning to Cynthia, "but I dislike parrots above all things, and this one gets on my nerves sometimes. It is a great pet of my wife's, however, so I have to put up with it."

With an attempt at a laugh he caught up one of the dishes from the table, and Cynthia heard him go down the passage.

He did not come back, and for a while the girl sat silent, scarcely thinking, merely giving herself up to the physical enjoyment of being fed and warmed.

Presently, however, she arose, and, telling herself that in the disorganized state of her cousin's household it was plainly her duty not to sit idle, she began to put back some of the things which had obviously been taken from the sideboard shelves. Looking at the cold beef, then remembering that Gillman had taken the other dish down the passage, she determined on a journey of discovery to find the pantry.

The passage was unlighted, but she managed to find her way, and with the heavy dish in her hand she stopped by the door before which she had fallen and tried the handle. It turned, but the door did not open. At the same moment a hand caught her arm suddenly from behind.

"What are you doing here?" It was Gillman's voice, but so changed and harsh that for a moment she did not recognize it. "What do you want?" he said, as he swung her round.

Even by that uncertain light Cynthia could see that his face was paling; she could feel that he was shaking from head to foot under the influence of some strong emotion.

She looked at him in amazement as she held out the dish.

"I only wanted to find the pantry; I was clearing the things away."

With a curious sound, half relief, half annoyance, Gillman's hand relaxed its hold and dropped by his side.

"I—I beg your pardon," he stammered. "I think my wits are wool-gathering to-night. I did not realize it was you. The pantry is down there," pointing to a door farther down. "This"—with a forced laugh—"is my private study, and contains the safe where most of our valuables are kept. It is never left unlocked."

"I see!" said Cynthia slowly.

She was trembling a little, the roughness of his tone had startled her; her lip quivered.

With scant ceremony Gillman took the dish from her unresisting hands.

"I will put this away; you go back to the fire."

"I think I will go to bed!" Cynthia said meekly. All the strength, partly born of excitement, which had upheld her through the journey, and through the strangeness of her arrival, had deserted her now, and her knees shook. She rested one hand on the wainscoting of the wall behind her.

"Do!" said Gillman curtly. "You know your way, do you not? Good night!"

His tone had all the force of a dismissal, and Cynthia's colour rose. As she passed through the sitting-room she heard the parrot's voice, husky but unabashed, in the darkness in which it had been plunged:

"Stop your snivelling now; I won't have it! Poor Polly—poor Polly wants Hannah!"

Chapter Three

"One! Two! Three!" The clock on the landing was striking the hour. Cynthia turned over on her bed with a restless sigh.

Though she was so tired when she came to her room that it was as much as she could do to undress herself and creep into bed, she yet found it impossible to sleep. As soon as she laid her head upon the pillow her mind became a prey to a thousand haunting fancies; and if for a moment her eyes closed she would start nervously and spring up in bed, a cold perspiration breaking out upon her forehead. In vain she told herself that she was nervous and foolish, that she was imagining she heard the sound of doors opening and shutting at the bottom of the house, the creaking of the boards in the passage outside her bedroom. She found herself unable to control her wandering thoughts and fancies, and she lay turning about from side to side in the great bed, the very size of which increased her sense of desolation.

As the clock struck she heard another sound, outside the house this time, to her great relief; it was distant and muffled, but she could not mistake it, so she sat up in bed and listened. The moon had risen now and was flooding the room with its pale radiance. Through the open window there came again the sound that had roused her. Some one was digging outside, putting out spadefuls of earth with a furtive deliberation that manifested a desire for secrecy. Cynthia sat still, her arms round her knees under the bed-clothes, her ears strained to the utmost to listen. The digging seemed to her to go on for an interminable time. At length, her courage returning with the moonlight, she sprang out of bed and hurried to the window. When she threw up the blind and peered out she could see no one outside, no sign of any living creature. But as she waited, wondering, a dog howled—a loud, long-drawn-out howl; the digging stopped, but the howling went on intermittently. Cynthia shuddered as she remembered that a dog's howling in the night is said to presage death, and she recollected her Cousin Hannah's illness.

As she waited, shivering by the window, she distinctly caught the sound of the outer door being opened; there was a joyous bark, a scamper upstairs, and then Cynthia heard a scratching and whining at a door level with hers down the passage. With a feeling of relief that here was something that she could understand she put on a warm dressing-gown and opened the door. By the bright moonlight that was streaming in through the uncurtained windows of the passage she could see the wire-haired terrier whom she had heard howling on her arrival; he was standing up on his hind legs now and pawing at a closed door, uttering piteous little whines at intervals. Seeing him, Cynthia's fears left her. She guessed that it was her cousin's door and that the poor little dog wanted to get to its mistress; but, fearful that it would disturb Lady Hannah, the girl went down the passage softly and tried to coax the dog away. Her efforts were without avail, however, and, fearful of being discovered, she had to give up the idea and return to her room. All was apparently quiet outside now. She crossed to the open window and stood looking at the calm beauty of the scene before her and drinking in the cool, fresh, night air. She let the breeze play over her heated cheeks; then, resolving to go back to bed and make one more attempt to sleep, she was turning away, when a movement attracted her attention, and, for a moment, she paused.

From out the shadows and the darkness, across the little patch of grass that lay in front of the window, a curious figure was moving carefully, avoiding the moonlight, it seemed to Cynthia, and keeping as much as might be in the shade. The girl watched it, held by a curious species of fascination, her face pressed against the window frame. Was it man or beast? she wondered, as she strained her eyes upon the curious irregular outline, upon the halting, jerky progression. One moment she felt certain it was a man, then her point of view changed as it moved onward and she doubted again. Then, just before it passed out of range of vision, it came for a moment into the light, and Cynthia saw that it was a man pushing something before him—a wheel-barrow, she fancied, piled high apparently with some heavy freight that he found a difficulty in moving.

She gazed at him in amazement, wondering who he could be and what he could possibly be doing, but in another moment he had disappeared among the trees, and she could see no more. Shivering and wide-eyed she crept back into bed. She had come to a house of mystery, it seemed to her, and she lay wondering what could possibly induce her cousin to remain, and what the man outside was doing, until by degrees her thoughts wandered and her eyes drooped, and she finally fell asleep.

When she awoke the sunshine was pouring into the room, the birds were singing in the trees outside. Everything looked bright and cheerful and commonplace. As she sprang out of bed, her fears of the night before looked foolish and unfounded, and she told herself that she had given way to foolish, silly fancies. She looked at her watch; the time was half-past eight, and she could hear that some one was stirring downstairs. With all dispatch she splashed in and out of the cold bath that stood behind a screen in the corner of the room.

As she was twisting up her curly chestnut hair she heard a step on the stairs, followed by a heavy bump outside her door, and Gillman's voice said:

"I have brought your trunk up; I thought you might want it. You can open it here, and after breakfast I will carry it into your room. I suppose it is yours? I see the name is Hammond on its label, not Densham."

"Oh, yes, it is all right! I put 'Hammond' because there were reasons; I must explain to Cousin Hannah. Thank you!" Cynthia stammered confusedly. "I can get at it beautifully there. Thank you very much, Mr Gillman!"

She waited until she heard him go downstairs, then glancing disgustedly at the brown cloth coat and skirt which she had worn the night before, and which looked travel-stained and dusty, she opened the box and brought out a blue serge skirt with a white silk jumper. It would be the very thing for the country, she decided. An empty breakfast tray stood on a bracket on the landing; evidently her cousin had had her breakfast, she thought as she ran downstairs.

The door of the room in which she had had her tea the preceding evening stood open; the interior looked pleasant and home-like; the sun was shining through the big bay window and gleaming on the pewter on the sideboard and the old copper pans on the wall. Spotless damask cloth was on the table, and a dainty tea equipage for two stood at one end; dishes of fresh butter and golden honey looked very tempting, and the freshly made toast and pale brown eggs in their snowy stand stood close by. Cynthia suddenly felt that she was intensely hungry. As she went towards the table Gillman came in at the opposite door.

"Ah, there you are!" he said heartily. "How do you feel this morning? Did you sleep well?"

"I don't think one ever goes to sleep very soon in a strange bed at first," Cynthia said evasively. "But I slept very soundly when I did get off."

"Ah, that was right!" The man's tone was light, but he glanced keenly at the girl's face as he placed a chair for her. "You were quite comfortable?" carefully supplying her wants. "I was a little afraid that I might have disturbed you. I found out quite late last night that there was something wrong with the potatoes—they were heating. I do not know whether you are aware that in this part of the country, at all events, we pack our potatoes in mounds. I had the pleasant task of opening two or three last night, otherwise they would have been ruined. I stupidly left the door ajar too, and Spot got in and disturbed his mistress."

"Oh, how tiresome!" Cynthia responded vaguely as she busied herself with the tea-urn. Her heart felt considerably lighter; she had tried to persuade herself that her fancy had exaggerated the incident of the preceding night, but the impression left on her mind had been a disagreeable one. Yet the explanation was so simple. "Sugar, Mr Gillman?"

"No, thanks." Gillman reached out and took the cup from her hand. "Your cousin does not seem so well this morning," he went on, balancing his spoon on the edge of his cup. "She has had a letter from her lawyers too, and that always upsets her."

Cynthia peeped out from behind her barricade of urn and spirit-lamp.

"I do hope she will be able to see me this morning!" she said, with real dismay in her tones. "I want to consult her, to ask her advice."

Gillman shook his head.

"I am afraid it will be impossible at present. She bade me give you her love, and say how sorry she was to have summoned you here on a wild-goose chase, and that she hoped later on, when she is stronger, you will pay us a longer visit."

Cynthia looked at him in open amazement.

"Does that mean that she wants me to go to-day, and without seeing her? Oh, Mr Gillman, that is impossible!"

A momentary expression of impatience crossed the man's face, and his thin, muscular hand made a sudden involuntary movement. Glancing at it, Cynthia saw that the brown skin was tense, that the knuckle shone white and strained.

"I hardly know what to say," he said with some obvious embarrassment. "You see for yourself that we are scarcely in a state to receive visitors and my wife has had a letter from Sybil Hammond, who will be here at midday. I am afraid two visitors—"

Cynthia dropped her egg-spoon.

"I—I don't know what to do, Mr Gillman," she confessed, her face crimsoning. "Cousin Hannah told me to come to her, and—and I have nowhere else to go. I thought at least I could stay here until I could obtain some sort of a situation."

Gillman looked almost discomposed.

"I did not quite realize the situation, neither, I fancy, did my wife; but I do not see how it is to be managed. Truth to tell, your cousin seemed fully determined on having Sybil Hammond to stay with her now, and I do not think that we could manage—" He stopped short and stared absently before him, his fingers now drumming idly on the table-cloth.

Cynthia with difficulty repressed her tears.

"Well, if it is out of the question I must put up with it," she said forlornly. "I—I think I might be able to teach little children. I wonder whether Cousin Hannah would allow me to give her name as a reference?"

Gillman looked slightly bewildered.

"Certainly she would, but I don't understand."

"No!" Cynthia said with a little catch in her voice. "I know you do not. I could have explained to Cousin Hannah; but since she does not want even to see me, perhaps I had better not bother her with my affairs. I dare say, after all, Bolt & Barsly would let me refer to them."

There was a vague, intangible change in Gillman's expression. For a minute or two he did not speak, but watched the girl's down-cast face in silence; then he said slowly:

"Ah, Bolt & Barsly! They are your solicitors as well as your cousin's?"

"I suppose they are the solicitors for the family," Cynthia assented. "I do not know whether they will be able to do much for me, but at least I can try."

"Do you mean that when you leave here you have no home to go to—that you are completely alone in the world?" Gillman questioned quickly, his restless fingers tugging mercilessly at his moustache.

Cynthia bowed her head.

"That makes no difference. Cousin Hannah asked me to come; I thought she wanted me. Now that I find that she does not"—gulping down a sob—"I must go away and try to find something else."

"Oh, this alters matters considerably!" Gillman said in a brisk, matter-of-fact tone as he rose from the table. "Naturally your cousin is the proper person for you to appeal to in the circumstances. I will go and explain things to her again, if you will excuse me for a few minutes."

Mindful of her experience of the night before, Cynthia made no attempt to assist in clearing away the breakfast things; it was quite evident, she thought, that her cousin's husband liked to do his work himself, and was rather inclined to resent any offer of help.

Her mind went back to her own affairs now. The outlook was anything but a bright one, and her face grew very melancholy. Her income was so infinitesimal that it would barely provide her with pocket-money, and in the few weeks that had elapsed between her mother's death and Lord Letchingham's proposal she had found that the lot of a penniless girl living on sufferance with relatives is neither an easy nor a pleasant one.

Even to herself she had never acknowledged until to-day how important that fact had been in bringing about her marriage. In present circumstances she knew that she could not return to the Fearons', that they would hasten to disclaim any connexion with her actions and to acquaint Lord Letchingham with her whereabouts. No! The only thing she could think of was to do as she said, and binding her solicitors to secrecy try to obtain a situation through them. The prospect was scarcely an attractive one, and she had counted so surely on her Cousin Hannah's help and counsel; she had felt so certain of her welcome. Tears of disappointment rose to her eyes.

She was wiping them away when Gillman opened the door. He walked over to the fire-place without affecting to notice her emotion.

"I have been talking things over with my wife," he began, "and now that she understands how you are situated she is distinctly of opinion that you must stay here for the present at any rate, until she feels strong enough to go into the whole question and discuss it with you. You and Sybil will be companions for one another."

Cynthia dried her eyes.

"It is very good of Cousin Hannah; but if I am no use to her I do not know that I ought to take advantage of her kindness."

"Oh, nonsense!" Gillman interrupted. "We shall be only too pleased to have you. My wife is scarcely well enough to see you this morning; still, perhaps, later in the day. However, now that is settled; and I want to know whether you have made any plans for to-day, because my wife suggests that if you have not, you should come with me to meet Sybil. Her train is due at Glastwick at a quarter to two. What do you say? We could take a picnic luncheon with us."

"I shall be delighted!" Cynthia said in a doubtful tone. "But surely we could not both leave Cousin Hannah?"

"Oh, Mrs Knowles will see to her," Gillman said easily. "She is a worthy woman; and my wife likes her. That is settled, then. I shall be ready to start in an hour, for it is a long drive."

Chapter Four

"ARE you ready, Cynthia?" It was Gillman's voice.

Cynthia raised herself from the bank, where, hidden among the glossy leaves, she had found a few late sweet-smelling violets. Her cheeks flushed. She was inclined to resent the free use of her Christian name; but Gillman, as he leaned down from his spruce dog-cart, looked so smiling and debonair, and so unconscious of his offence, that her displeasure melted away.

She walked down to him quickly.

"Surely it is earlier than you said you would start?"

Gillman flicked his whip carelessly.

"A trifle perhaps; but Mrs Knowles has arrived, and it is well to be in good time—the road to Glastwick is a rough one."

"It is indeed!" Cynthia agreed, with a rueful recollection of the previous night's joltings.

She climbed into the dog-cart beside him and submitted to have the rug carefully wrapped round her. The road was, as she had surmised the night before, little more than a winding track across the moorland, but the dog-cart was better provided with springs than had been the case with her conveyance of the previous evening, and she was able to admire the wonderful blue haze over the distant hill as she gazed round her at the great gorse-covered expanse.

Gillman could make himself an amusing companion too, she found, and some of the astonishment which she had felt at her cousin's infatuation for him died away as she listened to his stories of foreign travel and life in the other hemisphere. Suddenly he stopped short and pulled up.

"Something wrong with the mare, I am afraid; she is going lame."

He got out and went round. After lifting up one of the front legs and subjecting the hoof to a close scrutiny he gave vent to a low whistle of consternation.

"The shoe is loose, I must have this seen to or she will never be able to manage the journey back."

"I am sure she will not," Cynthia agreed, with conviction.

Gillman looked round in perplexity, then his face lighted up.

"After all, things might be worse; there is a blacksmith's over there on the other side of those rocks; and he will soon be able to put the shoe right, but it may take some time, and we must be within a mile of Glastwick now. I wonder whether you would mind walking on while I go over to the smith's? I shall probably overtake you long before you get to the station, but if I should be delayed will you go on and meet Sybil?"

Cynthia smiled.

"With pleasure," she said. "The only drawback to the plan is that I should not know her if I saw her."

"Oh, I do not think that you will have any difficulty," Gillman went on as he helped her down. "There are not many passengers and I think you will easily recognize Sybil from her likeness to my wife. She is small and fair like all the Hammonds."

"Oh, well, I will do my best; it will not be very serious if I do speak to the wrong person!" Cynthia said, and laughed. "Then we are to wait till you come, I suppose?"

"Please!" Gillman drew the reins over his arm. "You can't make a mistake in the road; just bear to the right when the path divides, that is all. I will be as quick as I can."

Cynthia watched him a moment as he led his horse over the rough, uneven ground; then she set off with a quick springy step. Her limbs felt cramped after the drive, and she thoroughly enjoyed the exercise and the exhilaration and the sense of freedom. The novel character of the scenery too engrossed her attention.

She found some strange fascination in its very austerity, in the bare rugged rocks that rose in heavy, irregular masses, in the great firs that stood here and there in solitary grandeur outlined against the clear northern blue of the sky; but after a time she began to think that it was strange that she saw no sign of nearing Glastwick. She felt that she must have walked more than the mile spoken of by Gillman, and it seemed to her that the country grew wilder and less cultivated. She walked a little more slowly, looking behind her to see if the dog-cart was in sight. She was, so far as could be seen, the only living person on the moor, however, and she began to feel nervous and frightened. She was half inclined to turn back, but after pausing and glancing round she told herself that she had probably under-estimated the distance she had walked, and that very soon she would see Glastwick Station before her. So she set off at a good pace once more.

After plodding on, it seemed to her for nearly another hour, she was obliged to stop and confess herself beaten. It was perfectly evident that Gillman had omitted some vital particular, or that she herself had mistaken his directions. She looked round now, in something like despair; to add to her difficulty she was by no means sure that she could find her way back to the spot where she had left Gillman. There were tracks across the moor in several directions, and, though as she had been directed she had borne carefully to the right, looking back all the paths seemed very much alike.

After scanning the landscape for some time she was relieved to see a thin blue column of smoke rising in the distance. She hurried along the path in its direction with all possible speed, and was presently rewarded by seeing before her a small ivy-covered cottage. In the pretty rustic porch an elderly woman sat busied with her needlework. A man was working in the garden.

Cynthia unlatched the gate.

"Could you tell me the nearest way to Glastwick?"

At the sound of her clear tones the man stuck his spade in the ground and looked up.

As he was about to speak the woman in the porch interposed.

"Glastwick? Why, you are a good four miles away, miss; and you look ready to drop now! Dear, dear!"

"Four miles?" Cynthia echoed blankly. "I—I must have been going in the wrong direction altogether! What in the world am I to do now? I do not believe I could walk there, and Mr Gillman will think I am lost and will not know where to come and look for me."

The woman's face stiffened.

"I beg your pardon, miss. Is it Mr Gillman of Greylands, you mean?"

"Yes, I am staying there," Cynthia said helplessly. "I was driving into Glastwick with Mr Gillman when the horse fell lame. He sent me on to meet some one at the station while he went to the blacksmith's, and I—well, I suppose I have lost my way."

The man had been resting one foot on his spade; he turned to her now.

"The blacksmith's on the Quesstrand side that might be. If you had turned to the left where the roads divided, and then kept straight on, you could not have missed Glastwick."

"To the left?" Cynthia repeated. "Why, I understood Mr Gillman—I mean I am sure he told me the right."

"That is where the mistake was made."

Looking at the speaker Cynthia was conscious of a strange feeling of familiarity, yet, glance back as she would, she could not place her memory of those dark, rugged features, those deep-set grey eyes.

"Well," she said forlornly, "I suppose there is nothing for it but to turn back, then. Probably Mr Gillman will be waiting for me at Glastwick."

The man took off his tweed cap and apparently gazed with deep interest in the lining. Cynthia glanced at him absently; he had a well-shaped head, she decided, and she liked the kink in his close-cropped dark hair. The voice, too, was deep and pleasant, and both it and his manner were those of a gentleman.

"You are not more than a mile and a half from Greylands itself now," he went on after a pause. "I fancy the better plan would be to go back and send some one to apprise Mr Gillman of your safety. Probably you would miss him if you tried to go back to Glastwick now."

Cynthia hesitated.

"I don't know what to do! Yes, perhaps what you suggest is best. I do not believe I am physically capable of a four-miles' walk. If you could tell me the most direct way to Greylands—"

"You keep straight on this path here until you come to the outlaws' Fen, then you turn; but the nearest way is not particularly easy to find. If you will allow me I will walk with you until you can see Greylands in the distance. Then you cannot make a mistake."

Cynthia looked dubious.

"You are very kind, but I could not think of troubling you."

"It is no trouble at all," picking up the spade and straightening himself. "As a matter of fact I have to go that way some time to-day."

"The young lady looks fair worn-out, though." The woman had come down the path and stood looking at Cynthia with an unusual amount of interest, or so the girl fancied. "If you could let me get you a cup of tea before you start, miss?"

"Thank you very much, but I must not stay; I am anxious to get back to Greylands as soon as possible. Mr Gillman may be getting alarmed about me. But if I might ask for a glass of water?"

"Or milk?" the woman suggested. She hurried into the cottage, and presently returned with a glass and jug of milk on a tray and an appetizing-looking cake. She cut a generous slice. "Now you will try and eat a bit, miss; it will put some strength into you."

Cynthia laughed, but the walk had given her a genuine appetite, and she felt very grateful for the refreshment and the rest as she took a seat for a moment in the little porch.

Her hostess looked at her.

"Lady Hannah does not enjoy good health now, I hear, miss?"

"I am afraid not," Cynthia assented, munching away at her cake.

"Nothing serious, I hope, miss?" There was a sort of subdued eagerness in the tone that grated upon Cynthia; quite evidently, she thought, the curious household at Greylands had excited comment even in this out-of-the-way spot.

"I hope not," she said gravely in a repressive tone.

At this juncture the man, who had gone into the house, reappeared. He had thrown off the jacket in which he had been working and now wore a Norfolk shooting-coat of the same texture as his knickerbockers and a tweed cap drawn down over his forehead.

Cynthia hastily finished her cake and milk and stood up, ready to start.

"You are very good and if you are sure I am not taking you out of your way—"

"Quite sure," he remarked laconically.

Cynthia turned to the woman. For a moment she hesitated, wondering whether she ought to offer any payment, but something in the kindly, wrinkled face seemed to forbid the thought, and she held out her hand with pretty friendly courtesy.

"Good-bye, and thank you so much."

"Good-bye, miss!" The woman paused in obvious embarrassment for a moment, then she went on, speaking in a nervous, jerky fashion: "If you would call again any time you are passing, miss, I should think it kindly. I am often very lonesome; and I haven't got used to these parts yet."

There was an underlying eagerness beneath the words that made an unpleasant impression upon Cynthia.

"Thank you very much!" she responded, her manner perceptibly colder. "I do not know how long I am staying with my cousin, and I expect during her illness my time will be very much occupied; but it is extremely kind of you to ask me."

The man held the gate open for her, and, looking at his stalwart broad shoulders and figure, Cynthia was struck anew with that haunting sense of familiarity.

"We are not so far from Greylands as you would imagine," he said as he joined her. "It lies on the other side of that pinewood."

A little breeze was rising now; it whistled through the branches of the firs and played around the little curls that peeped from the brim of Cynthia's hat. The girl drew a little breath of relief as they skirted the wood and she caught sight of the chimneys of Greylands in the distance.

Her companion looked at her compassionately.

"You must be tired out; but you will soon be there now, if you can only keep up a little longer."

"Oh, yes, I shall do very well!" Cynthia asserted bravely as she plodded along at his side.

She was finding that the London-made shoes she was wearing were by no means adapted to the rough moorland walking, and she inwardly resolved to provide herself with some stout country boots as soon as possible.

The man soon accommodated himself to her pace, but as he strolled along by her side he did not seem to be very communicative. For the most part he kept his eyes fixed straight in front of him in a dreamy, contemplative fashion, with his dark level brows drawn together in a frown, as though he were absorbed in some knotty problem. Cynthia wondered who he was and in what relation he stood to the woman in the cottage. He scarcely looked like her son, she fancied; and she began to speculate as to what could be the reason that brought the pair to settle down at that lonely cottage on the moor.

She had not arrived at any probable explanation, when he broke the silence.

"I hope you were not shaken to pieces in that cart yesterday?"

Startled, she looked at him in surprise.

"Why, how did you know?"

The stern lines of his face relaxed as he glanced at her astonished face.

"I was at the station when you arrived."

"Why, yes!" Cynthia broke into a laugh. "I remember now. You were talking to that station-master? I thought I recollected your face; but I could not recall where I had seen it. It has been puzzling me."

"Has it?" He gave her a quick glance, which Cynthia, absorbed in her discovery, did not note. "I gathered that you did not expect to find Lady Hannah such an invalid as she apparently is?"

"No, I did not," Cynthia said honestly. "You see, I had heard from her so short a time before. She asked me to come and see her; she must have written just before—"

"Before?" he repeated, turning to her. There was something compelling in his glance.

"Before her attack," Cynthia finished. "She is suffering from some sort of paralysis, you know."

"I did not know." His tone was one of shocked concern. "When?"

Cynthia suddenly awoke to the fact that she was discussing her cousin's intimate affairs with a perfect stranger.

"I do not know exactly," she replied coldly. "Oh, there is the gate of Greylands! I can find my way now, quite easily. Please do not let me take you any farther. Thank you very much!"

She stopped and made a half gesture to hold out her hand; the man paused also and looked curiously disconcerted.

"Yes, you cannot mistake the path now," he said brusquely. "Good afternoon!" And, raising his cap, he turned quickly on his heel.

Cynthia looked after him a moment in some surprise. His abrupt taking her at her word seemed to put her in the wrong; she felt as if she had been guilty of some discourtesy, and her cheeks burned.

However, it was impossible to alter matters now; he was striding back at a great rate; and even if Cynthia's dignity had permitted her to try to overtake him it would have been impossible in her present condition.

Her feet were becoming additionally painful; she positively limped as she opened the gate and made her way across the field and through the surrounding trees to Greylands.

As she approached the side-door she heard a quick, light step in the passage, and a girl with a dish in her hand came to meet her. The girl looked surprised.

"Did you want to see Mr Gillman?" she asked.

Cynthia guessed who the stranger must be.

"No; that is—at least I am staying here. I am Cynthia Densham, and you—"

With a little cry of joy the girl set the dish on the ground and sprang towards her.

"I am Sybil Hammond!" holding up one soft downy cheek to be kissed. "How glad Cousin Henry will be! He has been in such trouble about you. We could not imagine what had become of you, and he has just driven back to Glastwick to make further inquiries."

"Oh, I am sorry!" Cynthia said concernedly. "I thought I took the turning he told me, but it led me quite in the wrong direction, and I have walked all the way back. I am so tired!"

"You poor thing!" Sybil said caressingly as she made Cynthia lean on her. "Never mind, you shall have some tea, and then you will feel better. I am just going to take Spot his dinner, but that can wait. He is chained up to-day, because he will go and worry and scratch at Cousin Hannah's door. He is so devoted to her, poor beast! Now, Cynthia—I may call you Cynthia, may I not, for we are almost cousins?—you are just to sit in that chair and let me wait upon you."

Cynthia submitted with a good grace. After a long, tiring walk it was very pleasant to sit back and watch this pretty fair-haired creature flitting about, setting the table in order for the meal with deft and fairylike touches. Cynthia's nature was essentially a beauty-loving one. Something in the dainty finish of Sybil's appearance, as well as in the small features, attracted her almost irresistibly, and she found herself looking forward with new zest to her stay at Greylands.

As Sybil brought her tea and persuaded her to eat delicate sandwiches of her own making, Cynthia's eyes were dwelling admiringly on the other girl, upon the wealth of artistically-arranged golden hair, upon the pretty smiling mouth and large hazel eyes—eyes that could melt into anger or glow with a strange reflected light of green and opal and pale transparent blue.

At length Sybil poured out another cup of tea and caught up a tray.

"I am sure Cousin Hannah must be dying for her tea; she is always so thirsty!"

Cynthia raised herself eagerly.

"If you are going to see Cousin Hannah, may I come too?"

Sybil hesitated a moment.

"Not yet, I think. I don't fancy she feels quite equal to an interview this afternoon, poor thing!"

"You are going!"

The girl laughed and, stooping, laid a bird-like kiss on Cynthia's forehead.

"What—not jealous, Cynthia? You see Cousin Hannah is used to me; I stayed with her six months ago, and I am a great favourite of hers."

"I do not wonder at that!" The words came from Cynthia involuntarily.

There was another silvery ripple of laughter from Sybil as she vanished through the doorway.

"What a duck you are to say so! And Cousin Hannah means to see you some time this evening, Cynthia."

Chapter Five

CYNTHIA opened the door of her room.

Her trunk had been carried in and stood at the bottom of the bed; she felt for her keys and crossed over to it. The big wardrobe was empty save for the dress she had worn on her arrival. She took it out and looked at its unbrushed condition with disgust; it was bedraggled and dusty round the hem, and on the sleeve of the coat near the elbow there was a big dark mark. Cynthia looked at the latter with surprise as she got out her clothes-brush and applied it diligently.

"Where did that come from, I wonder?" she soliloquized. "Did I get it in the cart? Oh, no! It must have been when I fell in the passage. I know I came down heavily on my elbow."

Brushing had no effect on the mark, so Cynthia took her sponge and some soap, and presently had the satisfaction of seeing that it was yielding. Then spreading it out upon the back of a chair to dry, she turned to the washstand to rinse the sponge. As she squeezed out the water she was amazed to see that it was a dull red. For a moment she gazed at it in bewilderment, then she rolled back her sleeve and looked at her elbow in the glass. Its dainty dimpled prettiness was disfigured by a nasty black bruise, but the skin was unbroken. As she stood gazing into the glass, her colour faded, she shivered violently from head to foot; a fainting sensation against which she fought in vain came over her. She caught at the dressing-table with one hand and glanced round the room with eyes dilated by a sudden unreasoning fear.

"It was nothing," she said to herself, with white, stiffening lips. "Perhaps the dog hurt its paw scratching at the door—or something. Certainly it was nothing."

"Cynthia! Cynthia!" It was Sybil's voice; she was knocking.

Cynthia caught up the basin and emptied it into the toilet-pail before she answered.

Sybil glanced quickly round the room before she entered.

"Cousin Henry has come back, Cynthia. He was nearly frantic about you. He was glad to hear you were all right; he says he can't think how you came to mistake his directions. Is this all the luggage you have?" her bright inquisitive eyes turning to the open trunk. "You should see the heaps and heaps I've brought! Cousin Henry was so cross—I made him bring two trunks with us, much against his will, and the rest have to come on by the carrier, or some such antiquated person. Now" —putting her arm through Cynthia's and drawing her towards the door—"Cousin Henry wants to speak to you for a minute or two, just to make sure that you really are quite safe and not too much exhausted, and then I am going to fetch you for a chat with Cousin Hannah."

"Oh, will she really see me? I am so glad!" Cynthia's tone was one of great relief.

"Yes, she is quite anxious!" Sybil said as with arms entwined they descended the stairs. "But, oh, Cynthia, she is sadly changed since I saw her last. She is so helpless but"—dropping her voice to a whisper as she saw the open door into the dining-room—"I must not speak in this strain before Cousin Henry. He feels it all so terribly, and it is all so important that he should keep up for her sake. Now I shall leave you to your scolding!" And with an elfin laugh she pushed Cynthia forward and rushed back.

Gillman was standing by the fire-place, apparently reading a letter and balancing himself backwards and forwards on his toes.

He looked up as Cynthia entered; she went forward timidly.

"I am sorry to have given you so much trouble, Mr Gillman. I quite thought—"

"Oh, my dear child!" The genuine concern in his tone made Cynthia forgive the familiarity of the words. "I have been so worried about you. I shall never forgive myself; but I did think if you bore to the left when the roads divided you could not make a mistake."

His evident distress disarmed Cynthia's resentment. She smiled a little as she raised her eyes.

"You told me the right," she remarked.

Gillman looked thunderstruck.

"Surely I could not have been so stupid? Oh, it is impossible. You must have misunderstood me."

"I think not," Cynthia said positively. "I am certain you told me the right."

"Well, really"—with a gesture of despair Gillman ran his hands through his hair—"I believe the distress and worry I have had lately must be turning my brain. To think that I should have made such a mistake! How can I apologize to you?"

Cynthia nearly laughed at the tragic reproach in his tone.

"Oh, please say no more about it! It must have inconvenienced you far more than it did me. After all, I had a very pleasant walk and the air on the moor was delightful."

"You are very good to make excuses for me, but how did you find your way? That path is rather complicated."

"I called in to ask directions at a pretty, ivy-covered cottage, and a man who was working in the garden offered to guide me," replied Cynthia disingenuously.

"Oh, I know where you mean!" Cynthia fancied for a moment that Gillman did not look pleased. "The people have only just come there to live. Well, I am very glad that matters are no worse, and that you found a guide of a sort. Now, I am just going up to see how my wife is, and then, if she feels equal to it, I am going to let you in for half an hour."

He smiled down on her as he spoke, and then with a little nod left the room.

Cynthia nestled in her chair with a sigh of content; she slipped her feet out of her shoes and held them out to the warmth of the fire, they felt so sore and swollen. As she contemplated them ruefully she thought that life at Greylands had promised to become distinctly more attractive since Sybil's arrival. She was pleased too that she was going to see her Cousin Hannah; it seemed to her that when she was able to explain matters to her cousin and ask her advice the worst of her difficulties would have disappeared. The parrot's harsh voice broke across her meditations:

"Poor Hannah! Now stop that snivelling! Poor Hannah!"

Startled, Cynthia turned. With its head cocked rakishly on one side, the bird was surveying her with one beady, unwinking, black eye.

"Poor Hannah!" it repeated raucously. "Stop snivelling, will you?"

As the last word died away Gillman opened the door.

"Your cousin would like to see you, Cynthia," he said.

With a heightened colour the girl shuffled into her shoes. "Poor Hannah!" the parrot interjected, almost, as it seemed to Cynthia, with sarcastic emphasis. She laughed as she stood up, in spite of her obvious embarrassment.

"Polly seems to think that Cousin Hannah is to be pitied for having this interview forced upon her," she said lightly.

Gillman frowned.

"I shall kill that wretched bird before I have done with it, I know!" he said. "I hate parrots and this is a particularly disagreeable one."

He held the door open and Cynthia limped through.

"What is the matter?" he asked, looking at her. "Have you hurt yourself?"

"Only in going out in shoes not fitted for walking across the moor."

"My fault again!" Gillman said penitently. "I do not know what you can think of me."

He certainly was distinctly good-looking, the girl thought as he led the way to the door which, from Spot's scratching, Cynthia had previously concluded to be her cousin's. He paused before he opened the door and bent his head nearer hers.

"I shall not leave you more than half an hour to-night, and you must try to avoid exciting her as she is very weak."

"Certainly, I will be very careful," Cynthia promised.

He turned the handle.

"Well, Hannah," he said in a loud, resolutely cheerful voice, "here is Cynthia, very anxious to see you!"

The room was a large one, handsomely furnished; a large alcove at the farther end formed a sort of dressing-room, pretty shaded lamps stood on the mantelpiece, a bright fire burned in the fire-place; but Cynthia only had eyes for the quiet figure that lay propped up by pillows in the great, hearse-like looking bed that stood in the middle of the room. She went forward quickly.

"Dear Cousin Hannah, how glad I am to see you!" taking one of the stiffened, unresponsive hands in hers and chafing it as she bent over and pressed a warm kiss upon the woman's cheek.

"Cynthia!" Lady Hannah said faintly, in a low, thick voice. "You should have written—you should not have come like this. Sit down, child, and tell me what brings you here?"

Feeling chilled and thrown back upon herself, Cynthia took the chair that stood by the bed.

Gillman leaned against the heavy carved oaken posts at the bottom.

"I think I shall leave you two to have your talk out now," he said. "You must give Cynthia a better welcome than that, Hannah."

"Don't be away long!" the invalid implored, the whispering, husky tones suddenly becoming agitated. "I don't like to be left with a stranger without you, Henry."

"Cynthia is not a stranger, and I shall not be away long," Gillman answered soothingly as he moved to the door.

His wife twisted her head round.

"Lock the door, Henry, and take the key away. Yes! Yes! You must!" her manner threatening to become hysterical as Gillman hesitated. "I have told you that I will not be left with the door unlocked!"

Gillman shrugged his shoulders and glanced deprecatingly at Cynthia.

"She always will have it so, and it is not for long," he answered as he passed.

As she heard the key turned in the lock Lady Hannah gave a sigh of relief.

"That is better. I hate to think that the door is not fastened, that anybody—anything could get to me, and I could not do anything—could not move—that I should lie like a log " her voice dying away in a sob of terror.

Cynthia glanced compassionately at the limbs lying so straight and motionless beneath the bed-clothes.

"No one will come to you. Mr Gillman—we all—would take care of that."

"Um! I do not know about that." The invalid moved her head restlessly. "Should you have known me, Cynthia? Am I like what you expected?"

Cynthia hesitated. This quiet figure, in which the head seemed to be the only thing alive, was so sadly unlike the Cousin Hannah whom she could dimly remember as a brisk, active woman who carried her about and nursed her as a child. She glanced at the small aquiline features a little drawn on one side, at the grey hair that was brushed back in bands beneath a quaintly-fashioned black lace headdress, at the large tinted spectacles that shaded the eyes, and paused.

"Well?" Lady Hannah went on irritably. "I know I was not a helpless log in those days! You don't remember me?"

"Yes, I do a little," Cynthia said slowly, "and I have heard of you often."

"What have you heard?" The tone was abrupt, almost harsh.

Cynthia bent forward.

"Dear Cousin Hannah, principally of your kindness to your relatives, I think. That was what emboldened me to come to you when I was in trouble—that and your letter."

There was a moment's silence and then the invalid said slowly:

"Ah, my letter! I had almost forgotten it. I wrote it when I was feeling ill and lonely. Henry is very good to me, but when you are ill a man is not everything, and I wanted some of my own blood, so I wrote to you. You did not come, so I then sent for Sybil. What is your trouble, child? I think—I have a feeling that I ought to know, but my memory is bad, I forget everything now; I—I can't recall it."

Cynthia's head drooped.

"I—I don't think you have heard of it, Cousin; Hannah, but when you wrote to me you said you were going to give me a present. A great change was coming in my life. I was—"

"You were going to be married," the low, harsh voice finished. "It is coming back to me now, Cynthia. That is your trouble, child? Your engagement was broken off?"

"No!" said Cynthia in a dull, shamed voice. "It—it was not broken off!"

"What do you mean?" Lady Hannah's tone sounded hopelessly puzzled. "It was not broken off, and yet you are here!"

Cynthia's head sank lower and lower. "An hour after the ceremony I found that he—my husband—had deserted and betrayed my greatest friend. I"—she put up her hand to her throat—"could not bear it. I left him. Then I thought of your letter—it only reached me that morning—and I came here. You will not send me away—you will protect me!"

Lady Hannah drew a deep breath.

"I—I don't know what to say, Cynthia. I never thought of this. He will be looking for you—your husband—and if he finds you, what can I do? I am only a poor weak woman—" beginning to shake violently. "I don't think you ought to have come, Cynthia."

Cynthia stood up, her hands loosely linked before her; she looked very tall and slim in the flickering firelight.

"If this is how you feel about it, Cousin Hannah, I am sorry I did; but," faltering, "I was so lonely and so frightened of him—Lord Letchingham. Your letter was very kind, and I thought you really wanted me. Perhaps I ought to have applied to my solicitors in the first place. However, it is not too late to remedy my mistake. I will go back to-morrow."

"Do not be foolish, child," Lady Hannah said fretfully. "It is not that. I do want you; but it is such an extraordinary position. I never thought of anything like this. However, you will stay here, while I think what is best to be done. My husband tells me that your trunk was marked 'Hammond.' I think while you are here you had better keep to that name; it will at least make it more difficult for you to be recognized."

"There is no need—" Cynthia began, her voice sounding cold and steady; somehow she felt even her cousin's weakness left her untouched; she wished more heartily than ever she had not come to Greylands. "I—if I had put Densham on the box I should have been traced at once, and Hammond seemed the only name I could think of," she confessed.

"Yes, it is best. Let people think that you and Sybil are cousins. Oh"—with a queer sound between a moan and a sob the invalid slipped down among her pillows—"I feel ill!" she gasped. "Call Henry. I—I think I am dying. Henry, quick, quick!"

Cynthia seized the bell-rope that hung beside the bed and tugged at it violently. Then she poured some water in a tumbler and tried to raise the invalid.

"Dear Cousin Hannah!" she pleaded. "Do let me give you a little—"

Her cousin turned her head away.

"No! No! Not you—Henry!"

At this moment, to Cynthia's great relief, she heard Gillman's step in the passage. He threw the door open.

"You were ringing?" he said. "Is there anything the matter?"

"I am afraid Cousin Hannah is worse," Cynthia said desperately. "I—she will not let me do anything for her."

Gillman gave one look at his wife's face, then laid his hand on her arm.

"Come, this will not do, Hannah!" he said quietly. "You know the harm you may do if you over-excite yourself." Then he turned to Cynthia. "You had better go downstairs; she will become quieter alone with me."

Something in his tone forbade argument, and Cynthia obeyed in silence. She heard Gillman lock the door behind her and caught the echo of her cousin's voice; then she went slowly back to the dining-room.

There Sybil found her when, half an hour later, she ran downstairs.

"Cousin Hannah was rather tiresome to-night, was she not?" she questioned, perching herself on the arm of Cynthia's chair. "Now I suppose she will keep Cousin Henry with her for hours; nobody can manage her like him, and he is so wonderfully patient with her."

"Yes, he seems very kind," Cynthia acquiesced slowly. "He—he is very unlike what I expected."

Sybil bubbled into airy laughter as she patted the cheek next to her with one pink finger.

"Oh, you are a funny girl, Cynthia! I—really I shall begin to think you are quite deep."

Chapter Six

"Come for a walk this morning, Sybil?"

"Can't!" Sybil playfully shook the flour from her hands in Cynthia's face. "I am going to make a pudding for dinner. There! You didn't know I was so domesticated, did you?"

Cynthia looked at her dispassionately.

"I do not expect it will be much of a pudding! You had better come, Sybil."

Sybil pouted, as with pursed-up lips she measured out a portion of butter.

"Rude person. No, it is no use teasing, Cynthia. I am going to make a great culinary success to-day, and you will not persuade me to put it aside even to frivol with you."

"Well, if you are really determined—" With a shrug of her shoulders Cynthia resigned herself to the inevitable. She turned from the big, old-fashioned kitchen to the open door leading into the neglected garden beyond. Notwithstanding the tangled growth of grass, the moss upon the walks, it looked very pretty in the bright sunlight, she thought. Coaxed out by the warmth, here and there a brightly coloured tulip was peeping forth. At the edge of the long, narrow borders the blue forget-me-not and the hardy London Pride were beginning to raise their heads. Farther away, over the tall hedge, she caught a glimpse of the flowering cherry-trees in the orchard. She drew a long breath of the delicious fresh air. "I think it is much too lovely to stay indoors, even to cook. You are very tiresome, Sybil! I wonder"—as a loud howl from the distance reached her—"whether I might take Spot?"

"You will have to take him on the lead if you do," Sybil responded as, having secured all her ingredients, she began to mix them together with a vigour that spoke volumes for the strength of the muscle in her white, shapely arms. "There he is," she added, with a backward jerk of her head at the wall. "He will tear back to Cousin Hannah's room if you don't, and he does worry her so."

Cynthia took the lead down doubtfully.

"I don't suppose he would follow me without, but he won't like it much, poor little dog!"

She went slowly round the house to the out-buildings; as Spot saw her coming towards him his howling changed to noisy demonstrations of joy. He sprang on his hind legs and tried to lick her face;

it was with difficulty that she got the chain off and the lead fastened to the collar. When that was accomplished she found, too, that it was no easy matter to persuade him to accompany her; with might and main he tugged at the lead, trying to induce her to return to the house, and it was only by putting forth all her strength that she was able to force him in the opposite direction.

As, almost exhausted, she turned to close the garden-gate she found herself face to face with a stout, hard-featured woman who was looking down on Spot with a bland smile.

"Going to take the poor creature out for a walk, are you, miss?" she observed. "Well, I am sure it is real charity in a manner of saying, for he must feel very lonely, now my lady is laid up."

"My lady!" Cynthia repeated in surprise. "Oh"—with a flash of enlightenment—"you are Mrs Knowles, are you not?"

"Yes, miss. I hope the poor lady is better now?"

"I hope so," Cynthia said doubtfully. "Mr Gillman thinks she is."

Mrs Knowles raised her hands.

"Poor thing! I doubt she will never be herself again. Little I thought when I see'd her only last week as ever was walking in these fields with Spot there how soon she was to be took. As the saying is, one is took and the other left. Now, my poor mother—"

"Mrs Knowles," Cynthia interrupted, "you are making a mistake. Lady Hannah was not out last week. She was not well enough."

Mrs Knowles drew herself up with dignity.

"Which, if you know better than me what was on the spot, miss, I have no more to say. Monday in last week, it were. She were in this very meadow, with Spot jumping round her that pleased like; more by token that very day our Janet came back from London, so I couldn't make no mistake about it. "

"Oh, I thought Mr Gillman told me she had been ill a fortnight, but no doubt I was wrong," Cynthia said, looking puzzled.

"Which you were, miss, if you thought that," Mrs Knowles remarked. "Me, not being a person given to making mistakes, and always having a liking for me lady, and she for me, if I may say it without boasting, I was not likely to be out in my reckoning; but I see Mr Gillman looking out for me, so if you will excuse me, miss, I will wish you a pleasant walk."

She bustled through the gate and up the narrow path. Cynthia turned down the meadow, the unwilling Spot still dragging heavily at the lead.

In vain the girl coaxed and scolded; the dog could not be persuaded to enjoy the walk, and at length, her arms growing tired, she resolved to take him back and make a fresh start alone.

Now that her steps were turned homeward Spot became quieter, and Cynthia had more time for thought. Mrs Knowles had puzzled her a good deal; she knew that she had made no mistake. Gillman had certainly told her that her cousin's seizure had occurred a fortnight previously; yet in this case how would it have been possible for her to be walking in these fields only a week ago? There was evidently a discrepancy somewhere, and, notwithstanding the woman's positive assertion, Cynthia could only suppose that she had made a mistake of a week.

By and by the girl's thoughts wandered off to her own affairs; what was Lord Letchingham doing, she wondered, with an irrepressible shudder as she recalled the scene in the train. That he would be searching for her she had little doubt, and though to the best of her belief she had successfully hidden her traces she feared it was impossible that her secret should remain for ever, and then she shrank like a frightened child from the thought of Lord Letchingham's wrath and its probable consequences.

As her mind became more wholly absorbed her hold on Spot grew insensibly slacker, and after passing through the gate into the garden, the dog, with one wild jerk, freed himself and started off as fast as his legs could carry him, not this time in the direction of the house, but into the belt of dark pine-trees which surrounded Greylands on all sides but one.

Roused from her reflections Cynthia ran after him, only to find her progress obstructed by a tangle of undergrowth and brambles.

As, her face flushed, with dishevelled hair and burrs clinging to her garments, she sprang on to an intersecting path she found herself face to face with Gillman, who was apparently strolling along with bent head and hands clasped behind him, buried in thought.

"What in the world are you doing here?" he inquired, his eyebrows drawn together in a forbidding scowl—a scowl that deepened as he listened to Cynthia's explanation. At its conclusion he muttered a fierce imprecation and hurried away in the direction in which Cynthia fancied the dog had gone.

The girl made her way to the house more slowly. As she opened the side-door she saw Gillman, with Spot, looking cowed and subdued, at his heels, emerge from the pine-grove.

He came up to her quickly; all the anger was gone from his face and he smiled at her openly.

"I beg your pardon," he began, with a little embarrassed laugh. "I am thoroughly ashamed of my little ebullition of temper, just now; but this fellow"—with a glance at Spot's down-dropped ears and drooping tail—"has a knack of upsetting any attempts of mine in the gardening line. I had just been moving some young oak saplings, and I knew that he would play havoc with them. It is very annoying to see one's work spoilt, you know," with a winning glance. "That must excuse my hasty departure, and the, I fear, unwarrantable words I used; but you will forgive me when I tell you that I was only just in time to prevent serious mischief—he was making straight for them."

"Naughty Spot!" said Cynthia, stooping down to pat him. "I can see you have had a scolding. I feel half inclined to give you one myself. It will be a good while before I take you out for a walk again, I can tell you."

"Now you are going to be fastened up in your kennel again," said Gillman grimly as the dog showed signs of desiring to bolt into the house. "No, you don't, old boy!"

"How devoted he is to his mistress!" Cynthia remarked as she watched him straining at the leash.

Gillman sighed, and said:

"She was just as fond of him when she was well, but now, in her helpless state, she is afraid that he might jump up on the bed, and I suppose, in her condition, it is quite natural."

"Ah, yes!" Cynthia said with a shiver. "It must be dreadful to be unable to move."

"Dreadful!" echoed Gillman as he strolled off in the direction of the stables, dragging the reluctant Spot in his wake, and Cynthia turned into the house. Sybil's voice greeted her from the dining-room.

"That is right, you are just in time! Is Cousin Henry there? Luncheon is ready, and I have; cooked it all myself. So there, miss!" with a dainty little pout.

Cynthia laughed as she ran upstairs to take off her coat and hat. When she came down again Gillman sat in his place at the table before a well-cooked joint.

"Did you really do that, Sybil?" Cynthia inquired incredulously.

"Every bit of it, except that Mrs Knowles watched the oven and that I had a little advice from Cousin Hannah," Sybil said demurely.

Gillman's brow darkened.

"Don't talk nonsense, Sybil!" he reproved sharply. "Your cousin knows nothing about cooking as you are perfectly aware."

The girl's face clouded over at the harsh words, and her pretty full lips pouted. After a minute or two she smiled across at Cynthia.

"I have had interruptions too. A man, quite a personable-looking man, has been asking questions—all sorts of questions."

Chapter Seven

DARK though it was, the first faint streaks of dawn were dimly visible through the big, uncurtained window. Cynthia, gathering the bedclothes around her, sat up in bed and listened, her great brown eyes searching the darkness, terrified.

She had awakened from a dream that she was in a dungeon; that two men, one of whom bore a strong resemblance to Gillman, were attempting to chain her down; that she was resisting them with might and main; she heard the clanking of the chains as they forced her back, and she realized her powerlessness in their hands. Then, with the very violence of her struggles to free herself, she awoke, great beads of perspiration standing on her brow—awoke to find that the sounds of jingling chains was real at any rate. Outside her door in the passage she could hear it plainly enough.

She made a quick involuntary movement to cover her ears with the blanket, but at the same moment there was a low whine and the sound of scurrying feet, and with a great sob of relief Cynthia arrived at the conclusion that Spot must have broken loose from his captivity, and, having managed to get into the house by some means, was endeavouring to make his way to his much-loved mistress. A loud scratching and whining told unmistakably that she was right.

She sprang out of bed and opened the door.

"Spot!" she called softly. "Spot!"

The dog, however, paid no heed to her; all his attention was given to trying to get into Lady Hannah's room.

As she stood there on the landing, expecting every moment to see Gillman appear, Cynthia found, by the rush of air coming up the staircase, that the door in the hall, which was so seldom used, must be standing open. Shivering, she drew back, and at the same moment Spot's attack upon the door became more violent and noisy.

Knowing how bad disturbance must be for the invalid Cynthia ventured out, and catching the end of the chain that hung from his collar pulled him, despite his struggles, into her own room. Then, shutting the door, she tried to calm and pet him, but in vain; he would do nothing but sit and howl tragically. Cynthia was at her wits' end; to keep him there or to let him go to her cousin's room appeared equally impossible.

After thinking for a time she hastily threw a warm shawl over her dressing-gown, and catching the short chain firmly in her hand dragged the reluctant Spot downstairs. The hall-door, as she had surmised, stood open; she pushed Spot through, and with some difficulty closed it after him, and then she hurried back to her own room. The silence in which the rest of the house was wrapped amazed her; apparently she was the only person whom Spot's clamour had even awakened. The fact of the open door, too, was distinctly disquieting; she wondered whether it was possible that Gillman, whose anxiety about locks and bolts always appeared to her a little excessive, had overlooked it, and then, in some way, it had blown open.

As she got back into bed, puzzling over the whole matter, she heard Spot howling distractedly round the house; gradually, though, the howling grew more plaintive, and appeared to be farther away. Then there was a sudden sharp yelp, and it ceased altogether.

Cynthia shivered and drew the coverings more closely over her as she nestled down among her pillows, and soon in a sound slumber she had forgotten Spot and his woes.

In the morning, however, he was recalled to her; at breakfast-time Gillman looked pale and worried.

"I cannot find Spot," he announced. "He must have broken out of his kennel, and goodness knows where he has got to. I only hope he will not worry the sheep. He has been after them before, and Farmer Spencer said he would make short work of him if he caught him at it again."

Cynthia had a guilty feeling that she would rather not explain her share in the night's transaction, and though Gillman glanced keenly at her reddening cheeks, and she had an uneasy suspicion that he thought she might have spoken if she would, she remained silent. After a while he turned to Sybil, with whom he was now apparently on the best of terms, and evidently did his best to shake off his depression and reply to her merry chatter in a similar strain.

When breakfast was over Cynthia rose.

"I wonder whether I might sit with Cousin Hannah this morning?" she remarked.

Gillman looked up from his letters.

"She asked for Sybil when I came down. Another time no doubt she will be glad to see you, but to-day—"

"Then I will wash up the breakfast things," Cynthia said, with decision.

Gillman laughed as he gathered up his papers.

"I am afraid I must thwart you again, for Mrs Knowles will be here in a few minutes, and she is a lady who dislikes any interference with her prerogatives."

He went out of the room as he spoke.

Cynthia crossed over to the window and stood idly drumming her fingers on the pane.

"I am sure I do not know what to do," she said disconsolately. Then, glancing out of the window, her expression grew more animated. "Sybil, I see something blue under the trees; I believe it is blue bells."

"I dare say it is," Sybil remarked listlessly. She had taken the opportunity afforded by Gillman's absence to transfer herself to his arm-chair, and was now lying back at full length idly watching the buckles on her smart little French shoes twinkling in the firelight. "Cousin Henry said they would be out in the fir-wood directly."

"Did he really?" Cynthia said animatedly. "Oh, I never thought of such a thing as blue bells in this cold north country! I must go and see them, Sybil. I have never seen a blue bell wood when the flowers were in bloom. I have never been in the country in the spring until this year."

"Well, it will give you an object for your walk," Sybil said languidly. "I wish I could come with you, but I suppose I must sit with Cousin Hannah." She said this reluctantly.

She had not moved, however, when Cynthia, dressed for walking, came downstairs.

"Good-bye!" Sybil called after her. "If you see any white bells mind you bring them back to me for good luck."

"No, I think I shall have to keep them myself—it is time my luck turned!" Cynthia said and laughed as she closed the door.

Outside the dewdrops were still lying on the grass, the scent of the cherry-blossom was sweet in the air; in the trees the birds were singing cheerily, glad with the promise of summer.

Standing on the short grass of the moorland, her head uplifted in the sunlight, Cynthia glanced back at Greylands; surrounded by the dark belt of trees it looked grim and sombre, strangely at variance with the life and colour around. Involuntarily the girl shivered. Then, reproaching herself for giving way to foolish fancies, she turned once more towards the woods.

There already, as Sybil had surmised, a thin line of blue was beginning to show beneath the firs, and as Cynthia unfastened the gate and let herself in, all alone though she was, she uttered a cry of delight. Though not yet fully out, the blue bells stretched like a peaceful undulating sea far away beneath the pines until they were lost in a vague, misty haze behind the dark stems. Their very immaturity only seemed to give them an added beauty, a more fairy-like charm.

She walked on down the narrow winding path carpeted with moss and withered pine-needles, feasting her eyes on the beauty around. At length the sight of a solitary white bell among the sea of blue reminded her of Sybil's parting words, and, treading carefully, she made her way to it. There appeared to be only one flower, which she gathered, and then, standing knee-deep amongst the drooping azure heads, she looked searchingly about her for more, and was presently rewarded by seeing another gleaming some distance away.

Going towards it she was surprised to find that she was close to the gate by which she had entered. She was wondering how this had happened when she saw a patch of white not very far from the palings that surrounded the wood; thinking that now she would be able to gather quite a big bunch for Sybil she hastened towards it.

Long before she came up to it she knew that it could not be white bells, that it was something more compact and solid. No; it was the coat of some white animal—a dog or a cat that was lying raised up on some little hillock. Half frightened she was about to turn back, when it struck her that there was something familiar about the black mark which she was now near enough to see upon the white back. She peered forward, then her face brightened.

"Spot!" she called softly. "Spot!"

There was no recognition of her voice, and she went forward.

"Spot! Spot!"

With a quick throb of fear she hurried up. Spot would never answer her more, she saw at a glance; he lay stretched cold and dead on the top of a molehill, a gaping wound in his head. With a cry Cynthia sank on her knees beside him.

"Oh, poor little Spot! Who can have done this?" she cried, great tears filling her eyes.

At the same moment she heard a deep masculine voice behind her.

"Is there something the matter? Can I do anything?"

Looking up through her tears Cynthia saw a tall man, who had apparently been walking along the narrow path that ran along the inside of the palings, and who was now crossing in her direction. She recognized her guide over the moors with a feeling of great relief.

"Some one has killed Spot," she said, her voice trembling. "Cousin Hannah's dog."

"What?" The man bent over the poor little dead dog for a moment in silence, then he raised his head. "Yes, there is nothing more to be done here," he said briefly. "How could this have happened? What brute could have done this—for you see the skull has been laid open. It looks like a blow from a pick or a spade, and the clayey soil is still sticking to the wound. That shows he was not killed here. He must have been brought, I should say, to the side of the wood and then thrown over."

"Poor little dog!" said Cynthia. "He was so fond of his mistress, and so anxious to get to her always. I cannot think how anyone could have had the heart to hurt him. Why, only last night—"

She stopped suddenly. With the mention of last night there had come the remembrance of the digging she had heard in the garden, of Spot's howling, of that sudden yelp! Surely, she said to herself, with rapidly whitening cheeks, it could not be then that Spot had died, and, if so, who had been working in the garden, who had struck that cruel blow? Repressing her sobs she struggled to her feet with an effort; the little bunch of white bells slipped from her hand and fell to the ground unheeded. "I—as you say, can do nothing here—I will go home and tell them."

She shuddered as she looked round; the sun was momentarily obscured behind a passing cloud; all the warmth and light had faded out of the landscape; even the blue bells looked grey and cold, she fancied.

"Thank you very much; you are very kind," she said forlornly. "I will go now!"

The man turned with her.

"May I walk as far as the gate with you? I see our ways are the same."

"If you choose," Cynthia said helplessly.

A gleam of pity shone in the man's deep-set eyes as he glanced at her downcast face, at her quivering lips, and the tears trembling on her long eyelashes.

"I am afraid Lady Hannah will feel the loss of her little favourite very much," he said abruptly.

"I am afraid she will," Cynthia assented, just glancing up at him from beneath her wet eyelashes. "Still, she has been rather afraid of having him near her in her present state, so—"

"How is she?"

Cynthia looked a little surprised at the sudden change in his tone.

"I think she looks rather better than I expected, but it is very sad to see her so helpless."

"Naturally it is." The man pulled his cap down over his eyes as the sun shone out again. "I had the pleasure of meeting her many years ago, when she was Lady Hannah Hammond," he stopped to explain with strained politeness. "She struck me as one of the people to whom a long period of absolute helplessness would be torture."

Cynthia forgot her trouble in her amazement.

"You knew my cousin? I had no idea—"

The man did not look at her as he spoke.

"It is years since I saw her. I think I had the misfortune to displease her, but I have been exceedingly sorry to hear of her illness. I called, partly on business and partly to inquire after her the other day, and I saw a young lady," glancing at her questioningly.

"Ah, yes!" said Cynthia, still puzzling over this curious announcement. "Sybil Hammond, another cousin. We are staying there together. I must tell my cousin I have seen you, Mr—"

"Heriot," he supplied, raising his cap, "James Heriot. If you will tell Lady Hannah how anxiously I ask for news of her and how glad I shall be to hear that she is better, I shall be infinitely obliged to you."

"Certainly I will!" Cynthia promised.

Arrived at the gate her companion opened it for her.

"It must be very pleasant for Lady Hannah to have you with her," he went on conversationally as she passed through.

Cynthia paused irresolutely.

"I do not think she cares much about having me," she replied truthfully. "She is fond of Sybil, I think, but at present she does not seem to be much interested in me."

Heriot's sombre eyes rested for a moment on the girl's fair face, upon the pretty flush coming and going beneath the transparent skin, upon the gleaming chestnut hair and long, upcurling lashes.

"I am surprised to hear that," he said curtly, yet with a directness that brought a wave of hot colour to Cynthia's face. She held out her hand.

"I am afraid I ought to go now. I must tell Mr Gillman about the dog. Did you know him too—Mr Gillman, I mean?"

Heriot bent low over the slim ungloved hand with a certain old-fashioned grace.

"No; Mr Gillman had not appeared on the scene when I last saw Lady Hannah. Do you know that you are very like what she must have been?"

Cynthia looked surprised.

"Do you really think so? I should not have guessed it. Now I can see a strong likeness in Sybil."

Heriot had closed the gate; he folded his arms on the top bar and looked at her meditatively.

"Sybil!" he repeated. "That is the young lady I saw at the house yesterday, isn't it? She does not remind me of Lady Hannah in the least. Now, you"—with another embarrassing long glance—"have almost the same contour of face, her expression even at times."

"Mr Heriot," Cynthia said suddenly, "you must have known Cousin Hannah very well. Where did you meet her?"

The man looked down and apparently watched her brown little fingers drumming on the wooden bar with interest.

"I had the pleasure of meeting Lady Hannah Hammond on several occasions," he replied after a pause. "The last time, if I remember rightly, was in Brussels."

"Oh, Brussels!" Cynthia repeated. "It was there she met Mr Gillman; but you do not know him, you say? I wonder whether you knew Sir Donald Farquhar?"

"Oh, yes, I knew him!" Heriot said but did not look up.

"Did you really?" Cynthia asked excitedly. "What did you think of him? What was he like? Did you know him very well?"

Heriot took his arms from the gate and stuck his hands in the wide, loose pockets of his shooting coat.

"I suppose I knew him fairly well. He was not much to look at. I did not think much of him," he answered, replying to her questions categorically. "I fancy he was a bit of a fool," he added, as the result, apparently, of a further contemplation of the subject.

"Oh!" Cynthia said disappointedly. "He does not sound very interesting."

"He is not," Heriot acquiesced. "I am awfully sorry about the dog, Miss Hammond. If you think Lady Hannah would like to have him buried in the garden anywhere—some people do, you know—I would bring him up to the house for you."

"Thank you very much!" Cynthia looked doubtful. "I don't know whether Mr Gillman will think Cousin Hannah ought to know. I must ask him; but in that case I am sure he would not wish to trouble you, he would send down for it."

The man glanced at her quickly.

"It would be no trouble. I have nothing much to do with my time at present, and I am often about here."

"Oh!" Although conscious of the studied indifference of his tone, Cynthia's colour deepened, and with a little gesture of irritation at her own stupidity she turned away.

"You are very kind; I will tell Mr Gillman."

She walked rapidly towards the gate, the wild broom and the gorse brushing against her skirts as she passed; the yellow kingcups gleamed golden in the sunlight at the farther edge of the little tarn lying blue and silent in the distance with pale meadow-sweet standing sentinel around it. At another time Cynthia would have revelled in the beauties of the scene, but to-day she felt worried and fretted and out of harmony; she was mentally upbraiding herself for her stupidity as she turned in at the garden gate.

Her unfortunate habit of colouring was a continual annoyance to her; and to-day, she told herself, she had behaved like the veriest schoolgirl. Heriot's kindness was evidently prompted by his friendly feeling towards Lady Hannah; her blushes must have made him set her down as foolish in the extreme. She opened the outer door quietly, fearing to disturb the invalid; as she walked down the passage she caught the echo of Gillman's voice—

"Yes, it is an awkward situation—one that shall come to an end as soon as possible, I promise you that; but in the meantime you will put up with it, you will do your best for my sake, Sybil?"

"Oh, there you are!" Cynthia said quickly. "Mr Gillman, such a dreadful thing has happened!"

The dining-room door was open, Gillman and Sybil were standing by the mantelpiece; at the sound of Cynthia's voice they moved apart. Sybil came to meet her.

"A dreadful thing? What do you mean, Cynthia?"

"Poor Spot is dead—he has been killed! He is lying in the pinewood," the girl replied breathlessly.

"Spot dead! Nonsense! You have made some mistake!" Gillman contradicted gruffly.

"No mistake at all," Cynthia affirmed indignantly, and she proceeded to relate the details of her discovery.

Gillman caught up his hat.

"This must be inquired into. By the palings, near the gate, you say? I will see to it at once. Do not tell your cousin until I come back!" And without more ado he hurried out into the garden.

Chapter Eight

"May I look at the paper a moment, Mr Gillman?"

Cynthia was sitting at the table, her writing-case was open before her, but she was nibbling meditatively at the handle of her pen, her eyes fixed absently on the fire. Evidently she found a difficulty in beginning her correspondence.

"With pleasure!" said Gillman as he tossed over his copy of a newspaper. "The worst of it is that it is a day old. Daily papers are an unprocurable luxury in these out-of-the-way regions."

Cynthia took it eagerly. How was it going on, the world she had left? She scanned the first page with interest. A foreign sovereign was staying in London, there was the usual account of festivities and decorations in his honour, and the conventional "leader" setting forth the reasons why this particular monarch should be received with special honour. Cynthia turned the sheet over listlessly: a party of British savants were visiting a Continental capital; a man and a woman staying at one of the principal hotels in the Strand had committed suicide. There was a graphic description of their personal appearance and of the few belongings found in their room.

Cynthia came to the conclusion that things were much as usual in London. She glanced idly at the literary news and then turned back to the other part of the paper. As she picked it up she saw her own name in bold black type, staring at her from the "agony column."

"Cynthia," she read, staring at it incredulously, "come back. Communicate at once with your distracted husband. Everything shall be explained. Your place is awaiting you.—Horace."

There could be no doubt that it was meant for her. The girl felt the colour ebbing from her cheeks as she read the words once more; they seemed to bring before her so vividly the fact that she could not escape from her past, that her husband was searching for her, that her present refuge would not serve to hide her from him for ever, that sooner or later she would be found and would have to face her life anew.

As she put the paper down with a little shiver and looked up, she found that Gillman's eyes were fixed upon her with an odd, scrutinizing expression, and though he averted his eyes instantly it gave her a disagreeable feeling that even her thoughts were not her own.

Gillman rose and moved to the sideboard.

"I wonder whether you would mind being left alone with your cousin this morning, Cynthia?" he said, as standing with his back to her he poured some liquid into his pocket-flask. "I have to go over to Glastwick on business, and Sybil has betaken herself off, goodness knows where. She may be back at any time, and Mrs Knowles will be in the house, but my wife seems to think she would like some one to sit with her. As Sybil is out I thought that you—"

"Why, certainly; I shall be delighted," Cynthia responded with alacrity. "I was just wishing that I could consult her about something."

Gillman screwed down his flask and turned to the door.

"That is all right, then? You will have your opportunity. I may be away till late, but I hope Sybil will not be long. You will not be nervous if you are left alone with your cousin for a while?"

Cynthia laughed and said:

"Not at all! Shall I go up to Cousin Hannah now?"

"Whenever you like," Gillman responded as he closed the door. "She will be very glad to have you. Good-bye for the present."

Cynthia sat still for a few minutes, trying to see some way out of her difficulties; then, taking the paper with her, she went slowly upstairs. Lady Hannah's door was locked, in accordance with her curious fancy, but the key was in the lock outside. Cynthia turned it after tapping lightly and went in. Lady Hannah was lying propped high with pillows, her head drawn back in the shadow of the heavy bed-curtains.

"Ah, is that you, Cynthia?" she said in her thick, indistinct tones, as the girl hesitated. "Come in. Can you draw down that blind over there? Henry insisted on leaving it up; he said the sunshine would do me good, but I cannot stand the glare, it makes my eyes ache."

There was not much glare, Cynthia thought, as she moved across and rearranged the blind obediently. Warm though the day was a fire burned in the grate and the windows were closed.

"I think you would be ever so much better if you had a little air, Cousin Hannah," she said impulsively. "If you would let me open one of these windows—"

"No, no, I will not," the invalid interrupted fretfully. "You are as bad as my husband; but I will at least have my room as I like! If it does not suit you I can do quite well alone."

Cynthia ventured to kiss the half-averted cheek.

"Dear Cousin Hannah, you know it is not that! It was of you I was thinking; but it must be as you please."

"Sit down then; I hate people fussing round me!" Lady Hannah said irritably and thanklessly. "Tell me what has become of everybody. Sybil is out enjoying herself, I suppose. She is an ungrateful young monkey!"

"She went out a little while ago," Cynthia said as she drew one of the arm-chairs near the bed and sat down, "but I do not suppose she will be very long. I am sure she is not ungrateful, Cousin Hannah; she is very fond of you."

"Umph, I dare say!" The invalid rolled her head round restlessly. "What have you been doing with yourself since I saw you?"

"Not very much," Cynthia replied truthfully, greatly to her own annoyance and for some unknown reason colouring vividly.

"You haven't thought better of leaving that husband of yours?"

"N—o," Cynthia faltered. "But he wants me to go back, Cousin Hannah. I have just seen a paragraph from him in the paper. It has made me very miserable," choking down a sob.

"Why?" Lady Hannah inquired cynically. "It shows you can return to him if you like, and if you don't, why, you must just stay with us."

"I don't know what I ought to do," Cynthia said despairingly. "Certainly I know I have taken those vows; but I think of Alice—she was such a pretty girl, and we were so fond of her, Mother and I—and he ruined her life—he deceived her!" She shuddered violently. "I cannot bear it! I cannot see him again! Oh, why did I not find out sooner!"

Her cousin did not make any reply; she moved her head restlessly from side to side. Cynthia sat for a moment or two absorbed in her own woes. She seemed to see her husband's face, reproachful, beseeching; then the tear-filled eyes and trembling mouth of her childhood's friend; then, all unbidden, mingling with these and blotting them out, a stern, dark face, a pair of deep grey eyes.

"Cynthia!"

It was her cousin's voice. Resolutely controlling her vagrant thoughts the girl bent over the bed.

"Yes, Cousin Hannah? Can I do anything?"

"I—I think the use is coming back to my hands a little," Lady Hannah said slowly. "My husband thinks so too; but until it does I wonder whether you would act as my amanuensis, Cynthia— whether you would write a few letters for me?"

"Why, certainly, I shall be delighted!" Cynthia said heartily. "Shall I get my desk now?"

"Well, I think I should like to send a line to Messrs Bolt & Barsly—" the invalid was beginning, when she was interrupted by a knocking at the front door, accompanied by a peal on the little-used bell.

Cynthia started, and Lady Hannah's head seemed to fall back.

"What—what is it?" she gasped. "What shall we do? I am frightened!"

"There is nothing to be frightened at," said Cynthia sensibly. "I expect it is only some one to see Mr Gillman on business."

Then her heart seemed to stand still as there was another loud, insistent knock, and the thought occurred to her that her husband had discovered her whereabouts and had come personally to seek for her. She had little time for misgivings on her own account, how- ever; her cousin was evidently in a state of tremendous nervous agitation, her lips were twitching, she was uttering little moans of terror. Cynthia tried to soothe and calm her, but with little success. There was another loud knock; evidently whoever might be at the door, he or she was not inclined to go away without any response.

"Dear Cousin Hannah," Cynthia said, laying her hand on one of the motionless arms, "I think, perhaps, I ought to see who it is. It may be something important. I believe out of the bay window I could see whether it is a tramp or anyone of that sort without leav- ing the room."

"Yes, yes! Look!" Lady Hannah said feverishly.

Cynthia drew back a corner of the blind and peered out cau- tiously. By dint of twisting her head to an almost impossible angle she managed to get a view of a tweed cap, of a familiar shooting jacket.

She drew back with an exclamation of relief.

"It is nothing—I mean it is only a man who lives in the neighbourhood. He called here the other day and saw Sybil."

"Oh, is that it?" Lady Hannah's tone became more composed. "Go and see what he wants, Cynthia."

The girl hesitated.

"I do not like to leave you, Cousin Hannah; and if no one answers the door surely he will go away."

"No, no! You must ask what he wants," the invalid reiterated feverishly. "Go, Cynthia, make haste."

Thus adjured, the girl had no choice, and she opened the door.

"I will not be long, Cousin Hannah," she said.

"Lock the door after you!" the invalid called out anxiously. "I—I cannot be left with the door unfastened, Cynthia!"

The girl obeyed her and hurried downstairs, wondering what could possibly be the reason of Heriot's persistency.

The front door was carefully locked and bolted. Cynthia had some difficulty in opening it, so securely was it fastened. At last, however, the bolts yielded and she turned the handle. Heriot was standing immediately before it. His face looked gloomy and set; it softened as he saw Cynthia.

"I beg your pardon!" he began. "I am afraid you will think I have been making an unwarrantable amount of clatter, but I have a message to deliver to Lady Hannah, and I felt sure that in her present state of health she would not be left alone in the house. I have been round to the other door, and as I was unable to make anyone hear there I determined, if possible, to succeed at this one."

Cynthia laughed in spite of herself.

"Well, you have managed that at any rate; but I do not know that you will find it very satisfactory, for Mr Gillman is not at home, I am sorry to say."

"I know Mr Gillman is out. I saw him driving towards Glast-wick. My errand is not with him: it is with Lady Hannah, and I wish to see her."

"Lady Hannah!" Cynthia repeated in surprise. "Surely you know she is not able to see anyone. I told you the other day how very ill she was."

"Yes, I know; I was deeply grieved to hear it." Heriot hesitated and, looking down in obvious indecision, kicked aside a stone that lay on the path. "The fact is, Miss Hammond, I have brought a message from Donald Farquhar. He is most anxious to be reconciled to his aunt. I have come in some sort as his ambassador, and it struck me that I should be far more likely to achieve my purpose in Mr Gillman's absence."

"In Mr Gillman's absence?" Cynthia repeated, amazed. "Surely, Mr Heriot, you understand that I cannot take the responsibility of admitting a stranger to Lady Hannah in her weak state?"

He looked at her in evident doubt for a moment. "A stranger? Well, no! At least if you could ask her whether she would see me—whether she would receive a message from Donald Farquhar, he would—I should at least know whether there really is a genuine objection to a reconciliation on her part. He has an idea—he has been told that she was anxious to be reconciled to him some little time ago, but that her attempts to find him were frustrated by Gillman."

Cynthia was obviously embarrassed.

"I do not know anything about it. I have never heard her mention him. Mr Gillman told me when I first came that her resentment at what he spoke of as his ingratitude was as keen as ever."

The man shrugged his shoulders contemptuously. "He would say so, no doubt; it is to his interest that the quarrel should be kept up. I have it on good and sufficient authority that three months ago she wished to recall Farquhar, and was only prevented by her husband. Miss Hammond, you will help us, if you can? For years Farquhar was like this poor lady's own son; you can imagine what it is to him to hear of her illness and not even to be allowed to send a message of sympathy."

Cynthia wavered between her certainty that she ought to avoid any excitement for the invalid and her sympathy with Sir Donald, sympathy which she, as well as the rest of the family, had felt for the young man at the time of Lady Hannah's extraordinary marriage. After a pause, during which Heriot watched the indecision in her face anxiously, she looked up.

"I will do the best I can," she promised. "I will at least see that your message reaches her safely. Will you come in?" She led the way to the drawing-room.

Heriot glanced round sharply, then he walked up to a large oil-painting hanging over the mantelpiece.

"There she is at twenty, Miss Hammond. Now don't you see the likeness to yourself?"

Cynthia looked at the portrait, which represented three girls in different stages of young womanhood. Glancing at the abundant chestnut hair, at the big brown eyes of the middle one of the three, Cynthia fancied for a moment that she did see a resemblance to herself; then her gaze wandered to the other figures.

"One of those is Lady Farquhar, certainly?" she said questioningly. "But the third—"

"The sister who died of consumption—Cynthia."

The girl gave a little cry of surprise.

"I must have been called after her, and I never knew."

Heriot turned.

"What, is your name Cynthia? Well, at any rate that will give me pleasanter associations with the name than I have had hitherto."

"Pleasanter?" Cynthia repeated.

He did not seem disposed to be communicative.

"Yes, it has never been a favourite of mine—until now!" He added the last two words after a pause in a perfectly matter-of-fact tone, but beneath his cold, direct gaze, to her intense vexation, Cynthia's eyes drooped and her colour rose.

"I will go and see what I can do with Cousin Hannah, if you will sit down, Mr Heriot."

Her heart was beating rapidly, her cheeks still flushing hotly as she ran up the stairs.

Lady Hannah turned her head as she entered.

"Well," she said anxiously, in her guttural, whispering tones, "what did he want? Has he gone?" Her breath was coming and going in little fluttering gasps as she spoke.

Cynthia looked at her pityingly.

"Not yet; he asked to see you, Cousin Hannah, but I told him I feared it would be impossible."

"Quite—quite impossible!" the invalid assented. "What did he want, Cynthia? Speak! I order you to tell me!" as the girl hesitated.

"He brought a message from some one who is very troubled about you"—Cynthia chose her words carefully—"some one of whom you used to be very fond. I—I think you must guess who I mean, Cousin Hannah"—as the head moved round restlessly, the fluttering breath grew deeper—"Sir Donald Farquhar."

"A—h!" With a harsh, discordant noise Lady Hannah interrupted her. "I will not hear it— I will not have that name mentioned! You—how dare you, Cynthia!"

The girl tried to soothe her, but Lady Hannah drew her head away.

"You have no right to bring him here; my husband will be very angry."

Cynthia stooped lower until her face was very near her cousin's; she caught the trembling, quivering hands and held them in hers reassuringly.

"Dear Cousin Hannah, indeed I did not bring him; I had no idea why he had come until he told me. I will send him away at once if you don't want to see him; but I thought, as he did, that perhaps you might be glad to send a message of forgiveness to Sir Donald?"

"Hush!" Lady Hannah's face twitched, and she fought for her breath. "Yes, I will send him a message!" she panted. "Tell him that

I will never willingly hear that name again, that I will never forgive him as long as there is any breath left in my body, that I hope never to see his face, that—"

She paused, exhausted, great beads of perspiration standing on her brow.

"I will send Mr Heriot away. He will write to Sir Donald that you have no wish to see him," Cynthia said gravely. There was to her something infinitely sad, infinitely tragic, in this spectacle of unrelenting animosity carried to the verge of the grave; and unconsciously she straightened her tall, slim figure and drew a little away from her cousin.

Lady Hannah's head moved from side to side impatiently.

"Yes, yes, go and tell him! Send him away!" she reiterated feverishly. "Make haste, Cynthia! Go, go!"

The mingled passion and entreaty in her voice were so insistent that Cynthia had no choice but to obey. Promising to be back as soon as possible she ran lightly down the stairs.

Heriot was standing as she had left him, still apparently absorbed in gazing at the portrait over the mantelpiece. He turned as she entered.

"Well?" he said expectantly as she paused.

"I am very sorry I have no good news for your friend," Cynthia replied simply. "Cousin Hannah bade me say that she would not send any message. She—her feelings towards him do not seem to have altered or softened at all; at least, I should imagine not."

The eager hopefulness died out of Heriot's eyes.

"You are quite sure she is under no coercion, that she is really expressing her own feelings?"

"Quite!" Cynthia replied with decision. "I did my best to make her listen, but to no purpose. She became terribly agitated at the very mention of Sir Donald Farquhar's name, and told me she would not hear it, and that she would never forgive him. It was very terrible!" shuddering. "What could he have done to give rise to such animosity?"

Heriot's face looked grave and perplexed.

"I cannot understand it at all! I know that a comparatively short time ago she was anxious to send for Farquhar."

"Well, I can do no more at present," Cynthia said positively. "I dare not! She threw herself into a state of agitation at the notion which must, I am sure, be very harmful."

"Then there is nothing more to be said. She does not strike you as being under any kind of influence, hypnotic or otherwise?"

Cynthia shook her head.

"I am sure she is not. I am afraid her anger with Sir Donald is genuine enough; but her agitation rather frightened me. I think I must go back to her."

"Yes, I must not keep you." Heriot held out his hand. "Thank you very much for your kind help! We must hope that time will alter Lady Hannah's feelings. I shall not fail to let Sir Donald know of your kindness to his aunt, and I am sure he will be very grateful to you." They crossed the hall; and at the open door Heriot paused. "If you should be walking across the moor my old landlady would be delighted if you would step in and have a chat with her," he said diffidently. "She has often spoken of you since that day you were lost—when you first came."

"I shall be delighted to come some day. I thought she had such a nice face. So she is your landlady? I wondered—" colouring ingenuously.

"Yes, I am staying with her for a few weeks," Heriot responded, with a certain awkwardness. "I knew her years ago, and she makes me very comfortable. I shall tell her that she may hope to see you, then?" His clasp of Cynthia's hand was somewhat unnecessarily lingering. "Thank you very much!" He paused as if about to say something else, changed his mind, and said "Goodbye!" abruptly.

Cynthia gazed after him for a moment in some surprise; there was an unexpectedness about him which she found singularly disconcerting, but the sight of his tall frame striding away in the distance was not illuminating. She closed the door, turned the key, and did her best to fasten the heavy bolts.

As she went towards the stairs she missed the little satchel that usually hung at her side, and remembered that she had laid it down in the dining-room. She turned back to fetch it; it lay on one of the little tables that stood near the fire-place. As she picked it up she was amazed to hear a sound upstairs—a sound which drove the blood from her cheeks—as of stealthy footsteps crossing the floor above. She listened a second—yes, unmistakably there was the creaking of a board. An instant's reflection convinced her that her cousin's room must be immediately above, and she remembered that she had left the door unbolted.

With a quick fear that some one—she did not stop to analyse—might have got into Lady Hannah's room and be terrifying the invalid she rushed across the hall and upstairs. As she hurried down the passage she distinctly heard a slight noise as of some article of furniture being moved; but when she ran into her cousin's room and looked round there was no one to be seen.

Lady Hannah glanced up in surprise.

"What is it, Cynthia? Wouldn't he go?"

"Yes, he has gone," Cynthia answered, gazing round her in a puzzled fashion. "But I thought— I fancied—"

"What?" the invalid's tone sounded suddenly sharp in the midst of its weakness.

"I thought I heard some one walking about overhead in this room while I was in the dining-room," Cynthia stammered, too thoroughly bewildered to realize the danger of alarming the invalid at the moment.

"What—in this room?" Lady Hannah's tone was full of terror and she twisted her head about from side to side. "Search! Look!" she gasped. "In the wardrobe; under the bed! Oh, Cynthia, I am frightened! It—you know I told you always to lock the door, and you did not; you left it open, and who knows who may have got in?

Quick, quick, look! Open the wardrobe door! Oh, if I could only get to it myself!"

As Cynthia obeyed her common sense came to her aid.

"No one could have got into the room without your seeing them, Cousin Hannah," she said. "I suppose," doubtfully, "I must have made a mistake."

"Look! Look!" the invalid commanded excitedly.

Cynthia threw the heavy wardrobe doors open and moved the dresses aside; they smelt musty, as disused clothing often does, but no living intruder was to be seen. Lady Hannah was evidently the possessor of an extensive wardrobe; there were gleaming, lustrous silks that might almost have stood alone, soft, rich velvets.

"Now look under the bed!" the invalid ordered fretfully.

"It is all right, Cousin Hannah," Cynthia said reassuringly as she lifted the valance, "there is nobody here. I must have been mistaken. It was very stupid of me!"

"Yes, yes, you were mistaken," Lady Hannah agreed more quietly, "but you should be more careful! I—I think I would rather be left alone for a time, Cynthia. Lock the door and put the key in your pocket; perhaps I may go to sleep by and by."

Cynthia looked at her doubtfully.

"Indeed I do not like to leave you alone, Cousin Hannah! May I not sit over there by the window? I will be quiet."

"No, no, I wish you would do as you are told," Lady Hannah said peevishly. "You do contradict so, Cynthia! Now, Sybil—where is she? I wish she would come back!"

Cynthia looked hurt.

"No doubt she will be back soon. I will leave you if you wish it."

"Lock the door and take the key with you," her cousin repeated feverishly, "then I shall know that nobody can get in."

Cynthia felt more than doubtful of the wisdom of this suggestion but, in face of the invalid's urgency, she had no choice but to obey. After carefully following Lady Hannah's directions she made her way to the dining-room and sat down to think over the situation, which was, as far as she could see, daily becoming more complicated. Her own position—that of a wife and no wife, an undesired dependant upon her cousin's bounty—was one which her own common sense told her would be untenable for long, and yet she was unable to make up her mind as to what her next step should be.

The sound of steps upon the stairs roused her as she was seeking to solve the puzzle, and she sprang to her feet, her eyes dilating with terror, her hand catching at the door. The echo of the refrain of a gay little French *chanson*, sung in Sybil's clear, blithe voice, made her look round in amazement.

Sybil threw the door open.

"Cynthia, will you give me the key of Cousin Hannah's room? She called to me just now as I went past."

Cynthia felt for it mechanically.

"How did you get into the house, Sybil?"

"You forgot to fasten the side-door after Cousin Henry. I had no difficulty."

"Did I?" Cynthia said, looking intensely puzzled. "I—I quite thought I had locked it."

"Did you?" said Sybil carelessly.

She passed the parrot's cage and inadvertently shook it. Much incensed, the bird sat up and preened itself.

"Poor Hannah!" it croaked, eyeing the girl vindictively. "Where is Hannah? Stop your snivelling, I tell you!"

"Horrid thing!" Sybil said, turning from it pettishly. "I shall make Cousin Henry get rid of it. I sneaked upstairs while you were holding that colloquy with the interesting young man at the front door, Cynthia. I—I was rather surprised at you," she added mischievously.

Chapter Nine

"I AM afraid I am very late this morning— I slept so soundly."

A. Gillman was crossing the hall as Cynthia came downstairs, and he smiled at her.

"I am glad you had a good night! As for being late"—with a little deprecating movement of his shoulders—"you know this is Liberty Hall; we only want you to please yourself in all things, my dear child!"

"Thank you very much; you are very kind!" Cynthia said hurriedly. There was something in the quasi-paternal manner that Gillman adopted at times that she disliked intensely. "How is Cousin Hannah?" she went on as he still waited.

The smile died out of his eyes.

"I am afraid she is not so well; the excitement of hearing that that young scapegrace Farquhar was attempting to open up communication with her again seems to have been too much for her. She can talk of nothing else since."

"I am very sorry," Cynthia said penitently, "but I did not know what to do. She made me go to the door, and then I thought I ought to tell her."

Gillman passed his hand over his forehead with a weary air.

"I was not blaming you for a minute, my dear Cynthia. I am sure, on the contrary, that you acted for the best, but the fact is none the less unfortunate. However, it cannot be helped."

Cynthia did not find this exactly a comforting speech.

"Do you think I may go to her this morning? It is a week since I have seen her."

Gillman pulled his moustache slowly for a minute before he spoke.

"I know it is; but I am not going to let even Sybil in this morning. I find that she is quieter alone with me."

"Mr Gillman," Cynthia said timidly, "don't you think that if Cousin Hannah is so ill she ought to have a doctor called in?"

Gillman's expression altered a little, and he glanced sharply at the girl's concerned face.

"I really do not know what to say," he began, toying with the hunting-crop he was carrying. "The specialists we summoned at the time of the attack were quite the highest authority we could obtain, and I am in constant communication with them and carrying out their treatment; but I do think it might be advisable to have a local man to watch the case also. The unfortunate part of it is, though, that my wife objects so strongly, and when she once makes up her mind it is no easy matter to persuade her to change it, as you know!" with a short laugh.

"I do, indeed!" Cynthia agreed heartily. "Still, in that case—"

"The whole affair seems beset with difficulties," Gillman finished with a sigh. "I do not know what to do for the best."

He passed on, and Cynthia went into the dining-room. Her solitary breakfast stood at one end of the long table; as she poured herself out a cup of tea Mrs Knowles entered, carrying the parrot's cage.

"I made bold to see if Polly would let me clean her out this morning, miss," she observed. "My lady was always that particular about it. I don't say it is as she'd have had it, but I done the best I could, and I do think the bird looks more comfortable. Poor Polly, there!" as she replaced it on its stand.

"I am sure it does," Cynthia said absently, buttering her toast and paying but scant heed to the charwoman.

That functionary, however, seemed in no hurry to depart; she straightened the sideboard cloth and put one or two little things into the cupboard.

"I have been wondering whether I might make so free as to speak to you, miss," she went on at last, twisting her hands together beneath her white coarse apron. "It is a matter that I have had on my mind for some weeks, in a manner of speaking, and I thought if you would allow me to ask your advice, miss—" She paused apparently for want of breath.

Cynthia looked slightly bewildered.

"Certainly, if I can do anything, Mrs Knowles."

"It is about my lady," Mrs Knowles proceeded volubly. "Mr Gillman, he says to me when I first come, 'Mrs Knowles,' says he, 'if her ladyship should ask you to take any messages or post any letters, you are always to bring them to me,' he says, 'and if it is advisable they should go I will post them myself.' Well, in course my wages being paid by him I obeyed him, as the saying is, but when she come to me and says, 'Mrs Knowles, I want you to post this letter for me; it is to my cousin as is going to be married, and it is just to wish her joy and to ask her to come and see me before the wedding if she can spare the time,' it did not seem to me as there could be any harm in it, me knowing as the master kept her close and did not encourage no visitors. It was only natural as the poor lady should pine." She paused and looked at Cynthia for encouragement.

Cynthia, on her part, felt curiously bewildered. She recalled her first feeling when she received her cousin's letter that Lady Hannah must be under some species of coercion, that she was appealing for help; and then she contrasted this impression with Lady Hannah's present attitude towards her. It appeared to her inexplicable.

"I think you were quite right, Mrs Knowles," she said at length, "but I cannot understand—"

"Which is not at all, miss," the charwoman proceeded, casting an anxious glance at the open door as if fearful of being overheard. "That being over and done with, I should not have ventured to trouble you with it; but the last day as ever she spoke to me before she was took the poor lady gave me another. 'Post this for me, Mrs Knowles,' she says, 'and I will make it worth your while.' I was just going to say I'd rather have no more to do with it, when Mr Gillman he come down the passage.

My lady, she were standing just where you are now and she says to me, so pitiful like, 'Put it away, quick, Mrs Knowles, for my sake.' I slipped it in my pocket, miss, and there it has been ever since. For when I got home that night one of my children was took ill with croup, and I never give the letter a thought—it would ha' meant walking a mile to the post, and I couldn't leave Tommy for a minute. Then—it's no use disguising it from you, miss—the letter went clean out of my head till I happened to put my hand in my pocket last night and felt it there. Then I made up my mind as I would take counsel with you. Here is the letter, miss," drawing it out and handing it to Cynthia. "You shall say whether I am to post it or not—you being the poor lady's cousin and there being often a look about you as reminds me of her."

Cynthia took the letter in her hand with an odd species of reluctance. It was directed in her cousin's handwriting to Sir Donald Farquhar, to the care of her solicitors, Messrs Bolt & Barsly, Lincoln's Inn, and the words "To be forwarded immediately" were underlined with two thick uneven strokes that seemed to tell of the writer's inward perturbation. Cynthia looked at it dubiously; the envelope was by no means improved by its sojourn in Mrs Knowles's pocket, and was further decorated by sundry smudgy imprints of a thumb and forefinger.

"I really do not know what to say, Mrs Knowles," she began in some perplexity. Then the remembrance of Mr Heriot's description of Sir Donald's anxiety for a reconciliation with his aunt recurred to her mind. This letter could be nothing less than a message of forgiveness, she decided, and it seemed to her that if before her seizure his aunt's thoughts had turned lovingly towards him assuredly Sir Donald ought to know it. "I—I think I should post it just as it is," she ended with decision. "After all, if she wished to write it to her own nephew, why should she not?"

"Which I have said to myself a many times, miss," Mrs Knowles said, taking back the letter carefully, and somewhat unnecessarily, considering its condition, in the cleanest corner of her apron. "Post it, I will, and it is to be hoped as me having forgotten it all this time hasn't made any difference. Thanking you kindly, miss!" as something passed from Cynthia's hand to hers. "I will walk down to the office with it soon as I have got my day's work over."

And she left the room just as Sybil came in from the hall ready dressed for walking.

She danced up to Cynthia.

"Lazy girl! Haven't you finished breakfast yet? You must make haste now, for I have set my heart on a good long walk this morning."

"I don't know that I feel inclined to go out today," Cynthia said absently, her mind still busy with Mrs Knowles and the letter. "Besides"—Sybil's disappointed face recalled her to the realities of the situation—"I do not think, since Cousin Hannah appears to be worse, we both ought to be out of the house at the same time."

A curiously impatient expression crossed Sybil's face.

"Oh, I am sure Cousin Henry can look after her!" she remarked slightingly, her pretty rosy lips pouting. "To tell you the truth, Cynthia, I am getting just a little tired of Cousin Hannah. She is so capricious and exacting."

There was some truth in this, as Cynthia knew, but something in Sybil's accent displeased her.

"At any rate, I shall stay in this morning, in case I can be of any use—" Cynthia was beginning, when Gillman opened the door.

"Ah! Going out for a walk, I see," he remarked. "That's right. It will do you both good."

"It would, but Cynthia is so tiresome," Sybil said pettishly. "She says we can't both leave Lady Hannah. You know, Cousin Henry, you said—"

"Oh, my dear child, this is absurd!" Gillman turned to Cynthia, and for one moment she fancied that there was a look in his eyes that betokened anything but amiability; his tone however was urbanity itself. "I shall be at home, and Mrs Knowles is in the house if anything is wanted. However"—as Cynthia's face showed no signs of yielding—"I want a note left at Flaxman's, the veterinary surgeon's; there is something wrong with the mare's leg, and I should like him to look at it. The nearest way is across the moor. I am sure Sybil would be afraid to go alone, for I know of old that courage is not one of her chief characteristics!" with a kindly laugh at Sybil's flushed face.

"I do not know that I am more of a coward than other people," the girl said defiantly, "but I think it is horrid of Cynthia—"

"Oh, I will go!" Cynthia yielded at once. "It is not nice to cross the moor alone. Sybil is much too pretty to do so, I am sure."

All Sybil's ill-humour left her and the dimples peeped out round her mouth.

"That is a nice speech, you are a nice old thing, and I forgive you all your reluctance now, Cynthia."

"That is all right, then!" the other girl remarked with a smile, as she went away to put on her hat and coat.

As Cynthia went up the stairs, though, insensibly her step grew slower. The more she thought of it the more curious did the episode of her cousin's letter to Sir Donald appear. It was quite evident from Mrs Knowles's story that Gillman had endeavoured to exercise a control over his wife's actions which must have been irksome in the extreme. That her cousin could willingly have submitted to such a system of espionage and surveillance as was implied by Gillman's warning to the charwoman that her mistress's letters were not to be posted Cynthia could hardly bring herself to believe. The more she thought it over the more curious it appeared. That Gillman seemed to be genuinely attentive to his wife now, and that she preferred his ministrations to those of anyone else, was perfectly obvious; but, open and above-board though everything appeared, Cynthia could not rid herself of an idea that there was some secret connected with the curious *ménage* at Greylands, some mystery the clue to which lay in her own hands, though so far it had eluded her.

She was still puzzling over the problem when she came downstairs, and her face looked grave and dissatisfied.

Sybil was eagerly awaiting her in the hall, note in hand.

"What a long time you have been, Cynthia!" she said impatiently. "We shall have to walk very quickly to get back before luncheon."

The sun was shining brightly; already the hawthorn-blossom was beginning to fade; May was giving place to June. The bright golden blossoms of the furze were investing the moors with a brighter, gayer aspect, and only the pines in the wood, the great firs that surrounded Greylands, looked sombre and gloomy.

Sybil ran about from one clump of gorse to another, uttering little cries of delight as her hands, safely encased in dogskin gloves, plucked great branches of the thorn-covered stems. In vain Cynthia reminded her that she would be wiser to wait until their return; she refused to desist until her arms were full. Then she came back to Cynthia, and taking little heed of the girl's abstraction chattered away with her usual abandon until Cynthia, looking before her, saw the cottage at which she had inquired her way when she was lost on the moor the first day after her coming to Greylands. To her surprise it looked shut up and deserted. She paused involuntarily.

"What is the matter?" Sybil asked crossly, annoyed that her conversation was passing unheeded.

"He has gone, then?" Cynthia said, still standing. "I mean, that is where that man came from that knew Sir Donald Farquhar—Mr Heriot. He must have left."

"A good thing too!" Sybil said pettishly. "I couldn't bear the man; he was always poking and prying about. He—he frightened me!"

"Frightened you?" Cynthia echoed, turning to look at her companion with astonishment. "What do you mean?"

Sybil pouted and shrugged her shoulders; her eyes looked dark and mutinous.

"Do not ask me questions with that inquisitorial air, Cynthia; I am not in the witness-box! I did not like him. I do not believe he knew Sir Donald Farquhar at all, and sometimes I used to think he had some reason of his own for making so many inquiries about us—that he might be a burglar or something of that sort in disguise."

"Absurd!" Cynthia said indignantly.

Sybil gave a meaning look.

"Oh, certainly, we know you would not believe any harm of him! But, in your circumstances, do you think so much interest is quite wise?"

"In my circumstances?" Cynthia questioned. "What do you mean? I do not understand!"

Sybil bit her lip; she glanced away in embarrassment; but recovering herself in a moment she looked up.

"In your circumstances, in my circumstances, in anybody's circumstances," she said innocently, "do you think it is quite discreet to pick up a man of whom one knows nothing, Cynthia dear?"

Chapter Ten

THE OFFICES of Messrs Bolt & Barsly were situated within the gloomy purlieus of Lincoln's Inn; the private room of Mr Barsly, the active partner of the firm, was regarded as a sort of Holy of holies. Thither clients who had made appointments with the principal were solemnly conducted; a very bold man must he be, or very highly placed in the world, who ventured, without having previously announced his coming, to demand an interview with the head of the firm. Yet one such courageous individual there was on a morning in early June. The impropriety of his request was made evident to him by the hesitation of the clerk who admitted him.

"Mr Barsly is extremely busy this morning, sir. If you have no appointment I am afraid it is useless," the solemn and bespectacled youth observed with an air of reproof.

His manner changed to some extent when he saw the name on the stranger's card; and he looked with increased respect at this muscular, broad-shouldered man, whose tanned skin, combined with his freedom of bearing, seemed to bespeak a life spent in the open.

"I will inquire, sir, if you will step this way," he said as he ushered the visitor into the dreary little waiting-room already occupied by a couple of impatient clients.

Mr Barsly was sitting at the writing-table in his private room, apparently engaged in paring his nails, when the clerk knocked at the door.

"Didn't I tell you that I was not to be interrupted for an hour, Williams?" he asked with some natural irritation. "I wish you would endeavour to remember what I say to you!"

"I beg your pardon, sir," the solemn youth responded, much abashed, "but the hour was nearly up, and I thought perhaps the gentleman—"

"Thought, thought!" Mr Barsly responded pettishly. "I wish you would do as you are told without thinking!"

He caught up the card the clerk had placed respectfully at his elbow.

"Sir Donald Farquhar!" he read aloud. Then his expression changed. "Ahem! I don't know that you have been so far wrong, Williams," he said generously. "Ask Sir Donald to come up."

He was absorbed in his papers on the desk before him when Farquhar was ushered in.

"Ah, Sir Donald," he said, as he rose, "I am exceedingly glad that you have come in this morning, though you find me overwhelmed by the pressure of business!"

"I am very sorry to interrupt," Sir Donald said as he took the chair opposite and deposited his hat and gloves on a neighbouring table, "but I am becoming increasingly anxious about my aunt. As I told you in my letter, I have been quite unable to see her or to obtain any answer to my letters; and it seems to me that it is time, considering how her property is being dealt with, that some more definite information was obtained."

Mr Barsly bowed.

"Quite so, quite so!" he said blandly. "We were precisely of your opinion, Sir Donald; I say 'were' advisedly, for having occasion to dispatch Mr Fowler, our managing clerk, early this week to Glastwick we instructed him to go over to Greylands and insist, if it were any way possible, on seeing Lady Hannah Gillman herself. He only returned last night, and his account of the interview—"

"He saw her?" Sir Donald interrupted eagerly. "What did she say? What did he think of her?"

"Certainly he saw her, Sir Donald, and received some very definite instructions with regard to her property. As far as Fowler could judge, she was quite as well as could be expected; but I think it would be better for you to hear his account and to judge for yourself."

Receiving a gesture of acquiescence he spoke down the tube, and in a minute there was a deferential knock at the door.

Sir Donald looked up with interest as Mr Fowler entered—a tall, reedy-looking man with a prematurely bald head, and weak red-rimmed eyes protected by blue glasses; his appearance hardly augured an unusual amount of intelligence, Sir Donald fancied.

"This is Sir Donald Farquhar," Mr Barsly began, with a comprehensive wave of the hand. "He is naturally anxious to hear your account of the visit to Lady Hannah Gillman."

"Ah, yes, I quite understand!" Mr Fowler blinked benevolently at Sir Donald over the tops of his glasses. "As far as I can judge, Lady Hannah appeared to be as well as can be expected from the nature of her attack. She is quite helpless, but I understand from Mr Gillman that definitely favourable symptoms have made themselves apparent lately, and he is not without hope that she may yet be restored to a certain amount of activity."

"She talked to you—she spoke to you of business matters?" Sir Donald interposed. "Did her mind appear to have been in any way affected by her illness?"

"Decidedly not!" Mr Fowler answered impressively. "She gave me the impression of being quite clear-headed, and as being, if I may say so, a lady with a very decided will of her own, whom it would be no easy matter to coerce."

Sir Donald nodded as he leant forward and gazed fixedly at the silver knob of his cane.

"So I should have thought," he assented. "But some information I received a short time ago has inclined me to the opinion that she is not a free agent—that her husband is keeping her in a species of captivity."

Mr Fowler looked at him for a moment in astonishment; then he shook his head decidedly.

"I should say that your informant has made some strange mistake, sir. As far as I could judge, Mr Gillman appeared to be devoted to his wife; and I should take her to be the leading spirit of the two. It seemed to me that he was anxious to please her and to carry out her directions in every way within his power."

"Did you see her alone?" Sir Donald asked abruptly. "Without Mr Gillman, I mean."

"Certainly, certainly! Mr Gillman went out of the room while she gave me her directions with regard to the business we have in hand for her. He was most particular that there should be no suspicion of his influence; in fact he told me privately that he was not in accordance with the course Lady Hannah had pursued lately, but had remonstrated with her in vain," Mr Fowler said.

It was quite evident that Mr Gillman had made an extremely good impression on Messrs Bolt & Barsly's clerk.

There was a pause. Sir Donald sat with his eyes fixed on the pattern of the Turkey-carpet at his feet; his face looked gloomy and dissatisfied. Mr Barsly restlessly turned over the pile of papers before him, as if to intimate to his client that time was passing. Mr Fowler gazed inquiringly at his principal.

At length Sir Donald broke the silence.

"Did it strike you that the household and the whole mode of living at Greylands were exceedingly curious for a woman in my aunt's position?"

Mr Fowler pushed his spectacles on to his forehead; seen without them his pale-blue eyes looked more than ever weak and watery.

"Lady Hannah appeared to me to have every attention, every luxury even," he said, embarrassed. "But now that you put the question to me, Sir Donald, her income would warrant a more expensive style of living. Still, there are people who prefer—"

Mr Barsly gathered together several envelopes and now fastened an elastic band round them with a snap.

"One minute, Sir Donald," he interrupted suavely. "As you know from our correspondence with you, for some time past we have been seriously uneasy about Lady Hannah; the way in which she was disposing of her alienable property caused us some considerable anxiety, and there was something about the tone of the letter in which she bade us prepare a deed of gift of the Greylands property to her cousin, Lady Letchingham, as well as in the tone of the letter in which she returned the deed duly executed, which made us feel that some inquiry must be made as to her health and the general condition in which she was living. No doubt the attack of paralysis which must have been impending accounts for much, and since Mr Fowler's visit we have felt—"

"Deed of gift of Greylands to Lady Letchingham!" Sir Donald interrupted. "I had no idea—"

Mr Barsly coughed.

"It may be indiscreet to take you thus far into our confidence, Sir Donald, but—well, it is done now. Lady Hannah gave us instructions that the deed of gift was to be forwarded to Lady Letchingham when she herself should direct, but from what Mr Fowler gathered in his interview, Lady Hannah has been seriously considering revoking the deed. The unfortunate differences which have arisen between Lord and Lady Letchingham seem to have had the effect of incensing her against her cousin. I understand she expressed herself strongly on the subject."

"I did not know any differences had arisen between Lord and Lady Letchingham," Sir Donald remarked indifferently. "It is early for that, surely."

Mr Barsly nodded in a melancholy fashion.

"It is indeed, but there the matter stands. As you are a relative, Sir Donald, there is no harm in telling you what is leaking out to the world now—that Lady Letchingham has positively declined to live with her husband."

"Has she?" Evidently Sir Donald was not interested in Lady Letchingham's proceedings. "I do not know anything of her. My aunt has two young cousins staying with her now."

Mr Barsly flashed a lightning glance at his subordinate; in his absorption the signal escaped Sir Donald.

Mr Fowler coughed.

"So I understood. I saw one of them—Miss—er—Cynthia; she appeared to be most attentive to Lady Hannah."

"Ah, yes." Sir Donald rose. "Well, I suppose nothing more can be done at present. It seems useless for me to write to my aunt, but I warn you I shall not be satisfied until I see her myself."

"It is very sad," Mr Fowler remarked in his mild, compassionate tones, "to see anyone reduced to so helpless a state as Lady Hannah. She is unable to move hand or foot. I saw how unhappy she looked when she spoke of her inability to write, and I thought that her pretty white hands, lying so still and useless, were a most melancholy sight." A slight smile curved Sir Donald's lips.

"I am afraid you are somewhat embroidering the truth now, Mr Fowler. As my aunt's hands have been crippled by rheumatism for years—sad, as I am sure it is, to see them helpless—they can hardly look either pretty or white, to quote your description."

Mr Fowler gazed at him in bewilderment.

"Lady Hannah's hands were smooth and white," he affirmed positively. "I thought how soft and unwrinkled they looked for an—er—elderly lady's. There was no sign of rheumatism about them—in their appearance, at any rate."

"Hands often alter in illness," Mr Barsly remarked didactically. "No doubt Lady Hannah is considerably paler after this long confinement in bed, and doubtless that has affected her hands also."

"Her knuckles were permanently enlarged. They could not alter," Sir Donald contradicted. "Well, I do not know what the secret of that strange household at Greylands may be. I suppose, however, that if my aunt is comfortable it does not concern me. Still, I shall not feel convinced that it is so until I have seen."

"Oh, my dear sir, I do not think there is any further cause for uneasiness—I do not indeed," Mr Barsly said, as he rose. "We, as you know, were, like yourself, inclined to be suspicious with regard to Mr Gillman's proceedings. The whole circumstances of the marriage, taken in conjunction with other things, were so extraordinary that we felt compelled to exercise perhaps an undue amount of precaution. In fact, I may tell you that Mr Fowler's journey North was undertaken principally on that account; but as his report was of so satisfactory a nature we see no reason for further misgivings, and are very glad to acknowledge that in the past we were mistaken. Still, it was a fault on the right side, Sir Donald, a fault on the right side!"

"Quite so, in my opinion," Sir Donald said brusquely. "I suppose there is no more to be said this morning, Mr Barsly. Apparently we have been on the wrong track all the time."

"I am glad to think so, Sir Donald, glad to think so."

Mr Barsly touched the electric bell at his elbow; as Mr Fowler moved forward to open the door for the young man the solicitor spoke again:

"Your pardon, Sir Donald! I believe a couple of letters for you have been forwarded to our care. As we have been in ignorance of your address for the last month, they are awaiting you here. Shall we send them to you, or will you—"

"Oh, I will take them, thanks!" said Sir Donald. "I do not suppose they are anything of importance."

"They are in the private safe, sir. Allow me!" Mr Fowler threw open a door in the wall, and from a tin box marked "Farquhar" produced a couple of envelopes.

"One of them looks distinctly grubby," said Sir Donald, touching it gingerly; then, as he noted the writing, his expression changed. "It is from my aunt," he said hurriedly. "Excuse me!" as he tore it open. "When did it come?"

Mr Fowler took the answer upon himself.

"Yesterday morning, I believe, sir."

Sir Donald glanced rapidly through the pencilled scrawl. As he read his grey eyes softened and grew very pitiful; but when he looked up and met Mr Barsly's gaze his mouth was set in grim, stern lines. He held the open sheet out to the solicitor.

"Read this, and then tell me whether there is not some strange juggling going on somewhere."

Mr Barsly took the letter in his hand with obvious reluctance.

"I hardly know whether I ought, my dear Sir Donald."

"Read it aloud," Sir Donald said abruptly. "Wait!" he went on as Mr Fowler moved towards the door. "It is possible you may be able to throw some light on this."

Mr Barsly read in a puzzled tone:

"GREYLANDS, *April* 18*th*.

"MY OWN DEAR BOY,

"I have written to you before, but somehow I do not think the letters have been allowed to reach you; I think that if they had you would have forgotten all that has stood between us, that has kept us apart this year, and come to your old aunt. It hurts me to say it, to confess it even to you who have been like my own son to me, but I have made a mistake, Donald, and I am very miserable, lonely and frightened—frightened I hardly know of what.

"If this letter reaches you, you will forgive all the hard words I said to you at our last interview, when my heart was sore and disappointed at the failure of a scheme that was dearer to me than perhaps you know, will you not? You will come to me and take me away?

"They will try to prevent your seeing me, try to prevent your communicating with me in any way, but do not listen to them, Donald. Insist on seeing me, and, oh, my boy, come soon, or something tells me it will be too late! For there is an ever-increasing dread hanging over me, and I am afraid—

afraid of what is coming. Good-bye, my own dear boy, and whatever the future may hold in store for us, believe that I am now and always,

"Your affectionate

"AUNT HANNAH."

Mr Barsly read the sentences out in his driest, most matter-of-fact tones.

"Well," Sir Donald said curtly as he finished, "what do you make of it now?"

Mr Barsly so far forgot his position as a legal adviser as to run his fingers through his remaining locks until they stood on end.

"I do not know what to make of it," he confessed in bewildered tones, laying it on the table and staring at it. "I do not know what to make of it all. It is a most extraordinary thing!"

Sir Donald turned to the clerk.

"Are you going to tell me now that my aunt is not under some sort of coercion?" he demanded.

Mr Fowler leaned over and gazed at the paper; then he stood up and blinked at Sir Donald over the top of his coloured spectacles.

"It is incomprehensible," he said slowly. He glanced at it again. Mr Barsly and Sir Donald watched him anxiously. Presently he looked up. "I can only suggest one explanation," he said in his diffident, halting fashion. "This letter was written six weeks ago. The attack from which Lady Hannah is suffering must have been hanging over her then; it is possible that it affected her views of things in general, and of her own position in particular, and that now that its effects are to some extent passing away she is able to look at the situation differently."

Mr Barsly was drumming on his desk with the fingers of one hand; his face looked absorbed and speculative.

"That explanation is scarcely an adequate one, I am afraid, Fowler," he said at length. "How do you account for the change in her feelings towards Sir Donald which is expressed in this letter?

You told me that, when acting in accordance with our instructions, you introduced Sir Donald's name, her anger with him appeared to have in nowise abated."

"Quite so, sir," Mr Fowler assented. "The very mention of Sir Donald's name appeared to excite Lady Hannah tremendously; she stated that she never wished to see him or hear of him again, and that she would never forgive him."

"Was Mr Gillman in the room at the time? Is it possible that he exerts some hypnotic influence over her to induce her to express his sentiments?" Sir Donald inquired.

Mr Fowler considered the question for a moment, and then slowly shook his head.

"No; I was alone with Lady Hannah at the time, or with only Miss"—with a little hesitation in his manner and a glance at Mr Barsly—"Miss Cynthia in the room, and, save for her excitement—I might almost say anger—at the mention of Sir Donald's name, Lady Hannah appeared to be perfectly cool and collected."

"Yet, in face of this expressed anger, she writes to Sir Donald in terms such as these?" Mr Barsly repeated, striking the open letter with his hand.

Mr Fowler opened his mouth, but before he could speak Sir Donald interposed:

"It is inexplicable; but it has settled one thing for me. I had almost made up my mind to give up attempting to gain admission to my aunt and go back to Tasmania. But now that I have seen this I have quite determined that nothing, however apparently definite, shall turn me from my purpose. I will not rest until I have seen my aunt face to face and heard from her own lips whether she is in need of help or not!"

He held out his hand and Mr Barsly took it.

"You will communicate with us again shortly, no doubt, Sir Donald?" he said, frowning a little. "We shall not fail to let you know anything that may help to elucidate the mystery. We have not attempted to disguise from you that for some time we have been seriously uneasy with regard to our client, Lady Hannah Gillman, but since Mr Fowler's interview we had really hoped that things were on a more satisfactory basis; now, however, since reading this letter, I do not know what to say—I really do not; but I do think it would be as well for you to delay your return to Tasmania for a while. As Lady Hannah's nearest male relative it would be decidedly better that you should be in England—that is to say, if any sort of restraint is being exercised upon her. I can hardly think it is so, but still—"

' "You may depend upon it I shall not go back to Tasmania without seeing my aunt," Sir Donald said, with grim determination, "or without wringing the secret of Greylands from her husband."

Chapter Eleven

"WHERE are you going, Cynthia?"

There was something almost affectionate in Gillman's tone, some nuance in his expression, from which Cynthia instinctively shrank.

She hesitated.

"Only for a stroll across the moor; the evening is so pleasant."

Gillman's eyes had an odd gleam in their depths.

"If you will wait half an hour I will go with you," he said.

A strange repellent shiver shook Cynthia.

"I—you see I am quite ready," she stammered, "and I promised Sybil not to be late."

Gillman kept his eyes fixed upon her confused face.

"So you will not wait for your old cousin?" he said, with his sudden smile. "Well, perhaps"—with a mischievous look—"there may be greater attractions on the moor!"

Cynthia drew herself up; her eyes flashed.

"I do not think I quite understand you!" she said, with dangerous quietness, holding her haughtily-poised head high. "If you mean—"

Gillman's tone changed.

"Oh, my dear child, I meant nothing!" he said hastily in his most paternal fashion. "Come, I am old enough, surely, to have a little joke?"

"Oh, certainly!" Cynthia said still stiffly.

They were standing near the orchard gate, and Gillman held it open.

"Well, I must not keep you. Possibly I may walk a little way to meet you later on. If I do, I shall bring Nero with me."

Cynthia's reply was inaudible as she passed.

Her path led through the belt of firs on to the moor close by the pine-wood. The weather was decidedly cooler to-day, and, as she hurried along, it fanned her burning cheeks. Her first dislike of her cousin's husband, against which she had struggled and which she had believed she had overcome, was returning in greater strength than ever; fight against it as she would, she found herself unable to subdue it. To such an extent had it grown that she told herself that it would render her further stay at Greylands impossible, and once more she racked her brains to think of some other refuge, and puzzled herself as to what she could do and where she could go.

Before she had been able to arrive at any decision, however, she found herself on the main road which led across the moor in the direction of Glastwick. She had proceeded along it for nearly a mile, when she saw some little distance in front of her a motorcar evidently disabled. It had come to a standstill, but was emitting a series of snorts and gurgles that testified to something being very far wrong with its internal machinery. As Cynthia drew nearer she saw that the chauffeur was lying at full length on his back beneath the car, evidently occupied in trying to remedy whatever was defective, while a couple of men in motor-dress were examining various nuts and cranks.

She was almost within speaking distance, when one of them stood up and turned round, straightening himself; then, catching sight of Cynthia, he came towards her, raising his cap courteously.

"Could you tell me whether there is any smithy or place on the moor where we could get help for this thing?" he asked, indicating the still snorting car by a backward jerk of his head.

Cynthia paused irresolutely.

"There is a smithy, I know, but I think it is a good way from here; I believe it is over there," she said, pointing in what she believed to be the right direction.

She made a pretty picture as she stood there glancing about her in indecision, the breeze toying with her hair lightly, lifting the little curls round her temples, her colour heightened both by her quick walk and her nervousness.

A swift gleam of admiration shot into the heavy eyes of the man watching her; it was pleasanter to stand here on the short springy grass and talk to a pretty girl than to assist his companions to get the motor right.

"Our chauffeur is a first-rate fellow and understands his business thoroughly," he went on conversationally, "but it seems that some nut or crank is missing, dropped on the road, and the difficulty is to supply its deficiency. Probably, however, we shall be able to do that at any blacksmith's. Perhaps it would be as well to send the man to see. Over there, I think you said," as Cynthia began to move on.

The girl bowed coldly.

"As far as I can judge from here; but I am a stranger to the neighbourhood, so I am afraid I am not a competent guide."

The man did not seem discouraged by her change of tone.

"I wonder also if you could tell me of any farmhouse near where we could obtain some refreshment?"

"I cannot!" Cynthia replied stiffly. Her eyes glanced at the stranger's short, stout figure, by no means set off to advantage by his loose motor-costume, at his heavy, unprepossessing face, and his coarse, sensual mouth and she moved on decidedly.

The man turned too.

"Oh, but can you not give me some idea—" he began to remonstrate with odious familiarity.

Cynthia quickened her steps indignantly. Then as she looked straight in front of her, something familiar in the attitude of the man waiting by the car struck her. Her expression changed; all the pretty colour that the man beside her had been admiring faded away; she came to a sudden standstill, her eyes wide open, dilated by fear, fixed on the waiting figure by the car. It must be some horrible mistake, she told herself; it could not be that she was looking at Lord Letchingham—at her husband!

The man who had spoken to her stopped too, evidently in surprise. He glanced at her disturbed face, and seemed about to speak, when the man by the car turned, and Cynthia knew that her worst fears were realized—it was Lord Letchingham who stood there looking at them!

As Cynthia still waited motionless, only her breath coming and going in great fluttering gasps, he moved a few steps towards them. At the same moment the man beside her spoke.

"I assure you we should only be too grateful if—"

With a sound that was like a sob of terror the girl turned, and with no very clear idea in her fright save that she must get away at all hazards, somewhere, she rushed away, panting as she ran, and stumbling over the rough moorland ground.

"I say, I hope I have not—" Cynthia caught the words; a backward glance showed her that the man had turned, that her husband had joined him, and that they were following her. The sight seemed to lend wings to her feet. She rushed on, her head bent, uttering little moans of terror as she ran, not knowing where she was going, only feeling that at all hazards she must get away from this man who owned her.

Lord Letchingham came up to his companion.

"Eh, Dempster!" he said, giving him a poke in the ribs. "What have you been doing, you sly dog? I thought you were going to ask about a blacksmith's shop. This"—pointing to the flying girl—"does not look as if that had been your only occupation, eh?"

The man he had called Dempster was still watching Cynthia.

"We were getting on like a house on fire until you began to think of joining us," he said fatuously. "You frightened my shy bird away, Letchingham. Perhaps she had heard something of your reputation!" with a meaning laugh. "Pretty girl she was too!" as he watched poor Cynthia's heedless progress.

"Who was she, Dempster? You don't put me off with fairy-stories of girls living on the moors. I did not get much of a look at her, but it seemed to me that I had seen her somewhere before."

"I hadn't," Mr Dempster remarked sententiously, "and it doesn't seem as if I should again when you are about, old fellow."

Lord Letchingham appeared by no means ill- pleased at these allusions to his gallantry. He screwed his monocle firmly in his left eye.

"I see why you were so keen on coming over this moor, Dempster. You won't blind me."

Dempster's face suddenly grew graver.

"It hadn't anything to do with this girl, at any rate; but I do not mind telling you, Letchingham. I dare say you remember a little girl named Meldrum, who used to act at the Alexandra—pretty little *ingénue* parts?"

"Delphine Meldrum? Remember, yes, I should think so!" Lord Letchingham repeated in a tone of interest. "I should think I do! She had the biggest eyes and the brightest smile in town. Why, half the young men were in love with her; she might have had the pick of them. I never heard what became of her."

"Nobody did," Dempster said solemnly. "She disappeared, told the managers she was tired of the whole thing, and took herself off, and that was all about it. They were in despair, for Delphine Meldrum was a safe draw, but that didn't mend matters. Well, Letchingham, while I was driving over this moor last week on my way to Glastwick Tower who should I see standing by the roadside but Delphine Meldrum herself."

Letchingham stared at him incredulously.

"What did you say, man? This was not Delphine Meldrum!"

"No, this girl is younger, and quite a different stamp, but the one I saw last week was little Delphine Meldrum! I recognized her without a shadow of a doubt, and what is more she knew me. She stared at me for a minute, her face turning white, and then, before I could pull up, she had turned and was scudding over the moor like a lapwing, or—or that one!" pointing after Cynthia.

Lord Letchingham's eyes twinkled derisively; he little guessed whose flight he was watching.

"Seems to be a little way they have down here. You were thinking of the Meldrum, Dempster, that was it—I remember hearing that you were numbered among her admirers—and you invested some country girl with her likeness. You would be the first to laugh at yourself if you could see the supposed Delphine Meldrum face to face."

"Give you my word of honour I hadn't thought of Delphine for years," Dempster said impressively. "Why, though the face was perfectly familiar, I couldn't even put a name to it at first. No! It was Delphine Meldrum safe enough, but what she is doing down here I can't conceive. I don't mind confessing to you, though, Letchingham, that it was partly on her account that I came across the moor this afternoon. I should be prepared if I saw her again, and I should like to know if she is happy and all that, for—er—Delphine was a nice little girl—a very nice little girl!"

Lord Letchingham laughed disagreeably.

"Oh, don't make excuses, Dempster! I quite understand; and this afternoon when you went off in such a hurry to this girl, you thought—"

"I thought in the distance she might be Delphine," Dempster acknowledged. "Good-looking little girl she was too, and we were getting on very well, until you came up and scared her away."

Lord Letchingham caressed his moustache, a smile lurking round the corners of his mouth.

"You see, Dempster, I—"

The chauffeur came up, touching his cap.

"Beg pardon, my lord, but I think I have put matters right, so that we can get back to the Towers!"

"That's all right, then, Brookes," Letchingham said thankfully. "I was beginning to think it would be a case of walking to Glastwick and sending some one out to you, for I do not see much chance of getting help out here on the moor."

Meanwhile Cynthia, rushing headlong away, did not heed where her steps were taking her; she only realized that at all hazards she must get away, she must put as much distance as possible between herself and the man whom she dreaded above all things on earth.

After that one backward glance she never turned her head, but hurried along, catching her gown on the gorse, stumbling over the rough ground, her breath coming in long-drawn sobs.

"What is the matter? Where are you going?" It was a man's voice; a man's hand was laid on her arm.

With a shriek of terror the girl tore herself away.

"Let me go! Let me go!" she cried.

"What is wrong? Where are you going?"

Cynthia's heart gave a great throb of relief as she recognized Heriot's voice.

"Oh, there was somebody, a man!" she began. "He—he frightened me!"

Heriot's eyes lighted up with anger.

"A man—where?" he asked laconically, his hand involuntarily gripping the handle of his stick.

"I—do—not—know!" she said, with a great breathless gasp between the words. "I suppose I have come a long way. I seem to have been running—for hours. They—they frightened me so terribly."

"Poor child!" Heriot's face was very pitiful. After another long look round he drew her trembling hand through his arm. "Lean on me; I will take you to the cottage; you can rest there. You are completely done up." He guided her carefully.

"I thought you had gone," Cynthia said, recovering after a few minutes. "The cottage was shut up.

"I have been away," Heriot said laconically, "and my landlady has been visiting friends. There she is—look."

Cynthia was surprised to see how near she was to the cottage; in her fright she had run a far greater distance than she had imagined. The elderly woman whom she had seen before sat in the porch knitting; everything looked exactly the same as it had done on the first day of her stay at Greylands.

Heriot unlatched the garden gate and drew her in authoritatively.

"You will be better when you have rested and had a cup of—er—my landlady's tea. Later on I will walk home with you, but in the meantime," grimly, "I will look round and see whether I can find anything of the gentlemen who have annoyed you."

Cynthia uttered a cry of alarm; her hot fingers clutched his arm imploringly.

"Oh, you must not—indeed, you must not! Promise me you will not! Besides you will not find them; they—they had a motor. By now they are far away."

"Well, in that case it is not much good looking for them," Heriot conceded reluctantly. "Mrs Smithson"—as his landlady, becoming aware of their approach, laid aside her knitting and regarded them with some surprise—"I have brought you this young lady, Miss Hammond, whom you have seen before; she has had a fright and is rather knocked up. You must give her a cup of tea and let her rest quietly a while."

"Bless you, sir, certainly I will!" Mrs Smithson responded heartily as she rose. "Eh! Dear, dear, miss, you do look bad!" she went on, raising her hands. "It was owing to that that I didn't recognize you at first, for I have often thought of you and wondered if you would come in to see me again. Sit down, miss"—drawing forth her chair—"I will soon bring you a cup of tea."

Cynthia hesitated and glanced round nervously.

"Would you mind—I would so much rather come indoors if you would let me?" she said pleadingly, her eyes looking big and frightened.

"Come inside and welcome, miss!" Mrs Smithson said. "Myself I am very fond of sitting in the porch; I see all that there is to be seen here anyway, but I know some folks never can abide having their food out of doors."

Cynthia could not help laughing in the midst of her agitation.

"It is not that at all; but if I sat there and that man came by again to ask the way or anything he would see me."

"You would be safe enough if he did, miss," Mrs Smithson remarked reassuringly. "Mr Heriot would take care of that; don't you trouble yourself! Why, I declare you are all of a shiver! You ought to have a dog to go about with you—there's nothing for keeping tramps off like a dog—"

"I think I must get Mr Gillman to let me bring Nero," Cynthia assented. "But he is a mastiff, so big and strong that I am half afraid of him myself. Now, Spot, the little dog they had when I came—the one that was killed—was a different matter."

Mrs Smithson looked troubled.

"Is Spot dead, miss?"

"Yes, Mr Heriot and I found him in a wood; somebody had killed him. Did you know Spot, Mrs Smithson?"

The expression of the woman's rosy face changed.

"I have heard of him," she said evasively. "Please come right in, miss; this is Mr Heriot's own sitting- room, and a pleasant enough room it is, though I suppose I should be the last to say it."

Cynthia agreed with her unreservedly as she followed her into the room at the right of the door; its raftered ceiling and quaint latticed windows, now thrown wide open, gave it a charming old-world air, while the brightly-polished table and the book-case and the light clean chintz with which the couch and chairs were covered presented an impression of dainty freshness which was delightful to the girl's tired brain.

Mrs Smithson drew the longest, most comfortable arm-chair up beside the open window.

"Sit down, miss, and I'll bring you a cup of good tea; that will be the best thing for you," she said and lingered a minute, bringing forward a little tea-table and arranging it beside the girl. "You'll excuse me, miss, but I was told that her ladyship had taken a turn for the better. I hope it is true."

"I do not see much difference, myself, thank you," Cynthia said listlessly, laying her head back against the cushions, "but she may be a little better perhaps. I know Mr Gillman thinks she is."

"I am sure I am glad to hear it, miss!"

Intent on her tea-making, the good woman bustled out of the room, and Cynthia was left alone.

At first she was too much exhausted to do anything but lie perfectly still; but after a while she revived, and, with some fear that she might be seen from the road, drew her chair back behind the curtains. Her eyes wandered slowly over the room; finally they rested on a picture over the mantelpiece, and, with a cry of surprise, she rose from her seat and went over to it. It was evidently a portrait of husband and wife, but what startled Cynthia was the feeling that the face of the lady seemed perfectly familiar to her; she looked at it again.

Yes, she had made no mistake; it was the same face, a little older, perhaps, of one of the three sisters portrayed in the large oil-painting in the disused drawing-room at Greylands. Hardly grasping the significance of this discovery, she was still gazing upwards and speculating as to the identity of the tall, dark man pictured behind the lady, with an odd feeling, too, that his features were not entirely unknown to her, when there was a step in the passage behind her.

She turned and saw Heriot standing in the door-way, a curiously embarrassed expression on his face as he watched her. As she met his eyes in a moment enlightenment came to her; she held out her hands; her face paled.

"You—you are not Mr Heriot," she said with instant conviction. "You are Sir Donald Farquhar!"

Chapter Twelve

THE MAN hesitated; there was a minute's tense silence; then he stepped forward and took the outstretched hands in his.

"Yes," he said slowly, "I am your cousin, Donald Farquhar; I have often wondered that you did not guess it before!"

A great bewilderment was struggling with the comprehension in the girl's eyes.

"I do not understand! Why have you not given your true name? Why have you been hiding like this?"

Farquhar looked down at her gravely.

"I have found it quite impossible to gain access to my aunt; from my correspondence with her solicitors I had learned that they were uneasy about the large demands she had been making for money, and I thought that by staying here under another name I might learn more about her and possibly obtain an interview with her; but I have not succeeded, as you know, so far."

Cynthia slowly drew her hands from his and went back to her chair. Sir Donald crossed to the mantelpiece and took up his position before it, leaning his broad shoulders against the high wooden ledge and smiling a little as he looked down at the girl's troubled face.

"I have often thought that my anxiety about my aunt must have given me away to you, that you must have guessed my secret."

Cynthia's eyes drooped.

"No, I never guessed; I never thought of such a thing!"

There was the sound of tea-cups cheerfully rattling on the tray, and Mrs Smithson made her appearance.

"I have made it strong, miss, and I have brought a few of the hot scones that Mr Heriot is so fond of," she said as she set her load on the table before Cynthia.

"You are very kind," the girl said absently.

Sir Donald laughed.

"Ah, Mr Heriot is done for!" he said. "Miss Hammond has guessed our secret—half of it, at any rate!"

For a moment Mrs Smithson looked embarrassed; then her countenance broke into smiles.

"Real glad I am to hear of it, Sir Donald!" she said with emphasis. "Now that Miss Hammond knows that we are here in my lady's interests she will help us all she can, I know, in a manner of speaking."

"Ah, now we must tell Miss Hammond the other half of our story," Sir Donald interposed. He turned back to Cynthia.

"You may have heard of Gleeson—my aunt's confidential maid, who was with her all through my childhood?"

"Ay, and before that—before you were ever thought of, Sir Donald!" the woman tearfully interpolated.

"Though my aunt had refused to hold any communication with me after our quarrel," Sir Donald pursued, "I wrote several times to Gleeson, who had always stood my friend, asking her to give me news of my aunt and to let me know if there was any sign of a reconciliation with me, but whether Gillman discovered that Gleeson was working with me, or whether her presence in the house interfered with his plans in some other way, I do not know, however that may be, her dismissal followed very shortly.

"When I went back to England my first care was to seek her out, and when I heard from her my aunt's story it struck me as so serious that, failing to obtain any satisfactory information about her through ordinary channels, I resolved to come down under another name and see what I could discover for myself. The idea commended itself to Gleeson as so eminently satisfactory that she resolved to do the same. This little cottage was to let; we took it, and *voilà tout*!" with a comprehensive wave of his hand.

Cynthia drew a long breath.

"You are Sir Donald Farquhar and Mrs Smithson —Gleeson?"

Mrs Smithson—or Gleeson—took the answer upon herself.

"Yes, indeed, miss! Many is the time since that day you came by and told us of my lady's illness that I have not been able to sleep at nights for thinking of what she might be going through, and me not there to help her!" She was wiping her eyes as she spoke. "I beg your pardon, miss! I had been in her ladyship's service for years; she had treated me almost as a friend, and it is sore trouble to me not to be with her now."

"I am sure it is," Cynthia said sympathetically; "but you must not think that she is not well looked after. Mr Gillman and Miss Sybil are most attentive and devoted to her, though I am sure she must miss you, and no doubt you would be a great help. I am sorry you left."

Gleeson put away her handkerchief.

"I didn't leave till I was pretty near turned out of the house by main force, miss. Mr Gillman, he was determined that nobody should be with her ladyship except himself. He resented her affection for me as if it had been a personal affront to him, and when he found out that my lady was talking to me of Sir Donald and wishing he was back, he made up his mind that I should go, in spite of all she could say. Poor lady! How she cried and clung to me when she heard I was going, for he turned me out of the house at a moment's notice. I begged her to leave him, to come with me, and for a moment I thought she was about to yield, and then he came on the scene. 'Why, Hannah, my love, what is the matter?' he says in that oily voice of his. 'I have just heard of a maid for you that seems most suitable. She will be able to do your hair better than Gleeson has done, for you know you have lovely hair, my dear.'

"She tried to smile at him, but I could see her lips tremble, and as I went away she whispered to me, 'I am frightened, Gleeson—so frightened!' Ah, many a time since my heart has ached thinking of those words!"

"She said exactly the same thing in her letter to me," Sir Donald confirmed. "I made up my mind then that I would not relax my efforts until I had seen her face to face and heard from her lips, in Gillman's absence, what she wished to do."

"Ah, you had the letter, then? I am so glad!" Cynthia said quickly. He looked surprised.

"What, you know?"

"She gave it to Mrs Knowles to post." Cynthia told the circumstances in which it was sent. "She expressed herself in precisely the same way when she wrote to me," she added, "but when I spoke to her about it she explained it by saying that it was written when her illness was coming on and when she could not realize what was the matter with her."

"Do you think that accounts for everything?" Sir Donald demanded abruptly.

Cynthia paused and wrinkled up her brows.

"I don't know," she said slowly. "It does not seem to me to be altogether adequate, yet I cannot form any other theory."

Sir Donald nodded gravely. His eyes looked absorbed and speculative as he mechanically watched the shaft of sunlight that fell athwart Cynthia's head and turned her glory of chestnut hair to burnished gold.

"It is my belief her ladyship wanted Sir Donald back almost as soon as he was gone," Gleeson interposed. "I noticed how she was fretting for him before we went to Brussels. Then Mr Gillman came on the scene; and from the first that ever he saw her he laid himself out to please her. He wanted the spending of her money, the villain!" she concluded vindictively. "It was just pure loneliness made her take him, poor lady! I made no doubt she has regretted it often enough since. However, here's your tea getting cold while you are talking, miss, and I am sure a drink of it would do you good."

She poured it out and brought it to Cynthia with a tempting plate of thin bread and butter. To please her the girl put the cup to her lips and then, surprised to find how thirsty she was, drank a little feverishly.

Sir Donald took a cup and stirred the contents absently.

"You saw Bolt & Barsly's clerk when he came over, he told me?" he said. "The interview seems to have been enough to convince him that matters were all right."

"Yes, I was in the room a good deal of the time," Cynthia replied, toying with a piece of the scone which had been so urgently recommended by Gleeson. "Cousin Hannah was terribly averse to seeing him. Mr Gillman had hard work to persuade her, but it did not do her any harm, and afterwards she said she was very glad she had done it."

"Dear, dear, yes," Gleeson went on volubly as Sir Donald relapsed into silence again, "that she would be, for she was always trying to write to Mr Barsly without Mr Gillman knowing! You'll excuse me, miss, but you do feature her; I noticed it the first time I saw you. No need to tell me she is a Miss Hammond, sir, I said to Sir Donald here; she carries it written in her face. I came to my mistress when she was not such a great deal older than you are now, miss, and the way you remind me of her is something wonderful! You will be one of Mr Basil's children, I made no doubt, miss—him as settled in Ireland?"

Cynthia glanced away from the woman's kindly interested eyes.

"I—yes, we were in Ireland," she replied evasively.

"I knew it!" Gleeson said triumphantly. "Eh, well, I remember your father, miss! A fine, personable gentleman he was, and a great favourite with my mistress; I'll go bail that it was the remembrance of him that turned her thoughts to you when she became ill!"

"I do not know, I am sure!" Cynthia said, plaiting two or three of the folds of her dress together. She shrank intensely from the friendly inquisition. Above all things she wished to keep her identity a secret; and her adventure of the afternoon, her knowledge that her husband was in the neighbourhood, had increased her previous desires tenfold. "It—it is very sad for Cousin Hannah," she went on quickly, anxious to change the subject. "She must feel her helplessness terribly after the active life she has led."

"Ay, ay, poor dear lady!" Gleeson shook her head mournfully.

"The spectacle of her helplessness seems to have impressed Fowler—Mr Barsly's clerk—considerably," Sir Donald went on. "One remark of his, though, struck me as rather overshooting the mark; he spoke of the pathos of seeing her pretty white hands lying helpless. Now—"

"I should just have laughed in the man's face," Gleeson broke in with withering scorn, "when I remember how the poor thing was crippled with rheumatism! If it hadn't been for that we shouldn't have spent our time wandering from one watering- place after another, and she might never have met that scamp Gillman, for, saving your presence, miss, I can't mince matters when I remember what he made my poor lady suffer while I was with her!"

Cynthia was sipping her tea, and, feeling intensely thankful that the conversation was thus diverted successfully into fresh channels, she looked up in surprise.

"Cousin Hannah's hands are pretty and delicate," she said, "I have often thought how beautifully white and unwrinkled they are for an old lady's, though she cannot use either of them—I mean that though she can just manage to sign her name, it's a matter of great difficulty; her power of grasping seems gone."

"Dear! You surprise me, miss!" Gleeson said slowly, her wrinkled face looking troubled and perplexed. "I'm not denying that one's hands may turn white in illness, but that knuckles distorted by rheumatism should regain their comeliness is what I cannot understand!"

Cynthia finished her tea without making any comment; then, after a short pause, she rose.

"I am very much obliged to you for the tea and rest," she said gratefully, "but I think I must be going back now, or they will be getting alarmed about me."

Gleeson began an animated remonstrance, but Sir Donald quietly picked up his cap.

"I will come with you," he said. "We will walk through the pine-wood where you found Spot's body. Was my aunt very much troubled when she heard of his death?"

"Yes, I think so," Cynthia replied doubtfully. "She did not say much to me. Mr Gillman had buried him under the oak saplings he has been moving in the plantation. Cousin Hannah did say that if Greylands passed into other hands she should make a stipulation that the poor little grave should not be disturbed; but she has not mentioned him to me lately. I have sometimes thought from little things I have noticed that her memory is failing her a good deal."

"That is very likely," Farquhar assented. "I believe that when paralysis has affected the body to the extent it has in her case it usually ends by attacking the brain, and of that loss of memory is one of the first symptoms. Poor old Aunt Hannah! You do not know how I blame myself for this quarrel, Miss Hammond! It is true she demanded an obedience which I was compelled by my own manhood to refuse, but I knew that her bark was worse than her bite, that very soon she would regret her hard and bitter words and be glad to have me back. I was angry too, though I vowed I would not retract until she sent for me, and I betook myself to the other end of the world in a dudgeon."

He pulled his cap down over his eyes and walked along by Cynthia's side, apparently absorbed in gloomy reflection. There was a pause; Cynthia's eyes wandered across the moor, strayed over the sunlit gorse, past the pine-woods to the clump of dark firs that represented Greylands.

"I am very sorry about it all," she said, "but perhaps it will come right some day. Even if Cousin Hannah in her illness remembers only her feeling of anger against you she must have forgiven you before —her letter shows that. I think—I am sure I have heard that when the brain is affected people are often angered with those whom in health they have loved the best." She glanced up wistfully at Farquhar as she finished.

Meeting the look of sympathy in her eyes, some of the hardness died out of his.

"Thank you!" he said softly. "You are very good to me, Cynthia— for I may call you that, may I not?"

A curious look, half fear, half repulsion, came into the eyes he was watching; an involuntary tremor shook Cynthia as she remembered the name that was hers by right.

"Yes, yes, please do!" she said hurriedly. "Always call me Cynthia—I like that best."

They were nearing Greylands now, and in the shadow of the pine-wood the girl stopped.

"Please do not come any farther now! Indeed, I would rather you did not!" as the man made a gesture of refusal. "If Mr Gillman saw us together he might be angry or perhaps suspect who you are, and I do think it would be better for Cousin Hannah's sake and everybody's that it should not be known at present."

"Perhaps you are right," Farquhar conceded reluctantly. He held her hand for a minute. "You will stand my friend now that you know all, will you not, Cynthia? You will tell my poor old aunt that I am not ungrateful for all her love and kindness; you will win some message of forgiveness for me; you will persuade her to see me again?"

"I will do my best," Cynthia promised, looking up at him with dewy eyes.

Sir Donald retained her hand in his.

"Thank you! Some day, if I find you alone in the house, as I did before, I think I shall put your promise to the test by asking you to let me go up to her room and plead my cause with my aunt in person!"

"I doubt whether I could," Cynthia said hesitatingly, "or whether I ought after what she said then. Since that day I have never been left alone in the house with her. Mr Gillman and Sybil never go out together."

"Ah, well, perhaps there may be an opportunity some day! In the meantime it is much to know that I have your sympathy, little cousin!" Farquhar stooped low over the slender, ungloved hand lying in his; then, as the brown fingers grew restive, he released them, and straightening himself, stood upright. "I shall stay here until I see you safe within the gate of Greylands, to make sure that you meet with no annoyance."

"Oh, but there is no need!" Cynthia said quickly. "Indeed—"

Farquhar made no reply; something in the set of his mouth told the girl that his mind was made up, and, with a slight shrug of her shoulders, she turned away. Sir Donald watched the slender figure until it disappeared from sight beneath the firs; then he slowly walked back to the cottage on the moors.

Gleeson was leaning over the little wicket watching for him; her comely face looked troubled. As Sir Donald came up she gripped his arm.

"Ah, Sir Donald, what have they done to my poor lady?"

Sir Donald's own face was dark, but he looked at her kindly.

"We must hope for the best, Glee! It may be all the illness, you know."

The woman heaved a long sigh.

"Ay, Sir Donald, it may be, but when I listened to the young lady talking my mind was busy at work. I could not help thinking and worrying, and I couldn't see daylight anywhere." Her voice sank in a whisper. "You heard what she said about the hands—my lady's hands that could never wear her ring because they were that swollen? I can't understand it, Sir Donald; and telling the young lady she wouldn't hear your name, when I know she had been fretting herself to death thinking that she wouldn't have the chance to make it up with you before I left. Sir Donald, that Gillman is a villain, that's what he is! There's no dirty trick he wouldn't play to keep you out of your rights, and—and if he thought my lady was turning to you again—it's my belief that he wouldn't even stop at murder!"

Sir Donald's dark face paled, and he interrupted her sternly:

"Don't! Be careful what you say, Glee! You—you let your tongue run away with you sometimes."

Chapter Thirteen

"I DON'T know whether you are one who believe in ghosts, miss?"

Cynthia paused.

"Ghosts? Why no, Mrs Knowles; do you?" The charwoman rolled her arms in her apron.

"I never did hold with such like, miss; but last night when you were out walking on the moor, which I'm sure I am surprised that you are not afraid of being kidnapped out there alone in the dusk!"

Cynthia laughed.

"I think I am safe enough. What happened last night, Mrs Knowles?"

The charwoman's large-featured face looked perplexed and undecided.

"I had been washing out some blinds, miss, for the landing, and I was a bit late, for it was getting dark, but thinks I to myself I will put them up, for they was wanted. I'd just got the old ones down and was running new tapes in the others, when some one come along the passage so soft-like I never heard her till she was right on me—a thin tall woman with a lot of white hair and spectacles."

"Lady Hannah?" Cynthia cried involuntarily. "Why, then she—"

"My lady, not a bit of it, miss!" Mrs Knowles said with decision. "'Twasn't anybody I'd ever seen before; I could take my oath of that, and I had a good look at her too, for she stopped a minute and looked right at me! Then before I had pulled myself together to speak to her, she was off up the stairs to the top rooms as quick and as quiet as you please."

Cynthia felt puzzled.

"What an extraordinary thing! What did you do?"

"I sat a bit till I got my breath back, then I went up after her, but no sign of her could I see. Miss Sybil, she was up there in her room, and she come and helped me to look, but it was no good. That was why I asked you if you believed in ghosts, miss."

"Oh, it must have been your fancy!"

Mrs Knowles picked up her broom and began to sweep the kitchen with great vigour.

"'Twasn't no fancy, miss. She was there as large as life!"

"Well, I can't understand it!" concluded Cynthia as she went into the dining-room. Sybil was doing some fancy-work and Gillman was reading the paper, but as Cynthia entered he threw it aside and went to the window.

"What does this mean?"

The two girls looked at him in surprise, but Sybil, as usual, was the one to respond:

"What does what mean, Cousin Henry?" She ran over to the window. "Oh, a carriage and pair stopping at the gate! Somebody must be coming to call!" clapping her hands. "Oh, what fun!"

"Fun, indeed?" growled Gillman. "You know perfectly well that your cousin and I came here to get out of that sort of thing! This is your doing, I suppose?" turning on Cynthia, who had joined them.

His tone was almost savage. Cynthia glanced at his face, dark with anger, in unqualified amazement.

"I know no more of it than you do! It is scarcely likely—I mean"—her voice trembling at the thought of her encounter with Letchingham—"surely no one I know has found me out here?"

Her eyes were full of terror as, keeping well in the shadow of the window curtains, she tried to see the occupants of the carriage that was slowly making its way over the rough road to the front of the house. There were two men on the box, but a glance was enough to show her that they did not wear the Letchingham livery, and her face brightened.

As the mysterious carriage passed the window, Cynthia saw that the two ladies—an elderly woman and a young girl—who occupied the front seat, and a rubicund youth, who was lounging with his back to the horses, were equally unknown to her.

"They are friends of yours?" Gillman questioned shortly.

She shook her head, but he looked strangely disturbed.

Sybil gave a curious laugh as there was a loud double knock at the front door.

"I wonder what they will think of our *ménage*? Mrs Knowles will present a curious contrast to their footman."

As she spoke, Mrs Knowles was heard clattering across the hall; evidently she had not thought fit to remove the wooden pattens in which it was her habit to swill out the back premises. Cynthia could not forbear an inward smile at the vision of her opening the front door, attired as she had seen her but a few moments before in a rusty black bonnet, and with an apron by no means spotless tied over her working gown, while a dingy shawl covered her shoulders.

Through the partially-opened door they caught the inquiry:

"Lady Hannah Gillman at home?"

"My lady is at home, but she ain't well enough to see folks," was Mrs Knowles's uncompromising reply.

The footman went back to his mistress, and there was a short colloquy, during which Gillman appeared strangely uneasy. Once he turned into the passage as if he meant to leave the house by the back door, but as the elder lady got out of the carriage he paused.

"Can I see Mr Gillman or Miss Hammond? I am Lady Duxworth, an old friend of Lady Hannah Gillman's." The clear, low tones were perfectly audible in the dining-room. "I did not know until yesterday that she was in the neighbourhood, and I am particularly anxious to see her."

Cynthia drew a deep breath of relief.

"Well, my lady," they heard Mrs Knowles reply apologetically, and evidently overawed, "my lady don't as a rule see folks, not feeling up to it, but I make no doubt for your ladyship it will be a different matter. I'll make so bold as to ask your ladyship to walk in while I—"

At this juncture Gillman, after taking a few steps down the room in the opposite direction, apparently made up his mind as to his course of procedure. He threw open the door and went into the hall.

Mrs Knowles dropped a curtsy.

"Here is the master to speak for himself, my lady," she said, as she retreated.

A tall, elegant woman, dressed in palest grey, with costly laces drawn over her shoulders and a tiny Parisian toque resting on her abundant silvery hair, was standing in the doorway. Gillman went towards her with his swift flashing smile.

"Will you not come in, Lady Duxworth? I must apologize for your unceremonious reception!"

Lady Duxworth looked at him in obvious amazement.

"I beg your pardon—I do not quite understand! I asked for Mr Gillman or Miss Hammond."

Gillman's smile was as ready as ever as he stepped back and held open the drawing-room door.

"I am so sorry that to-day my wife is too ill to see anyone!"

Lady Duxworth's expression was one of puzzled bewilderment.

"Surely you cannot be—"

The next moment the door was closed, and the girls could hear no more. It seemed a long time to Cynthia, with the fear that the visit might in some way refer to her husband's presence in the neighbourhood, but it was not in reality more than ten minutes before Gillman came out looking grave and troubled.

"It seems that Lady Duxworth was a friend of your cousin's long ago; she is very disappointed that she is not able to see her to-day, but, in deference to the doctor's orders, I dare not let her go up. She is anxious to become acquainted with you both, though, and I have promised that one of you shall go over to lunch with her at Duxworth Towers, which, it seems, is within driving distance. It must be you, naturally, Cynthia!"

The girl drew back.

"No, no, I cannot go! Sybil, you—"

Gillman frowned.

"Nonsense, nonsense! Do not be silly, Cynthia! Lady Duxworth tells me that they are quite alone except for the young man who is outside in the carriage, Lord Arthur St Clare, and she is anxious to have a talk with you about your relatives."

"Well, I can't tell her anything about them!" Cynthia said in her desperation.

She looked to Sybil for support, counting upon that young lady's expressed love of gaiety; but Sybil basely deserted her.

"I do not think Cousin Hannah would like me to be away the whole day."

"I am sure she would not!" Gillman answered. "It must be Cynthia. Come, we must not keep Lady Duxworth waiting. She wants to see you both," as Sybil seemed to hang back. "Here are the girls, Lady Duxworth!" he went on as he marshalled them into the drawing-room.

Cynthia looked up timidly at the fashionably garbed woman, but she found her hands taken in a soft warm clasp.

"Oh, my dear, you are so like Hannah Hammond when we were girls together—and she was my greatest friend!" Lady Duxworth exclaimed. "I must give you a kiss for her sake." She drew the girl towards her, and Cynthia for her part fully responded to the gracious ease and charm of manner. "You are Basil Hammond's daughter, I hear," Lady Duxworth went on. "I remember him well. You must tell me about him."

Cynthia blushed vividly, but Lady Duxworth was turning to Sybil.

"Why, my dear, I should never have guessed you were a Hammond—from your appearance at least! And where do you come in?"

Sybil's candid eyes were smiling into the great lady's; her hand lay confidingly in Lady Duxworth's.

"My father was a cousin of Lady Hannah's too— William Hammond. He went out to Australia when he was quite young."

"Ah, that accounts for my never having heard of you!" Lady Duxworth looked a little puzzled. "Yet I fancied the ramifications of the Hammond family tree were fairly well known to me in the old days. Now I want to carry you both off to lunch, but Mr Gillman is very cruel and declares he can only spare one. Which is it to be?" She glanced smilingly at Cynthia.

The girl looked manifestly embarrassed.

"You are very kind, but I think Sybil—"

"I cannot leave Cousin Hannah," Sybil said quickly.

Gillman looked from one to the other with a smile.

"I think it must be this one," he said, patting Cynthia's shoulder. "My wife has learnt to depend more on Sybil, possibly because she is accustomed to illness."

"That is settled, then," Lady Duxworth said as she smiled. "You must tell me all about your cousin, Cynthia. I am longing to hear. Now, how soon can you be ready, my dear?"

With the pretext of putting on her hat Cynthia made her escape from the room. She sighed as she ran upstairs. With all her heart she shrank from the proposed visit, which, in face of Gillman's expressed willingness, she found it impossible to avoid; the fear that in some way, notwithstanding Lady Duxworth's evident lack of suspicion, it might lead to her discovery by her husband was strong upon her.

As she stood before the glass she heard the sound of voices outside—Sybil's light laugh mingling with a man's deeper tones; and, looking out, she saw that the girl in the carriage was leaning forward and talking eagerly, while Sybil, standing near the door, was chattering away in her usual airy fashion. The man who had come with Lady Duxworth was laughing and replying to her sallies, watching her at the same time with, as Cynthia fancied, an almost disconcerting amount of attention. Some instinct made Cynthia hurry with her dressing; she paused at Lady Hannah's door as she went downstairs, but it was locked as usual, and she could hear no sound within as she knocked softly.

Lady Duxworth and Gillman came to meet her.

"That is right, my dear, you have been very quick!" the former began approvingly. "Come out now and let me introduce you to my young people. Marion, this is Cynthia Hammond. Now, mind, I expect you two to be as great friends as Lady Hannah and I were at your age."

Lady Marion laughed.

"It seems to be all settled for us, then," she said as she made room for Cynthia.

Lady Duxworth turned to the young man who was lounging beside the door.

"Arthur, I want to introduce you to Miss Hammond—Lord Arthur St Clare, my dear."

Cynthia and Lord Arthur bowed, and after a momentary pause the latter turned quickly back to Sybil, his round, smooth, boyish face wearing an expression of open admiration not unmixed with perplexity. Gillman came forward to assist Lady Duxworth to the carriage, and stood chatting with her a while.

"How disappointed Hannah will be not to be allowed to see you!" he said as he closed the door. "But you understand that I must obey the doctor's orders. As soon as I have his permission you shall be her first visitor, when you come back."

"Which will not be before November, I am afraid," her ladyship remarked and sighed. "As I told you, we leave to-morrow for this round of visits, and then Lord Duxworth has been ordered to try Homburg for his gout. Altogether I do not suppose we shall be here again till we come for the November shooting. I know Lord Duxworth will not miss that."

"In November, then, we shall look forward to seeing you again. By that time I hope my wife will have made great progress. The specialist gives us hope—indeed, I may say certainty of it."

"I am so glad! What specialist did you have? I always think Dawson-Clewer the best for this sort of thing."

"I quite agree with you, but unfortunately—"

Gillman was leaning forward and arranging the rugs; the end of his sentence was inaudible. He stepped back and raised his hat. "Good-bye, Lady Duxworth. My wife will write to you as soon as ever she is able. Au revoir, Cynthia."

As the coachman drove cautiously down the rough road Lady Duxworth laid her hand over Cynthia's.

"My dear, I cannot tell you how sorry I am to hear of your cousin's illness. It is so good of you to come to nurse her, but it must be very depressing work for two young girls. I wish I could have brought your cousin away too."

"Nursing does not seem to have depressed her," Lord Arthur interposed. He glanced back at the house. "Curious thing, I could have sworn I had seen her before, yet I can't place my recollection at all."

"Oh, my dear boy, one meets every one in society!" Lady Duxworth shrugged her shoulders and dismissed the subject. "She is very pretty," she went on, turning to Cynthia. "Was her father a brother or a cousin of yours?"

Cynthia hesitated; her difficulties, which she had plainly foreseen when Gillman insisted on her accepting the invitation, were beginning already.

"I do not fancy he was either; but I really know very little about the Hammond family," she replied truthfully.

Her embarrassment was perfectly patent, and Lady Duxworth looked a little surprised.

"I wish I had known earlier that you were all at Greylands. It seems such a pity not to find it out until our last day, when we have been at the Towers for a month, for I could—at any rate while I was here—have made things a little livelier for you. Really, Greylands looks to me as though it might be haunted, with all those dark trees around. I wonder at Lady Hannah's liking for it, yet Mr Gillman tells me it was entirely her choice to settle down there."

"Yes, I suppose it was; she seems to like it."

"There is no accounting for taste," Lord Arthur remarked sagely. "One man's meat is another man's poison, don't you know."

"Arthur always has a proverb to suit every occasion," Lady Marion remarked, with a low ripple of laughter.

"Wish I had!" Lord Arthur defended himself. "Awfully useful things, proverbs. I used to hear my nurse quote them when I was a kid, and that sort of thing sticks, don't you know."

Cynthia felt as though she had been out of the world for years. She sat silent, well aware that to the rest of the party she must look *gauche* and unformed, yet unable for the life of her to join in the merry badinage that went on.

She was glad when the long drive was over and they pulled up before Duxworth Towers.

"Ah, Duxworth and Petre are back, then!"

Lady Duxworth said as they got out and saw a motor farther on.

"What should you say if they have brought a friend of yours with them, child?" with a smile at Cynthia.

"A friend of mine?" Cynthia faltered, shrinking behind as her thoughts flew to Lord Letchingham. "I don't understand."

"Well, don't look frightened!" Lady Duxworth patted her arm. "It is nobody very formidable. What do you say to a cousin?"

"A cousin!" Cynthia looked up and saw that one of the men coming down the steps was Farquhar; the other two she rightly judged to be Lord Duxworth and his son.

Farquhar held out his hand with a smile.

"So you actually managed to storm the enchanted castle and bring away the Princess!" he said to Lady Duxworth. "I give you my compliments."

"Oh, yes, that was comparatively easy," Lady Duxworth assented as she drew Cynthia with her into the hall. "But I was not allowed to see my old friend. I was agreeably surprised in Mr Gillman, though, after all that I have heard; he is a very handsome man and has really charming manners."

"Yes," Cynthia said doubtfully. "Certainly he is much younger than Cousin Hannah, otherwise I do not know that there is much—"

"Much fault to be found with the marriage," Lady Duxworth concluded briskly. "I dare say you are right. Our neighbours always know our business better than we know ourselves."

"Every man knows where his own shoe pinches," murmured Lord Arthur, in the background.

Meanwhile Cynthia, still feeling bewildered and apprehensive, was being greeted and welcomed by Lord Duxworth and Lord Petre. The former, a curious contrast to his tall, slim wife, was a short, stodgy little man, with a pleasant red face and red hair and side whiskers. As Lady Duxworth finished her speech, Lord Petre turned to his mother.

"Gillman!" he repeated. "Gillman, did you say? Why, I met a man of that name the year before last. It was when I was at Monte Carlo. He was an attractive sort of fellow, but an infernally bad hat, or so it was rumoured. It was said that he used to scrape acquaintance with all the silly young fools who frequent the tables and take them home to his villa and get them to play *écarté* till they had lost every penny they possessed. He had a pretty little wife with him too. I fancy she had her share in attracting visitors to the house; but I don't suppose this would be the same?"

"Highly improbable, I should think!" Lady Duxworth remarked in a repressive voice. "Gillman is not an uncommon name. Will you come in to luncheon, Cynthia? I am sure after your long drive you must be hungry!"

They all trooped into the dining-room, laughing and chattering gaily, and Cynthia took her place at the carefully appointed table between Lord Duxworth and Sir Donald. She felt as if the events of the past few months—her marriage, her flight from Lord Letchingham, and her sojourn at dreary Greylands—had been a dream, and she was back again at the Fearons'—Cynthia Densham once more. Sir Donald's voice at her elbow broke in upon her reverie. He was smiling at her with amused eyes.

"I began to despair of meeting you again. I have haunted the pine-wood for the past week in vain, so at last I took counsel with Lady Duxworth."

Cynthia looked at him.

"Do you mean that you—" Her expression was distinctly unfriendly.

Sir Donald hastened to make his peace.

"I was so anxious to hear of my aunt," he pleaded diplomatically, "and it is only through you—"

Cynthia was not inclined to be easily placated.

"I thought I told you that I was at Greylands because I particularly wanted to be quiet?"

Sir Donald looked crestfallen.

"I did not think a quiet visit like this and a quiet chat with your own cousin could be counted as gaiety."

"Did you not?" Cynthia's tone was cold, and she did not smile as she met his penitent gaze. After a moment's deliberation she turned to Lord Petre. "You were saying that the Mr Gillman you knew—"

"It is a funny thing," Lord Arthur St Clare broke in in his peculiar low-voiced drawl from his seat beside Lady Marion, "but I feel sure I have met your cousin before, Miss Hammond; her face is quite familiar to me, though I cannot remember in the least where I saw it."

"Indeed?" Cynthia said vaguely. "I do not know. I fancy Sybil has only been in England about a year. Before then she lived in Australia."

"She is extremely pretty," Lady Duxworth said authoritatively. "But she is not in the least like the Hammonds."

"Well, I am certain I did not meet Miss Sybil for the first time this morning," Lord Arthur went on argumentatively. "Though I can't place her at present, I never forget a face when I have once seen it, though I am a terrible duffer at names."

Lord Arthur was evidently a recognized butt, and Lord Petre began to rally him upon some mistakes into which his boasted memory for faces had led him. Sir Donald and Lord Duxworth and even Lady Marion joined, but amidst the storm of chaff and raillery Lord Arthur preserved his expression of imperturbable good nature.

"Give you my word, I never forget a face I have seen," he reiterated as they rose from the table, "though I never can—Oh, by Jove!" His face looked suddenly serious.

"What is it, Arthur? Have you suddenly remembered where you met her?" Lord Petre inquired with mock interest. "Come, tell us where it was!"

A sort of puzzled amazement was dawning in Lord Arthur's pale-blue eyes.

"I—oh, it is very easy to make mistakes; a fellow can never be sure that he is right!" he stammered evasively.

Lady Duxworth laid her hands on Cynthia.

"Now you are coming with me, dear. I want to hear all about your cousin, and you must tell me all you remember about your dear father and what you have been doing since you lost him."

This was precisely what Cynthia most desired to avoid, but she had to resign herself to the inevitable, and the next hour was to her a veritable ordeal. Her knowledge of the private history of the Hammonds was of the slightest, and in reply to Lady Duxworth's questions she had to draw in a great measure upon her imagination. With regard to Lady Hannah, however, considering the friendship that had formerly subsisted between her and Lady Duxworth, she was more explicit. Lady Duxworth looked more and more incredulous and puzzled as she went on; it was evident that she found the accounts of the life lived by the invalid at Greylands almost incredible.

"Somebody certainly ought to interfere!" she said decidedly at length. "It is impossible that a woman of Lady Hannah's position should really choose to live in that way without any servants or establishment. I wonder some of her relatives—"

"I don't think she has any nearer than cousins. The present Lord Hammond, besides being a minor, is only her cousin's grandson,"

Cynthia said doubtfully, "and it would be no use applying to him. There is only Sir Donald Farquhar," she added, blushing vividly, to her great annoyance, "and she will not see him!"

Lady Duxworth smiled as she drew her own conclusions, coupling the blush with Sir Donald's anxiety that she should invite his cousin to pay her a visit; but her face sobered again.

"Ah, I am so sorry to hear that!" she said quickly. "You must try to alter it, Cynthia. Poor boy, she was always so fond of him, and he was devoted to her, and it hurts him terribly that she should turn from him now. It must be your part to make peace, Cynthia dear!"

Cynthia looked mutinous.

"I do not know that I can do anything," she said.

Lady Duxworth felt disappointed; the likeness she saw in Cynthia to her old friend had attracted her in the first place, but now, glancing at the girl's firm mouth and sparkling eyes, she was inclined to wish that the more plastic-looking Sybil had been the one to accept her invitation.

"It must be as you please, certainly," she said coldly. "But one can hardly help sympathizing with Sir Donald—or at least it seems so to me."

Seeing her change of expression Cynthia felt a quick throb of compunction.

"I am sure—" she began hastily.

But the time for confidences was past. The door opened and Lady Marion's bright face looked in.

"Have you not finished, mother? Tea is waiting."

Cynthia would have drawn back, but Lady Duxworth rose.

"We have quite finished."

She went out through the open window to the tea-table, which was set on the lawn beneath a broad-spreading cedar, and Cynthia followed, feeling miserably that she had alienated one who might have proved a valuable friend.

Sir Donald hovered around her at tea-time, but all his attention failed to win a smile or a glance, and he stood by her looking gloomy and disconsolate.

Lady Duxworth, though far too great a lady to let her guest feel neglected, was yet fully able to make Cynthia recognize that she had displeased her, and it was with great relief that the girl saw the carriage that was to take her back to Greylands drive round.

After she had taken leave of her host and hostess Sir Donald leaned over her as she sat in the carriage and, under pretext of arranging the rug, managed to touch one hand.

"Have I offended beyond forgiveness?"

"Certainly not, Sir Donald!" Cynthia answered primly. "It was only that I thought you knew I came into the country for quiet; but it does not matter."

Sir Donald's eyes looked troubled; they dwelt wistfully on the small, averted face.

"I did not understand! I am very sorry; I am afraid I thought only of my own pleasure in seeing you."

Something in his tone melted Cynthia's resentment; a flicker of colour passed over her cheeks, and her eyes drooped.

Sir Donald's spirits rose as he noted the signs.

"You will forgive me, Cynthia?"

The girl gave him one shy glance.

"Perhaps—oh yes"—hastily as the coachman flicked his whip—"certainly I will!"

Chapter Fourteen

"Poor Hannah! Stop your snivelling, then! Who loves poor Hannah?"

"Who loves you anyway I should like to know?" Sybil inquired captiously, contriving to give the parrot's tail a tweak that made it emit a loud discordant shriek of rage and set it dancing about its cage. "I shall strangle that bird one day, I know, Cynthia."

The other girl looked up from her book with a smile.

"No, you won't; Polly's bite is sharp enough to protect her. What a baby you are, Sybil! The parrot would not be half such a nuisance if you did not tease her."

Sybil came over and perched on the arm of her chair.

"One must do something. I am not, like you, always happy if I have got my nose poked inside some musty, fusty, old book. What have you got there—Browning? Ugh!" wrinkling up her straight little nose. "Where did you find it?"

"In the drawing-room. I thought I might bring it out to read it. It is Cousin Hannah's and Mr Gillman must have given it to her— see!" She turned to the title-page. "'To my darling Hannah, from her devotedly attached Henry,'" she read. "Sybil, what are you doing?"

For Sybil, leaning over her, had suddenly snatched the book from her hand and flung it face downwards on the ground.

"Disgusting!" she said hotly, her eyes flashing, her cheeks flaming. "I wonder how she dare?"

Cynthia looked at her in amazement.

"Well, ridiculous as the expression may sound to you, I suppose a man has the right to address his own wife as he pleases!" She picked up the book. "I believe you have broken the back, Sybil. What will Cousin Hannah say?"

"I don't care." Sybil's tone was almost sullen. "Absurd old idiot! As for him—"

"Well, at any rate, if they like to write the silliest nonsense in the world we cannot prevent them," Cynthia argued sensibly.

"Can we not?" Sybil's mood had apparently changed; she laughed shortly as she sprang off the arm of the chair, with a suddenness that threatened to upset Cynthia, and went over to the open window. Cynthia, looking at her, saw that her breath was still coming quickly, that one of her feet in its small high-heeled shoe was tapping impatiently on the floor. Marvelling what could be the cause of her emotion, Cynthia sat silent; surely she thought the spectacle of Gillman's apparent devotion to his elderly wife was no new thing.

She was about to speak, when Sybil uttered a low exclamation and leaned forward.

"It is—it must be a circus procession coming across the moor! Oh, come, Cynthia, let us go down to the gate and look at it!" she said, running towards the door.

"A circus procession?" Cynthia repeated incredulously. "Nonsense!"

"It is! Don't I tell you it is?" Sybil affirmed impatiently. "If you look out of the window you will see the horses—such a string of them! A woman in a habit covered with tinsel is riding one; and then the vans—all covered! There are such a quantity! Do make haste, Cynthia; they will be at the gate in a minute!"

Cynthia hung back and said:

"I do not think I will come. I—I don't care for circuses; and I can see just as much as I want to from the window."

"How tiresome you are! I am sure it would be a treat to me to see even a funeral in this dull hole!" Sybil cried angrily. Then, with a twirl of her elaborately-flounced petticoats, she banged the door loudly.

After a minute or two Cynthia rose and looked through the window languidly. Only a very cursory glance could be obtained, through the fir-trees, and soon her attention wandered to the parrot, which, enraged by Sybil's treatment, was now clawing angrily at the wires of its cage, its feathers ruffled as it uttered shrill, raucous sounds of wrath.

"Pretty Polly, poor Polly! You do not forget your mistress, do you?" the girl said softly.

But the bird was in no mood for blandishments. It bit savagely at the extended fingers, and Cynthia drew back.

The circus was still passing. Through the open window she caught the sound of the animals' tramp, of the men's voices as they shouted to their charges; there was no sign of Sybil's return.

Cynthia smiled as she recalled her excitement. There was a triumphant squawk from the parrot. At length its efforts had met with their reward; it had succeeded in pulling out the bar which fastened the door of its cage, the door flew open, and, with its head cocked on one side and a wicked look in its round black eyes, it walked out and through the window.

Cynthia, whose thoughts were far away, hardly realized what was happening until it was balancing itself on the sill; then, with a quick exclamation of dismay, she sprang forward to catch it. But Polly had not gained its liberty in order to lose it again so quickly. With a fierce dab at the outstretched hands it flew away, right out of her reach, across the strip of grass before the window, and settled in one of the lowest branches of a pine-tree opposite.

Cynthia threw the window farther up and sprang out; long before she could reach her, however, Polly had recognized discretion as the better part of valour, and had flown to a higher branch right over her head. There the bird sat, preening her feathers, with guttural chuckles of satisfaction, regarding Cynthia cautiously out of the corner of her unwavering eye. The girl was in despair; in vain she tried to coax, but Polly was impervious to cajoleries. At length she saw it was impossible to think of getting the bird back alone, and she made up her mind to ask Sybil to help. She hurried down to the gate; there was no sign of Sybil, and instead she encountered Mrs Knowles's portly presence.

"La, miss, you do look flustered! Is there anything the matter?" that worthy inquired.

"The parrot has got out of its cage and I can't catch it!" Cynthia explained breathlessly. "Where is Miss Sybil?"

Mrs Knowles's rubicund countenance twinkled up in a broad smile.

"Eh, I never see such a one as Miss Sybil!" she said. "She was that excited when the circus was going by there was no holding her in. They are taking the horses and the elephants to drink at the pond over there, and nothing would do for Miss Sybil but she must go and watch them. What was it you were saying about the parrot, miss? My lady will be rare and put about if anything happens to it."

"I know she will!" Cynthia said ruefully. She was watching the animals as they trooped off across the moor to the pond, and thinking, with some natural exasperation, that surely Sybil at her age might have known better than run off after the animals like a child. Her irritation would not mend matters, however, and she turned round disgustedly and went back to the house.

"Come and try if you can help me, Mrs Knowles!" she called over her shoulder.

Mrs Knowles followed her, panting.

"Which I shall be glad if I can, miss," she said breathlessly, "knowing the store my lady set on it. Not that I can say that I am much of a hand at climbing trees, my head being apt to turn giddy on a height."

They came in sight of the parrot, busily engaged in cleaning its feathers on the branch where Cynthia had last seen it. It cocked its head as they looked up and regarded them rakishly. Cynthia could not forbear a laugh.

"Mrs Knowles," she said, "what are we to do?"

"Pines are not the easiest of trees to get up, I should say, judging by the looks of this one," Mrs Knowles said reflectively. "If we had a ladder now you could go up it, miss, and I might make shift to hold it at the bottom. I believe I saw one in the stable a day or two ago as Mr Gillman had been using over there for something. Maybe you and me together could carry it here, miss."

"We might try; it seems the only plan," Cynthia said doubtfully.

They went round to the back of the house, found the ladder where Mrs Knowles had indicated, and carried it back, notwithstanding some difficulty, the parrot meanwhile remaining an apparently interested spectator of the proceedings.

As soon, however, as they had reared the ladder against the tree, and Cynthia, having put on a pair of thick gloves and armed herself with a woollen shawl, was preparing to make the ascent, with a sound like a sarcastic chuckle it flew off and this time alighted on the outhouse in which various garden tools were kept.

Cynthia stepped down again.

"What is to be done now?" she asked despairingly.

"Well, if you ask me, miss," replied Mrs Knowles, "I should say it is a deal safer to go up and catch the bird just where it is and rest your ladder on solid bricks and mortar than on a nasty treacherous tree."

"I don't know." Cynthia looked up dubiously. "I wonder if we left the cage on the lawn and went away whether Polly would not go in herself?" she debated.

"Not she, miss! No, you just go up as quick as you can, miss. We shan't make any noise, and we shall have Polly back in the cage without my lady being any the wiser."

Cynthia thought it would be the best plan. She moved the ladder and Mrs Knowles held it at the bottom, while Cynthia, carefully and not without some feelings of trepidation, climbed up. At the top, as the charwoman had suggested, it was possible, by catching a branch of an adjoining tree, to swing herself on to the roof. The parrot eyed her with a curious sidelong leer, she fancied, but possibly it was tired of its spell of liberty, for it submitted without much struggle to be caught. Cynthia managed to throw the shawl firmly round it, and was about to turn back when, looking up, she saw that she was opposite to Lady Hannah's window. She paused a moment in amazement. The blind was not drawn down closely as usual, and from where she stood she had a distinct view of the interior of the room. The bed stood opposite the window, and the bed, as she saw plainly, to her intense bewilderment, was empty. There were signs of recent occupancy, as the bedclothes lay in a tumbled heap; not only, however, was Lady Hannah not in the bed, but as far as Cynthia could see, she was not in the room at all.

The whole of the bedroom, with the exception of the alcove, was perfectly visible, and there was no sign of any living creature at all. Something in the look of the matter-of-fact orderliness of the room, of the empty bed and easy-chairs, of the array of medicine bottles standing on the table, struck Cynthia with a terrible sense of ill. Where could her Cousin Hannah be, she asked herself, with chattering teeth as she stared round.

"Cynthia"—it was Sybil's voice, but so changed and hoarse that at first Cynthia did not recognize it—"what are you doing up there? Come down at once!"

"It is my lady's parrot as has got away, miss, and me and Miss Cynthia has been trying to catch it," Mrs Knowles took upon herself to answer. "There is its cage which we have been trying to coax it into. It is my belief that to hear that bird was lost might have done my lady some mischief, and Miss Cynthia got up there as light as you please."

"I am sure Cousin Hannah would be very cross if she knew you were scrambling about on the roof, Cynthia—parrot or no parrot!"

There was a strange note of fear underlying the anger in Sybil's voice.

Mrs Knowles laughed.

"La, my lady won't know nothing about it, will she, miss?"

Cynthia, looking strangely white and shaken, was descending the ladder, holding the shawl firmly fastened round the parrot in one hand, while she steadied herself against the rungs with the other.

"No," she said slowly, "no, she will not know."

Sybil looked at her sharply.

"She must have heard you; I believe she could see you from her bed."

Cynthia made no reply, but turned her back on the other girl and busied herself putting the parrot into its cage and fastening the door securely with Mrs Knowles's help.

When Polly was once more in safe custody Mrs Knowles lifted the cage.

"Now I think the sooner it is put back in the dining-room the better, young ladies. No, I can carry it myself, thank you, miss!" as Cynthia would have helped her. "I can see the climb has upset you. I know just how it is. If I got up there my head would be all of a swim, but for carrying and such like there is nobody better than me, though I says it as shouldn't."

She went off round the corner of the house to the back door and Cynthia and Sybil were left alone.

Sybil was the first to break the silence.

"I do not know what Cousin Henry would say!" she remarked resentfully, two hot red spots burning on her cheeks. "The doctor told us that the least shock might have the most serious consequences in Cousin Hannah's weak state; we have been taking the greatest pains to keep her as quiet as possible, and here you go and do just the very thing most calculated to alarm her. What would she think when she heard all that noise and then saw you on the roof! Why, you might have fallen down and killed yourself!"

"Cousin Hannah did not see me," Cynthia answered steadily, shivering a little as she spoke, "because—oh, Sybil, I couldn't understand it!—she is not in bed at all!"

"Not in bed at all!" Sybil echoed, her tone insensibly catching some of the solemnity of the other's. It was her turn to become pale now, and the angry colour in her cheeks faded slowly into a ghastly pallor. "What do you mean? Where is she?"

"That I do not know," Cynthia replied, watching Sybil's face. "I could see all over the room except just that part by the alcove, and assuredly she was not there. She—sometimes I have suspected it before, Sybil, once I heard steps in the room above—she is not so helpless as we think, and she can move about when she likes!"

There was a curious hard glitter in Sybil's eyes as she glanced quickly at Cynthia's puzzled face. For the first time, as the girl met her eyes, she was conscious of an overwhelming shrinking repugnance, and she drew back involuntarily.

"I think you are making some strange mistake," Sybil said. "I will go up and see what she is doing. Wait here, Cynthia!" And she hurried off.

Cynthia did not attempt to follow her; she was so bewildered and dazed by the fact of her cousin's absence as to be for the moment almost incapable of moving. Sybil was not long away; and as she came towards her Cynthia saw that she was still looking strangely disturbed.

"The door was locked as usual," she said, "but the key was not there. Cousin Henry must have taken it and then gone out and forgotten. I knocked, but there was no answer. What are we to do?"

"I do not know," Cynthia said absently. She could not forget the strange thrill that had shaken her, as she looked into that apparently unoccupied room. She felt another odd thrill of repugnance as Sybil put her arm through hers and drew her on to the grass.

Sybil turned and looked at her; she had regained her careless smile; her expression was as innocent and childlike as ever.

"You are cold, Cynthia, and I think it is so hot to-day. I hope you have not taken a chill?"

With an effort Cynthia managed to free her arm.

"Oh, it is nothing! I am quite warm, really."

Chapter Fifteen

SYBIL did not appear to notice Cynthia's rebuff; she sprang across the lawn and stood gazing through the trees.

"The last of the vans is not out of sight yet. I shall try to get Cousin Henry to take me over to see the performance," she said as she shaded her eyes with her hand.

Cynthia made no reply; the sense of mystery that had been with her since her coming down to Greylands was heavy upon her now. In vain she told herself that she was nervous and hysterical and fancied things, that she was inclined to magnify trifles. Her conviction that there was something radically wrong, that all was not open and above-board at Greylands, grew and strengthened, and with it there was borne in upon her mind a terror, a shrinking as from something indescribably evil that was altogether inexplicable.

The aversion to Gillman of which she had been conscious from the first seemed now to have extended to Sybil, and with an irrepressible shudder she moved quickly to the house.

Sybil soon caught her up.

"Do you know what I am going to do, Cynthia, if Cousin Hannah really is shamming? I am going to find her out!"

"How are you going to do that?" Cynthia's steps did not slacken and Sybil caught her arm.

"Do not be so tiresome! You will have to help me. You will have to come with me. I mean to get on the fowl-house roof, and if she is really not in her room I will tell you my plan. I do not believe I dare climb up myself, and you will have to help me."

Cynthia was by no means enamoured of the scheme.

"I thought you said the sight of anyone clambering on that roof was enough to kill Cousin Hannah?" she said uncompromisingly.

Sybil pinched her arm.

"How tiresomely literal you are! If Cousin Hannah is not there at all, as you say, it will not hurt her because she will not know anything about it. If she is, we will be as quiet as mice in getting up, and I am only just going to take the tiniest little peep. You will help me, won't you, Cynthia? Don't be cross, dear! I know I was horrid when you first told me; I couldn't believe it, it seemed so improbable. Now, if I must confess, I am most fearfully curious. It would be so funny if Cousin Hannah had been taking us in all this time!"

She raised herself on tiptoe and touched Cynthia's cheek with her hand as she spoke.

As Cynthia met her pleading smile she felt a touch of the old glamour; the spell that Sybil had exercised over her was broken, but it was not yet wholly forgotten. She even smiled a little as Sybil drew her towards the ladder.

"Well, as I feel sure that she is not there—"

"You will help me?" Sybil gave a graceful little pirouette of joy. "You are a dear, Cynthia! Now be very careful—no noise!" as she put one foot on the first rung.

Cynthia steadied the ladder carefully. Sybil went up lightly and swung herself on the roof with catlike agility. With an elaborate show of caution she peered forward at the window; then, turning she went through a joyful little pantomime.

"Come up, Cynthia!" she exclaimed. "Yes! Yes! You must! Be quick!"

After a moment's hesitation, with a curious feeling that she was taking part in some play, Cynthia climbed up.

"Oh, Cynthia, you *are* silly!" Sybil exclaimed as they stood clinging together. "To think that I was foolish enough to believe you! Cousin Hannah is there safe enough! I think I see how you came to make the mistake, though. The bedclothes are all hunched up in the middle, and she is lying half concealed by the curtain with her back towards us; her big frilled nightcap looks just like another pillow."

Cynthia gazed at her blankly.

"I tell you she was not there a few minutes ago!" she said positively.

Sybil pouted.

"How obstinate you are, Cynthia! Look for yourself instead of arguing," she said, giving her a playful little push.

Cynthia obeyed mechanically. As she leaned forward on the penthouse roof the other girl clutched her hand in a tight feverish grip.

"There she is, I tell you; you see, you are mistaken!"

Leaning forward, Cynthia looked in. Her first impression was that the room was exactly as she had seen it a few minutes ago, save that now, on the farther side of the great untidy heap of bedclothes, there lay a figure, though little of it could be seen— merely a vague outline, the back of the nightcap, one hand resting on the bedclothes. Cynthia's eyes wandered round the room. Suddenly they were caught by a chair standing by the bedside; something about it made her look again—and she knew instantly that it had been moved since she saw it before.

Sybil jerked her arm impatiently.

"Well, you see she was there all the time! You see you were mistaken!"

"Yes, I see her now," Cynthia said slowly after a little pause.

She turned her head unexpectedly, and surprised a strange exultant expression in the other girl's face. With a sudden certainty that in some way she was being tricked she bent forward again.

"Certainly she is there!" Sybil's tone was a little forced, a trifle impatient. "You are so fanciful, Cynthia! Why, you almost infected me," with a light laugh, "though I knew better in my heart, and I was certain poor Cousin Hannah could neither move hand nor foot."

Cynthia was still looking intently at that quiet form on the bed. The idea occurred to her that it might be a lay figure put in to represent Cousin Hannah, but that theory had to be dismissed, for, looking intently, it was possible to see a slight motion as of breathing. As the last phrase left Sybil's lips however the other girl started violently and drew forward recklessly.

Sybil pulled her back.

"How careless you are, Cynthia! You nearly upset us both!"

Cynthia shivered from head to foot; she caught her breath sharply; then, with a strange, frightened movement, she stepped back and hurried to the ladder. Catching sight of her face as she passed, Sybil saw that all the bright, healthy colour had faded, that even her lips looked a dull grey. She followed quickly.

"What is the matter, Cynthia, are you ill?"

Cynthia did not answer as she caught the branch and let herself down. When both girls stood on level ground once more Sybil glanced at her anxiously.

"What is it, Cynthia? Do you feel faint?" putting one arm round her caressingly.

Cynthia drew herself away swiftly.

"Don't please, Sybil! I feel hot—suffocating!" thrusting the heavy mass of hair back from her brow. "Surely there must be thunder about! It is terribly close."

Sybil regarded her pityingly.

"Poor old girl! The climb must have been too much for you! It was thoughtless of me to insist upon your doing it a second time, but I was so keen on your seeing that you had made a mistake."

"Yes, yes!" Cynthia said hurriedly. "It—it was the climbing, I—I'm not used to it. I do not think I shall come in yet, Sybil," as the girl turned towards the house. "I will walk round the garden a while. I feel as if I must have fresh air."

"You are sure you are able?" Sybil questioned anxiously. "I must go in because I have set my mind on making some scones for Cousin Henry's tea, and he may be in any moment. Don't you think you had better come in with me and rest?"

"No, no, I couldn't!" Cynthia responded incoherently, again putting aside Sybil's arm. "Please let me do as I like, Sybil!"

"Oh, certainly if you put it that way!" Sybil's tone was half offended. "But do not expect me to look after you if you are faint, for I shall be busy in the kitchen for the next half-hour."

"I shall not faint," Cynthia said decidedly as she moved off across the grass.

Sybil danced away in her usual light-hearted fashion; before she turned the corner of the house, however, she paused and cast one quick, searching glance at the tall, slim girl walking slowly down the lawn. At the same moment a corner of the blind in the room opposite the tool-house was lifted cautiously, a pair of eyes gleaming with malignant hatred looked out, a malediction was breathed into the silent air.

All unconscious, however, Cynthia pursued her way to the gate, and as she entered the belt of firs Mrs Knowles came in sight down the path that led from the kitchen. She quickened her steps as she saw Cynthia.

"It was rare and lucky we managed to get Polly back, miss," she began in her usual spasmodic fashion. "I can't say as she looks a bit worse for her outing!" with a laugh. "She was a-calling out 'Poor Polly! Poor Polly!' and a-asking for my lady as cheerful as you please when I come away."

"Yes, I'm glad we caught her," Cynthia responded absently.

Her lack of attention in no wise disconcerted Mrs Knowles; she set the basket she was carrying on the ground, and, bringing out a voluminous pocket- handkerchief, began to mop her face energetically.

"It is hot work catching parrots, isn't it, miss?" she remarked apologetically. "Especially when you are not so young as you was. I was saying just now to Miss Sybil as she ran into the kitchen, so anxious about her cakes, 'Ay, it is easy to see you have not been chasing parrots all over the place!' I said. She will have to put her best foot foremost too, as the saying is, about the making of those cakes," parenthetically, "as if they are not ready when the master calls for his tea he will not wait a minute for them. I never see a more impatient gentleman!"

"Perhaps he will not come in just yet," Cynthia remarked, somewhat overwhelmed by the torrent of words and intent only on making her escape.

"Oh, he come in some time ago!" was the unexpected answer. "I see him coming into the house before me when I was carrying Polly back to the kitchen, and while I was hanging her up and making her as comfortable as I could he was talking to Miss Sybil in the hall. Pretty cross he was too, though I couldn't hear what he was saying, but I knowed by his tone. He is a gentleman with a temper, he is, as I make no doubt my lady has found out to her cost. Begging pardon, though, miss, for alluding to it before you!"

Cynthia hardly heard the last sentence, so absorbed was she by the information thus unexpectedly imparted.

"Miss Sybil told me when she came back that she could not get into Lady Hannah's room, because Mr Gillman had gone out with the key in his pocket."

"Mr Gillman was in the hall a-talking to her when I hung Polly's cage up," Mrs Knowles affirmed doggedly. "I couldn't be mistook in his voice, miss, I have heard too much of it. Besides, I see him myself, with my own eyes, a-walking in before me. Miss Sybil must have forgot. She is a rare feather-headed one, she is!" she finished, her tone appearing to indicate that she considered the last-named quality as highly praiseworthy.

Cynthia's face looked puzzled and absorbed, and she did not reply for a minute or two. Mrs Knowles watched her expectantly. At length the girl's decision was taken; at all hazards she must consult Farquhar—must ask his advice.

"Could you take a note for me or get one sent, Mrs Knowles?"

Mrs Knowles looked round consideringly.

"I might send Tommy, miss, after I have given him his tea, if it isn't too far. It is no good me saying I will go myself, for I find the walk up here moils me to death, but if Tommy would do he could go and welcome."

"It is to Mrs Smithson's on the moor over there." Cynthia pointed vaguely in the direction. "Do you know the house? She has not been there long."

Mrs Knowles nodded.

"I know, miss. That will be all right!" she said reassuringly.

Cynthia tore a leaf from the little chatelaine hanging by her side and scribbled a few words in French upon it.

"Give that to the gentleman at Mrs Smithson's, please!" she said, handing it to the woman. "And that"—dropping a shilling into her hand—"is for Tommy."

"Which wasn't necessary, though thank you kindly for it. I'll see he takes the note, miss!"

Chapter Sixteen

IT WAS an almost oppressively hot morning, yet here in the pine-wood, beneath the shadow of the great branches, it was cool and pleasant; the sun filtered down through the leaves and chequered the paths covered deeply with withered pine-needles. To Donald Farquhar, as he waited, leaning against a tall straight fir-trunk, whence he could catch a glimpse of Greylands' gate, the morning seemed endlessly long.

For three-quarters of an hour he had waited there, hoping every moment to see a slender figure emerge from the dark belt of trees, but so far without success. He took out his watch and looked at it dolefully; he would stay a quarter of an hour longer, he decided, and if Cynthia had not come by then he would give it up for this morning, at any rate.

As he put the watch back, however, the gate opened and Cynthia came quickly across the pine- wood. Farquhar threw aside his cigar and went forward to meet her.

"I am so sorry to be late!" she began breathlessly, as she laid her hand in his. "What must you think of me? After asking you to come punctually at eleven o'clock too! I thought I should never get away—Sybil was so tiresome wanting to show me all sorts of things. I did not want her to guess why"—with a slight flush—"I mean I wished to consult you about—without anyone knowing at Grey-lands," she added, her face becoming serious.

Farquhar held her ungloved hand in his a moment longer than was really necessary.

"Anything I can do for you, my dear cousin?"

Cynthia's eyes drooped.

"You are very good; it is about Cousin Hannah."

Instantly Farquhar's expression became more alert.

"About Aunt Hannah? Has she expressed any wish to see me?"

"No, I have hardly seen her lately." Cynthia hesitated. She fancied that Sir Donald might help to solve the new perplexity of hers, but now, face to face with him, the various notions that had crowded into her brain in the past few hours seemed too fantastic, too unreal, to be imparted even to him, so she temporized.

"Would you think Cousin Hannah a person to do any very extraordinary things? To make up her mind to deceive people; in fact, to—to make them do what she wants?"

Farquhar looked slightly puzzled.

"She is distinctly fond of her own way. In the old days she generally said what she wanted and got it. Except with me on one occasion; but I dare say things are different now. Poor old Aunt Hannah!"

Cynthia looked troubled; her eyes watched the young man's questioning face wistfully.

"I can't understand it at all. But—but," with obvious hesitation, "I cannot help thinking—I have very good reasons for thinking—that Cousin Hannah is by no means so ill or so helpless as we have been told. That, however, does not explain everything."

Farquhar's face was very grave; his sombre eyes were fixed on the girl's face.

"Will you tell me exactly what you mean?" he said gently.

They had turned and were walking along the path that led right through the wood. The blue bells were all over now, their leaves were turning yellow and drooping disconsolately, while everywhere the tall bracken fronds were springing. A fallen tree-trunk lay where it had been blown down. Farquhar paused.

"Will you sit here for a few minutes and let us think things out?"

Cynthia poked her sunshade into the dry moss at the side of the path as she seated herself.

"It is very puzzling," she said, and sighed. "Why should Cousin Hannah want people to think she is helpless when she is not?"

"I cannot believe for one moment that she would—unless Gillman is compelling her to do so for his own ends," Farquhar said thoughtfully.

Cynthia shook her head.

"I cannot think that it is that. She talks of her helplessness when I am alone with her; it seems impossible to ascribe it all to Gillman's influence, and it is as difficult to understand as the resentment she expresses towards you after that letter."

"Ah!" Sir Donald drew his brows together, "that is a constant perplexity to me. How I blame myself now for having taken her at her word, for going away! But for that she never would have married that man and—"

Cynthia's eyes were full of sympathy.

"It is very sad for you," she said softly. "You were very fond of her?"

He looked away across the wood, through the endless vista of tree-trunks.

"She was the only mother I have ever known," he responded simply. "Do you wonder that I cannot bear to think of her ill and alone, in that man's power? That it was impossible to yield to her wishes I see now as plainly as I did then, but I might have been gentler—I might have waited until her anger had passed."

There was a minute's silence; Cynthia was mechanically tracing a pattern with the point of her sunshade among the fallen pine-needles. At last she spoke:

"It is always easy to see afterwards how much better we might have done. I am sure from her letter Cousin Hannah saw that she had been to blame as much as or more than you."

There was another long silence; then Sir Donald glanced at the girl's averted face.

"I have sometimes wondered whether I might tell you—whether you would care to know how it all came about."

Cynthia's colour deepened a little, and her eyes, as for one brief moment she raised them to his, looked clear and steadfast.

"I shall be very glad to hear if you care to tell me."

"I was an idiot!" Sir Donald began, with hearty self-contempt, absently striking out at an unoffending head of bracken with his cane. "In the first place it was the usual story. I was not the first fool to be caught by a pretty face with little else to recommend it, but my aunt could not forgive it." He waited a moment.

Cynthia felt suddenly chilled; surely it was colder than she had imagined, she said to herself with a slight shiver. Here, under the trees, where the sun could not penetrate, it was gloomy, damp almost.

"Yes," she said slowly. "So that was it—was why you quarrelled, was it?"

Sir Donald was not looking at her now; she glanced at the firm lines of his mouth, at his lean, dark cheek.

"That was it, partly," he agreed. "And then she wished to arrange my life for me. I do not know whether you have ever heard of the Denshams—Herbert Densham was Aunt Hannah's cousin on the mother's side."

Cynthia started.

"Yes, I—I think I have heard of them," she murmured faintly.

"Then you know that Aunt Hannah was engaged to Herbert Densham at one time?" Farquhar proceeded. "Something came between them, I do not know what, though I fancy Aunt Hannah always blamed herself. It was all broken off, and Densham married some one else. He died years ago, leaving a widow and a daughter. I wonder whether you remember my telling you that I disliked the name of Cynthia?"

"Yes, I remember." Cynthia's voice was very low.

"Well, this girl's—Herbert Densham's daughter—name was Cynthia. My aunt told me that it had long been a scheme of hers that I should marry her—Cynthia Densham. She told me that she was going to invite the girl to pay her a long visit, and ordered me to prepare myself to enter into an engagement with her."

Cynthia sprang to her feet, with an inarticulate sound of indignation.

"She could not—she never dared!" she cried, her cheeks flushing.

Sir Donald looked at her in some surprise.

"You are very good to bestow your sympathy upon me, Cynthia," he said softly. "It seemed to me too an outrageous thing that she should try to settle my life for me after this fashion. I was younger and hot-headed, and I told her so. She could never stand contradiction, and she threatened me with disinheritance unless I obeyed her. I retorted, telling her to do exactly as she pleased with her money, but that I intended to choose my wife for myself, and that nothing should induce me to contemplate marrying Cynthia Densham."

"I should think not!" gasped Cynthia, stammering in her indignation. "She—I am sure she—"

"Oh, she was furious!" Sir Donald went on, supposing the pronoun to refer to his aunt. "She said many very bitter things to me, and I resented them; matters went from bad to worse until she ordered me out of the house, and the situation seemed irremediable. The rest you have heard. I have wondered sometimes of late whether now that she knows how her *protégée* has turned out she is glad that I thwarted her scheme?"

Cynthia's wrath threatened to suffocate her during this speech, but her unqualified amazement at the last speech gave her breath.

"Turned out!" her eyes flashing. "Turned out! I do not understand you!"

"Oh, I see you have not heard all the story!" Sir Donald went on, with a smile: "well, directly after her mother's death, this girl, who was quite young, remember, became engaged to Lord Letchingham, a man old enough to be her grandfather, of whose reputation the less said the better. Only a short time ago they were married, but already, my Lady Letchingham, having got all she wanted in the shape of the title and the assured position, is declining to live with her husband or take up her responsibilities as his wife. I am sorry for poor old Letchingham. I am told that the whole thing has aged him terribly."

Some of Cynthia's colour ebbed as he finished.

"Lady Letchingham—you do not know—you do not think of her!" she said.

Farquhar laughed and said: "I must confess that I do not regard her as worth talking about, but do not let us talk of her again. I hate to hear her name on your lips. I hate to hear you defending her when I know that you cannot—that it is not possible that you should understand what she has done. Now you know why I told you I disliked the name of Cynthia, and why I was sorry you bore it. It was hitherto associated with Lady Letchingham, the woman whom I most utterly despise; but now and for the future pleasanter memories are linked with it. For your sake, little cousin"—his voice sinking to a caressing whisper—"I shall learn to love the name."

Cynthia put her hand to her throat; every pulse was thrilling with indignation, but underlying her anger she was conscious of a strange new gladness, a feeling that she could not analyse, of which she in no sense realized the meaning. She turned away and Sir Donald hurried after her. As he glanced at her drooping face, flushing and paling by turns, at her trembling lips, he told himself that he had been too precipitate, that he must wait, he must not frighten her, the shy, sweet girl whom he had learnt to love so dearly during these few short weeks of their acquaintanceship.

"Well," he said quietly, "after all it is I who have been bothering you with my affairs all this time. I have never given you an opportunity of telling me why you have reason to think that my aunt is not so helpless as she appears."

With an effort Cynthia collected her scattered thoughts.

"I was trying to catch the parrot," she began incoherently, "it had got on the coach-house roof, and when I went there after it I had a view of Cousin Hannah's room. I could see her bed plainly—and it was empty—she was not in the room at all."

"The bed was empty!" Farquhar repeated amazedly. "Where was she? I do not understand!"

"I do not know where she was—I could not see her at all," Cynthia replied, a little catch in her voice, notwithstanding her efforts to control it. "As far as I could ascertain she was not in the room; I could see all over it except a sort of alcove near the window. If—if she was in the room she must have been there. The—the door was locked, Sybil said; she tried to get in."

Farquhar looked entirely bewildered.

"If she can walk in and out of her room, lock and unlock her door, her illness must be the veriest sham," he remarked.

Cynthia sighed. With all her resolution she fought against the shock of Farquhar's extraordinary story and his opinion of her conduct, and strove instead to turn her thoughts to the enigma that had baffled them so long.

"Yes, I know that," she assented. "We got up there afterwards, Sybil and I, in a few minutes, and the bed was not empty then."

Sir Donald looked a little puzzled.

"What, she had returned?"

Cynthia hesitated; a contraction in her throat threatened to strangle her words. Again that terrible feeling of something evil came over her; she shrank, half frightened at the sound of her own voice.

"Somebody was there," she said, in a low, hoarse whisper, "but—it was this that I wanted to tell you this morning, this was why I sent to ask you to meet me—and now I am almost afraid to say it—afraid that you will only laugh at me—that you will—"

Farquhar watched her agitation in manifest bewilderment.

"I do not think that you need fear I shall do anything but listen with the utmost attention to anything you may have to say to me," he said gravely. "Will you not trust me, Cynthia?"

"Yes, yes! I will—I do!" the girl said confusedly, twisting her fingers together nervously. "Only this seems so improbable that you might well ridicule the idea. I"—drawing nearer to him and lowering her voice—"do not believe that the figure in the bed was Cousin Hannah at all."

"What!" Farquhar's accent was expressive of the utmost amazement.

"Yes, yes!" Cynthia went on, with feverish haste. "I—I am sure I am right, Sir Donald. It was not Cousin Hannah; it was some one masquerading in her place; I am quite certain because—do you remember asking me—"

"Cynthia! Cynthia!"

It was Sybil's voice; and with a guilty start Cynthia sprang away from her companion. Absorbed in their conversation neither of them had heard the other girl's approach. Sir Donald raised his hat gravely.

"Oh, Cynthia," she began breathlessly, "we have been looking for you everywhere. Cousin Hannah wants to see you, and she was so cross when you could not be found. Cousin Henry sent me all over the place, but I could not discover a trace of you until at last Mrs Knowles said a man who was getting up some peat on the moor told her that he had seen a young lady in the pine-wood. Then I came after you as quick as I could and here I am!"

"I see you are!" Cynthia's tone was distinctly annoyed, and her face did not relax as she met the other's smile. "I will follow you very shortly, Sybil."

"Oh, I am dreadfully sorry to seem so importunate, but really that will not do at all!" Sybil declared, linking her arm through Cynthia's. "I dare not go back without you. Cousin Hannah was making such a fuss, and you know they said she was not to be excited."

Cynthia saw that all opportunity of asking her cousin's advice privately was gone, so she resigned herself to the inevitable with as good a grace as possible, and held out her hand to Sir Donald.

"Good morning, Mr Heriot!"

He had turned to accompany them, but her glance forbade it and he bowed gravely and stood back reluctantly. As soon as he was out of earshot Sybil gave a gleeful little skip.

"So I have caught you, Miss Sobersides? Now I know what all these country walks mean! Well, he is not bad looking!"

Cynthia disengaged herself coldly.

"You are talking nonsense, Sybil. Mr Heriot did me a great service once, and naturally I speak to him when we meet."

Sybil laughed mischievously.

"So you go out to meet him sometimes, do you? It is all right, Cynthia; you need not blush and I will not tell Cousin Hannah. If there were any question of a *mésalliance* she might be angry; but in your case—"

Cynthia stopped short; several times it had struck her that Sybil had guessed her identity, yet Gillman was apparently unaware of it.

She could not imagine how the girl had discovered her secret unless Lady Hannah—

"What do you mean, Sybil?" she asked sharply, "it seems to me it—you are fond of hinting."

"Hinting—I?" Sybil shook her mop of fair hair back from her eyes. She looked up innocently at Cynthia from beneath the shade of her sun-bonnet, which she affected sometimes as the proper thing for the country. "What do you mean?" she asked demurely. "I can't understand."

Cynthia kept her eyes fixed on the dainty, piquant face, on the blue eyes that met hers without the suspicion of *arrière-pensée*.

"You said that Cousin Hannah would object if there were any question of *mésalliance*, but in my case—"

"You would have more sense, certainly!" Sybil finished gaily. "You might have known that. Do make haste, Cynthia! Cousin Hannah was fidgeting so when I came away, fearing that some harm had happened to you."

Cynthia quickened her steps, but she drew distinctly away from the other girl, and Sybil, hunching up her shoulders in displeasure, kept to her own side of the path.

They hurried to the house. Cynthia would have gone straight to the stairs, but as she opened the door into the hall Gillman appeared, looking worried and anxious.

"Be as quiet as possible, please," he said curtly. "Your cousin has just fallen asleep."

"I thought she wanted me," Cynthia said blankly.

"She did," Gillman said in displeased accents, "and she worked herself up into such a state of excitement when you could not be found that I was quite alarmed. But when I saw you coming out of the pine-wood, and could set her mind at rest, she quieted down at once, and now, as I tell you, she has just dropped off to sleep. It will do her more good than anything, and I am most anxious that she should not be disturbed."

Chapter Seventeen

"May I sit with Cousin Hannah this morning, Mr Gillman? It is so long since I saw her."

Cynthia's tone was very wistful. Gillman looked at her searchingly as he closed and locked the door of his wife's room.

"Not just now, later in the day perhaps. She is just dropping off to sleep, and after her bad night I am anxious that she should not be disturbed."

Cynthia went on to her room quickly and Gillman turned downstairs. Cynthia took a volume of Carlyle and sat down by her open window; but to-day she found it impossible to keep her attention fixed upon the intricate sentences. Her thoughts would turn to her own affairs; her encounter with her husband, as well as Lady Duxworth's visit the preceding week, had complicated matters by convincing her that the security which had been the charm of Greylands in her eyes was exceedingly precarious, and might come to an end any day.

She had already written to Messrs Bolt & Barsly, asking them to help her obtain a situation, but their reply had been ambiguous in the extreme, and so far nothing of a satisfactory nature had been concluded. The idea of applying for the post of English governess in a foreign school had occurred to her, but she was nearly without money for the journey or for the necessary advertisements and she had at last unwillingly determined to beg Lady Hannah to make her a small loan which should be returned at the earliest moment possible. But for the last few days she had not been able to see her cousin, and her scheme was therefore in abeyance.

Very soon she was obliged to give up the idea of reading and the book dropped from her lap. Lying back in her chair, her eyes wandering to the tall pines outside, to the tiny white flake-like clouds that were floating slowly across the deep blue of the sky, she gave herself up to a fruitless speculation as to her future which, so far as she could see, was daily becoming gloomier.

The sound of voices on the lawn outside broke across her meditations. She heard Sybil's laugh—a trifle shrill to-day, she fancied—then a man's voice, assuredly not Gillman's. Beneath the window they apparently paused and to Cynthia's amazement she recognized Lord Arthur St Clare's drawling, languid tones, quickened though they were to-day by a certain interest.

"I was positive that I had made no mistake, don't you know? But I cannot conceive how you managed it. However, where there's a will there's a way, I suppose."

Sybil's laugh sounded a little forced, Cynthia fancied.

"Oh, it was not difficult! My people were in Australia, you know. You have promised to respect my secret, however. You will not tell Cousin Henry or Cynthia?"

"You may trust me to the death!" Lord Arthur responded fervently. "If—if there is one quality I respect more than another it is pluck, Miss Sybil."

Becoming aware that she was listening to what was certainly not intended for her ears to hear, Cynthia rose and shut the window. The voices outside dropped to a whisper, but in another minute she heard Gillman come round the house and join them, and presently Sybil ran upstairs and tapped at the door.

"Cynthia, Lord Arthur St Clare is here; do come down!"

"I do not want to see him," Cynthia said, and looked at the girl, wandering what could possibly be the secret between her and Lord Arthur.

This afternoon Sybil was looking prettier even than her wont; she was wearing a white dress that threw into strong relief the vivid fairness of her complexion, her golden hair and wonderful blue eyes.

Cynthia glanced at her admiringly.

"I like the way you have done your hair, Sybil. You do look sweet! I am sure Lord Arthur won't miss me; he will have eyes for no one but you. What is this?" bending forward to look at something that was sparkling among the lace at the girl's throat.

"Oh, my pendant! Is it not pretty?" Sybil held it out, still attached to its thin gold chain.

Cynthia took it in her hand and looked at it curiously. It was a Maltese cross of finest filigree work, with five magnificent emeralds encircled by brilliants.

"It is perfectly charming!" she said admiringly. "Where did you get it, Sybil? Is it a family possession?"

"Yes, it belonged to—" Sybil began.

Mrs Knowles was puffing outside with a tray of clean linen on her extended arms.

"By your leave, young ladies!"

As the girls stood aside the charwoman's inquisitive eyes glanced at the bright object in Cynthia's hand; then her expression changed, and she stopped short.

"La! You do not mean to say that my lady has given you that there, Miss Sybil? I couldn't ha' believed that she would ever have parted with it. Many a time I have seen her wearing it, and she has told me she valued it more than anything else in the world. It was given her years ago by one she loved, she told me once, and she should treasure it as long as she lived for his sake, and when she died it was going back to his family. Well, well! I have been saying it ever since you come, Miss Sybil, that the way my lady has took to you has been something wonderful, and now to think of this! I wouldn't ha' believed it unless I had seen it with my own eyes!"

Sybil shrugged her shoulders and snatched the emerald pendant from Cynthia's hand with a quick, jerky movement.

"Don't be so stupid, Mrs Knowles!" she said pettishly. "I never said my cousin had given it to me. Your tongue runs too fast sometimes. I took a fancy to this and Cousin Hannah is letting me wear it."

Mrs Knowles paused in the doorway of the next room.

"So does other folks' tongues run on a great deal faster than they need sometimes," she said resentfully. "I am not the only person who talks, as you may find out some day, Miss Sybil. As for lending you that there—it was my belief that my lady's mind must ha' been weakened by her illness afore ever she did that, knowing the store she set on it, and as how she told me after her death it was to go to the gentleman's family, and their name began with a D, I am very certain."

Then Mrs Knowles disappeared into the room with all the dignity she could assume.

Sybil made a wry face.

"Stupid old thing! As if Cousin Hannah could not lend her pendant to anybody she pleased! I love emeralds!"

She ran down the stairs apparently forgetting her anxiety that Cynthia should accompany her.

Only too glad to have escaped the interview with Lord Arthur, Cynthia went back to her room; then, as she heard Sybil close the drawing-room door, a new thought occurred to her. She was, above all things, anxious to consult her cousin, and since her conversation in the pine-wood had been interrupted by Sybil she had had no further chance of taking him into her confidence. Sybil had developed a great fancy for walking. Cynthia had lately found it impossible to get out without her, and though on several occasions they had encountered Sir Donald, their intercourse had, of necessity, been restricted to the merest commonplace.

It struck her that to-day, while Sybil and Gillman were both occupied with Lord Arthur, she had an admirable opportunity of getting out of the house unseen, and, if possible, making her way to the cottage.

She caught up her hat and pinned it hastily on her loosened hair; then, scarcely giving herself time to think, she ran down the stairs and out of the back door.

There was a slight breeze; the air was distinctly cooler than it had been during the last few weeks; but to Cynthia, hurrying along, it felt almost hot and close. Every now and then she looked behind, fully expecting to see Sybil trying to catch her up; but there was no one in sight and at length she reached the cottage.

As she went up the garden path Farquhar came to the porch. He looked surprised as he hastened to meet her.

"Cynthia, what is it? Is there anything the matter?" he asked.

"Nothing fresh," the girl said as she gave him her hand. "It was only that to-day I was able to get away alone, and I wanted to tell you what I had noticed in Cousin Hannah's room that day."

Farquhar led the way into the little sitting-room.

"I am most anxious to hear," he said gravely, "but you must first rest, you look tired."

"I have been hurrying," Cynthia said feverishly, as with a pleasant sense of relief she dropped into a chair that he wheeled forward. "I was afraid that Sybil would overtake me. Sometimes of late I have fancied they have guessed who you are, that they want to prevent my telling you anything that may help you."

Farquhar took the low chair next hers.

"Yet if matters are as they say—if my aunt is absolutely decided in her refusal to see me—why should they fear me?"

"I do not know; it is inexplicable." Cynthia's tone was puzzled and distressed.

Farquhar drew his chair a little nearer hers, and his gaze rested on the girl's face with a look of protecting tenderness.

"I do not like you being there in that house, Cynthia," he said. "Yet how can I urge you to come away, knowing that without you my poor old aunt would be left alone, helpless in that man's hands, since Sybil seems to be entirely under his influence?"

Cynthia stirred restlessly beneath his gaze, her colour deepened, she bit her lip in embarrassment.

"I do not know that I am much good to her. Really, I very seldom see her, and it is only Sybil that she seems to care for. But you know that I wanted to tell you"—she lowered her voice and looked round anxiously as if afraid of being overheard—"I mean why I was so puzzled and frightened when I looked through Cousin Hannah's window the second time—I was going to tell you when Sybil interrupted us that morning. There—there was somebody in the bed I told you, but—but do you remember asking me about her hands?"

This apparently sudden transition amazed Farquhar.

"Certainly I do! But what—"

"When I first saw the figure in the bed," Cynthia went on quickly, "I did not think that I had made a mistake before. I felt sure my cousin was not in the bed then, but I did imagine that she had got back to bed. Now—now I do not know what to believe, for as I was looking in I saw that one hand was lying on the counterpane, and this hand, instead of being small and white like Cousin Hannah's, was big—at least twice as big as hers, and brown like that of a person who had been much in the open air. I cannot understand it!" She gazed at Farquhar with, troubled eyes.

He looked puzzled and disturbed.

"It is very strange," he said. "Possibly some stoppage of the circulation might account for it. In cases of arrested circulation the hands are often swollen and discoloured."

Cynthia looked unconvinced.

"No, I am sure it was not that!" she declared positively. "I was afraid that you would not believe me; but it was not Cousin Hannah's hand at all—I am certain of it! It was entirely different in every way."

Farquhar did not answer immediately. His eyes looked grave and hesitative. Quite evidently his mind was busy with his new problem.

"How can you account for it, then?" he questioned.

"I can't pretend to explain it at all," Cynthia confessed in a troubled tone. "I can only tell you what I saw. I thought, perhaps, you could help me to an explanation."

"The one I have just put forward seems to me the only feasible solution," Farquhar remarked. "Even if you suppose my aunt capable of playing a trick and having a substitute in her place—a hypothesis which I must confess, with my knowledge of her, appears well-nigh impossible—who could she get to undertake such a part?"

"I don't know!" Cynthia hesitated, her colour fading a little. "It has occurred to me that some one else—some one I have never seen—is concealed in the house," she said nervously. "Mrs Knowles once told me that she had seen somebody, an old lady, walking in the passage. Do you think that Cousin Hannah has some one else in the house and changes places with her sometimes? I feel frightened when I think of it."

She moved a little nearer Farquhar with the involuntarily confiding gesture of a child who fears she knows not what.

Farquhar's face was very grave.

"This is getting too much for you. The whole atmosphere of Greylands is bad for you and is getting on your nerves. Ah, Cynthia, I cannot bear to leave you there! Will you let me take you away?"

There was a touch of passion in his voice as he laid his hand protectingly over hers.

Cynthia raised her face with an expression of blank surprise.

"You are very kind," she began, "but—"

Then, as she met his gaze, suddenly comprehension came to her. The hot blood swiftly flooded face and neck and temples, her eyelashes drooped, and with a quick, shamed gesture she snatched her hand away and covered her face.

Farquhar bent over her, a gleam of passion in his eyes, a new caressing note in his voice.

"Have I frightened you, Cynthia? Did you not know that I have grown to care for you very dearly? That—"

"Ah! No, no!" With a sob that held a note of irrepressible pain Cynthia interrupted him. "I never knew—I never thought of such a thing. How should I? You must not—indeed, you must not!"

A touch of red burned on Farquhar's forehead at the sight of the girl's distress, of her evident shrinking from him. He drew himself upright.

"I am afraid it is too late for that, Cynthia. I cannot help loving you. Your soft brown eyes, your little tender, adorable ways, have stolen into my heart. I cannot tear them out—I would not if I could. But if my love means nothing to you, Cynthia, if it only troubles you, I will say no more. Only it seems to me that a love like mine must meet with some return. I will be very patient, Cynthia, if you will give me just one ray of hope."

In the light of his words, as by a lightning flash, the secret of her own heart was revealed to Cynthia. She realized the meaning of the vague, indefinable content that Farquhar's presence had always brought her, and she shrank appalled from the knowledge of what it meant. With a moan of irrepressible anguish she cried:

"No, no! It is no use—you must not!"

All the passion, all the fire had died out of Farquhar's face and in its stead there shone an infinite tenderness, an added gravity.

"Is that so? I think I understand. There is some one else—some one worthy of you."

"Ah, no! It is not that. There is no one else! There never will be—but—"

At something in her tone hope sprang once more to Farquhar's breast, a new glad light leapt into his eyes.

"If there is no one else, you cannot forbid me to hope, Cynthia," he said steadily. "Ah, do not shrink from me, dear!" the light in his face turning to triumph as he saw how her eyes refused to meet his. "I have been too sudden. I have startled you, my sweet! But you will let me teach you to care for me?" Then, as the girl shook her head, he bent over her again and captured the fluttering hands in his and stood up, drawing her with him. "Don't play with me, Cynthia! If you will look me in the face, if you will say, 'I do not love you, Donald,' I will go away and never trouble you again."

For a moment Cynthia waited, silent, motionless, striving with all her might to brace up her resolution, to resist the gladness that thrilled through every pulse in her body at the touch of his hands, at the sense of his nearness. Then, with one last supreme effort, she raised her eyes.

"I do not love—" she began; then, as she met his look, the words faltered and died on her lips. Again the swift hot colour flamed in her cheeks and her eyes veiled themselves in their long lashes.

Farquhar's arms closed round her, and he drew her head to his shoulder.

"Ah, you couldn't, Cynthia!" he whispered, his lips touching the strands of her loosened hair. "Sweetheart, your eyes told me the truth. Now it is a different lesson you must bring your lips to repeat. Say 'I love you, Donald.'"

For one brief second Cynthia had not attempted to resist the pressure of his arms. She had rested against him quiescent, her breath mingled with his, the touch of her soft hair had been upon his cheek, but now she broke from him, and, putting out her hands, she pushed him away.

"Oh, what does it matter?" she cried miserably. "What does it matter if I do, since it is no use—since you must forget me?"

At the sight of her white stricken face, Farquhar's arms dropped to his side.

"Why, Cynthia? Since we love one another nothing else matters."

"Does it not?" the girl asked drearily. "I do not seem to be able to think clearly now, but I know—I know"—with a little sob—"that it is impossible!"

"Why?" Farquhar asked. "Dear, tell me what this mysterious something is that stands between us!"

Cynthia put her hand to her head.

"I don't seem to understand anything now—only that it is all wrong. No, no!"—shuddering from him as he would have taken her hand. "No, no! I cannot! Let me go!"

She turned unsteadily to the door; Farquhar followed her, but she motioned him back.

"Not now! Indeed, I must be alone, I must think!"

Chapter Eighteen

"Yes, it was a bright thought. You are a real help. I believe it will be the very best thing!"

"I am sure it will!" Sybil said and laughed gleefully. "Confess I do better than you; but"—her tone sobering—"I wish I knew. Do tell me!"

"Hush, little fool!" Gillman said savagely. Cynthia caught the words as she came across the hall. Before she reached the door Sybil hurried out of the dining-room without noticing her and rushed quickly up the stairs. Gillman stood at the sideboard decanting wine; the parrot from his distant perch regarded him rakishly.

"What are you snivelling at now?" he demanded with an air of exasperating politeness; then, changing its tone to one of deepest commiseration, "Poor Hannah! Who loves poor Hannah now?"

With an angry sound Gillman set down his bottle and decanter, caught up a heavy cloth, and dashed it over the cage, then, with a gesture of irritation, he strode out of the room.

Left alone Cynthia crossed to the window. In the morning sun-light her complexion looked pale and wan. There were dark purple shadows beneath her eyes; her hair, instead of being arranged in its usual artistic disorder, was drawn back carelessly into an untidy, unbecoming knot at the back of her head. Her face and attitude alike were expressive of the deepest dejection. She had spent the long sleepless hours of the preceding night tossing about from side to side of her great bed, but, review the situation as she would, she had found little enough to cheer her.

Undesirable enough as it had seemed before Farquhar's decla-ration, the discovery of her own feelings towards him had rendered it impossible. For Farquhar's sake, as well as her own, she saw that her departure from Greylands must take place at once.

Resolving not to delay it by a single day, she caught up an old time-table that lay on the desk.

Gillman's voice called her away.

"Cynthia! Cynthia! My wife is asking for you."

With a momentary feeling of annoyance the girl went upstairs.

Gillman stood at the door of his wife's room. Lady Hannah lay far back in the shadow of the curtains, the big lace frill of her nightcap as elaborately goffered as usual, but her face looked smaller and more pinched, Cynthia fancied, and her lips were twitching nervously.

Cynthia went up to the bed, and stooped as if to kiss her cousin, but the invalid spoke sharply.

"No, no! Do not touch me—keep away!"

Thus repulsed, Cynthia drew back quickly.

"You wanted me, Cousin Hannah?"

"Did I?" the invalid said fretfully. "Oh yes"—as if recalling it with an effort—"I want you to write a letter for me. Sybil is busy and, besides, your letters are more legible. Hers are the veriest scrawls. Look on that table beside you; you will see a little epistle from Félicité Duxworth."

"From Lady Duxworth?" Cynthia picked it up. "Oh, yes, you want me to answer it, Cousin Hannah? Shall I tell her you are better?"

"Yes! No! I don't know what to say," Lady Hannah said uncertainly. "I feel just the same, but my husband assures me that I am better, and there is no doubt that I can move my leg a little."

"Enough to get out of bed?" Cynthia inquired impulsively.

The blue spectacles were moved sharply in her direction, and Lady Hannah sighed deeply.

"Ah, no! That is out of the question. Sometimes I doubt"—the low hoarse tones seemed to catch and rattle in her throat—"whether I shall ever walk again, but still an improvement is something. You will find paper and ink on the desk, child."

Cynthia looked where she indicated, and finding a blotting-book and all the necessaries, sat down to the table. Her cousin had just begun to dictate the letter when the door opened.

"You—you did not lock it!" Lady Hannah gasped. "I told you, Cynthia, that I would not be left without the—"

"I am sorry," Cynthia said penitently, "but it is only Mr Gillman, see!"

"I am sorry to interrupt!" Gillman began genially. "What is it, Hannah? Door unlocked? Oh, well, there is no harm done, and I will fasten it after Cynthia has gone! I am sorry to disturb you, Cynthia, but you are wanted downstairs. A gentleman! Ah," smiling mischievously as the girl's colour rose, "I think you know whom I mean? You should have told me you expected a caller when I asked you to come up here. I should never—"

"I did not expect anybody," Cynthia broke in desperately, her thoughts flying to Lord Letchingham. Was it possible that he had discovered her retreat?

"Will you please tell me who it is, Mr Gillman?" she asked.

Gillman looked at her a minute, as if enjoying the spectacle of her distress and confusion; then his face relented.

"Don't frighten yourself, child; it is not an ogre. It is that young man from the cottage on the moor—Heriot, isn't his name?"

Cynthia rose to her feet with a short, unsteady laugh as the guilty colour flamed in her face.

"I—I do not want to see him!" she said confusedly.

"I am afraid you must. I told him you were at home and that I would fetch you. Naturally I did not dream that you would raise any objection."

There was a hard look in Gillman's eyes as he glanced across at his wife.

"Really, Cynthia," she inquired fretfully, "why should you mind? After all, I don't think I shall write to Félicité Duxworth to-day. She has taken no notice of me for years, and I do not know why I should concern myself with her now. Besides, I am tired. You worry me, Cynthia—I like Sybil best!"

Cynthia's lip quivered as she turned to the door; it seemed hopeless to try to win to her cousin's affections, she thought. Such love as she had to give was evidently bestowed upon her husband and in a lesser degree upon Sybil. Cynthia was daily made to feel that she was only an interloper.

"Very well, Cousin Hannah," she said in a subdued voice. "I—I am sorry I have bothered you." She went down the stairs slowly and paused outside the dining-room door. What could Farquhar possibly want with her, she wondered. Was it merely to prosecute the suit he had urged upon her the preceding day, or had he made some fresh discovery that would help to elucidate the mystery in which the relations between Lady Hannah and her husband were involved? Telling herself that it was no use to wait outside when a moment's interview would probably set all speculations at rest, she turned the handle of the lock.

Farquhar was standing near the fire-place; the clear, merciless light from the window fell full upon his face, and it was curiously white beneath its tan. There were new, hard lines around the mouth, and the eyes were stern and grave. In his hand he held an open letter. As Cynthia came slowly into the room he held it out to her.

"Is this true?" he demanded, his voice sounding harsh and strained. "It—it—tell me it is a vile lie, Cynthia! You are not—you cannot be—"

The girl made no attempt to take the letter from his hand. She drew back and regarded it with wide- open, dilated eyes.

"What does it say?" she asked.

Farquhar's eyes were fixed upon her face.

"It says that you are not Cynthia Hammond—not the girl I have loved. It says that it has pleased Lady Letchingham to come down here, to masquerade as an innocent country girl—to make us think—"

"Ah, stop!" Cynthia stretched out her hand imploringly. "Indeed, it was not like that! Let me tell you—let me explain!"

A quiver passed over Farquhar's face; his eyes did not relax their merciless scrutiny of the girl's shamed, miserable face.

"I do not think I care for explanations, thank you! This thing is true!"

Cynthia slowly bent her head and said:

"I am Lord Letchingham's wife, but, Donald, I—"

Farquhar drew a long breath. There was a moment's tense silence; then he spoke slowly and deliberately:

"That is over, then! I congratulate you on your histrionic powers, Lady Letchingham. At any rate, in the future I shall have the pleasure of knowing that I must have contributed in no small degree to your amusement. I feel sure," sarcastically, "that it must have prevented your stay here from being in any way dull."

"No, no!" Cynthia caught at the table for support. "You know it was not that. I never thought—I did not understand—until yesterday!"

Farquhar laughed harshly.

"I can understand that I upset your calculations. It must have been most inconvenient. I can only plead as my excuse that I had not the smallest, the faintest idea of the farce that was being played."

Every word went through Cynthia's heart like a sword-thrust; but, though she shrank and quivered beneath them, with a supreme effort she rallied her courage. At all hazards she must make him understand. Moving timidly nearer, she looked at him, at the wrathful eyes in which there lay no faintest hint of softening, at the dark, rugged features that had grown dearer than she knew until his words had rent the veil from her eyes. A sob rose in her throat.

"You must hear!" she said feverishly. "Yes"—as he made a gesture of refusal—"you shall hear. I insist upon it! I—I did not know what I was doing. I had not the slightest idea to what I was pledging myself when I promised to marry Lord Letchingham—"

"That is so easy to say, is it not?" Farquhar interposed with an ironical bow. The anger, the sense of humiliation that had assailed him when he first read the letter of his anonymous correspondent, threatened to overwhelm him now. He was conscious of nothing but a blind, insensate desire to strike at something, to hurt some one. With a thrill of savage joy he saw how Cynthia winced after each bitter word.

Cynthia went on hurriedly, and resolutely crushed back the fear that was driving the blood from her cheeks. When he heard all, she told herself, he would understand, he would forgive.

"He—he had been very good to us, to my mother and me, and when he told me he loved me, when he asked me to marry him, I was glad. I thought it would be a home, a refuge, for already I had learnt how hard the world is to a penniless and friendless girl. He was very kind. Then, when it was too late, when I had bound myself for life, I found that he was not a good man. I—we had one great friend; somebody, some man, had ruined her life. When—when I married him I found that this man was Lord Letchingham—was my husband. I was frightened, terrified, too horrified to think clearly. My only idea was that I must get away from him, from this man to whom I had pledged my life. I had no one to whom I could turn for refuge; but Cousin Hannah, in a letter I had received only that day, had begged me to come to her. It seemed to me a special opening provided for me, and when I knew you were my cousin I thought there could be no harm in talking to you until yesterday. I never knew that we—that you—" Her voice died away in a long strangling sob. She fought with her tears for a minute or two; then, as he remained silent, she bravely raised her eyes. "You understand how it was now?" she said wistfully. "You will forgive?"

Farquhar had been wounded to the quick; his pride and his affection had been alike hurt; he hardened his heart against the pretty, wistful face, against the sweet, pleading voice, and a bitter smile curved his lips.

"I think I understand perfectly, Lady Letchingham, thank you!"

The pain in Cynthia's eyes deepened.

"You will forgive me, Donald?" she faltered, with a beseeching glance, as she ventured to lay her hand on his arm.

Farquhar started and almost flung it from him.

"No!" he said, speaking with cutting emphasis in his wrath. "No, I will not tell that lie even to gratify you, Lady Letchingham. I do not forgive you! I shall never forgive you! I will never look upon your face again!"

Chapter Nineteen

"OH, I must have those wild roses!" Sybil sprang up a steep bank and tried to reach some overhanging flower-laden branches.

"Did you ever see such a delicious colour, Cynthia? In the wild ones, I mean; they are quite a deep blush pink."

"They are lovely!" Cynthia said absently. She did not attempt to follow Sybil, but waited listlessly below.

Sybil managed to pull down the branch of the rose-bush with the crook of her umbrella, and was soon busy rifling it. Suddenly, as it sprang back, she uttered a cry.

"Oh, how it has scratched my wrist! I did not think brier-roses had such sharp thorns!"

Cynthia smiled faintly.

"Why, certainly they have! But that is a nasty cut," as Sybil exhibited a long, jagged wound, from which the blood was oozing rapidly. "Here, let me tie my handkerchief round it."

Sybil made a wry face, but she submitted to having her wrist bound up with a good grace.

"Anyhow, the roses are worth it!" she remarked contentedly, as they went on. "It is the first time I have ever had the chance of gathering wild roses in England for many a long year, so I must pay for my pleasure."

Cynthia looked a little surprised.

"How long is it since you came back from Australia?"

"Eleven years," Sybil replied, still eyeing her spoil proudly. "I mean"—correcting herself with a quick laugh, as Cynthia uttered an amazed exclamation—"eleven months. The roses were all over by the time we got into the country, for I stayed a while with some friends in London. I loved that too after the bush."

It was not often that Sybil was disposed to be so communicative about her past, and Cynthia, notwithstanding her absorption, was roused to a certain amount of interest.

"I must have been with the Fearons in Chester Square then. Where did you stay?" she asked.

"Oh, I do not remember! Somewhere over in the wilds of Stepney," Sybil replied evasively. "My people were far too unimportant to live in the West End. We shall have to make haste, Cynthia, or we shall be late for luncheon, and Cousin Henry is expecting some one on business. Do you know that Cousin Hannah wants to sell Greylands? They are thinking of going South as soon as she can be moved, and she says she shall get rid of the place altogether, as she is tired of it."

"I don't wonder, but I had not heard they were going to part with Greylands yet. I should not have thought Cousin Hannah likely to be in a fit state to be moved for some time."

Sybil shrugged her shoulders.

"If she makes up her mind to it she will get away somehow, by hook or by crook. I never knew anyone with a stronger will, and perhaps a change might do her good, though she would require an invalid carriage."

"Yes, she would," Cynthia acquiesced, with little show of interest.

In truth her own affairs were enough to occupy her now. The problem of how she was to gain enough to make life possible was as far as ever from being solved. The one or two advertisements to which, after much cogitation, she had ventured to reply, using Messrs Bolt & Barsly's name as reference, had failed to meet with any response, and now she was face to face with the fact that her cousin's departure from Greylands would make her needs far more pressing and immediate. Sometimes in the long nights the plan of applying to her husband would suggest itself, only to be rejected with horror.

Then the remembrance of Farquhar's dark face would recur to her, and at the recollection of his bitter anger and scorn she would bury her hot face in the pillows.

To-day, however, as she turned up to Greylands with Sybil she was not thinking of either of the two men who had crossed her life and helped to lay it about her in ruins. Though she told herself that she had no hopes of any future happiness, that her lot must of necessity be a cheerless one, all the vigorous young life in her fought against the desperate conviction. Even in her most despairing moments she could not help feeling that some day, somewhere, light would shine upon her path once more. With this fresh knowledge, however, she could not disguise from herself that her future looked dark indeed, and she decided that no time must be lost in making the appeal to her cousin upon which she had already decided.

Fortune favoured her this morning. Mr Gillman's expected visitor did not arrive until after luncheon, and after hesitating a minute or two after Cynthia's request to be allowed to sit with her cousin until tea-time, Gillman gave a gracious consent.

"Not both of you, though," he stipulated. "Sybil must stay down to be at hand in case this man should want any explanation of family matters that I am not able to give him."

Cynthia had only a passing glimpse of the stranger; it struck her that Gillman was anxious to hurry off.

She found Lady Hannah looking much as usual; she greeted Cynthia with one of the odd, wry contortions of her mouth which passed for a smile.

"So the customer has come, I hear, and I suppose Sybil is flirting with him, as she has deputed you to sit with me in her stead."

"I do not think so; I do not know where she is," Cynthia said truthfully. "I think she came upstairs after dinner. Cousin Hannah, I want to ask you, could you recommend me to anyone who wants a governess? I think I could teach quite small children, or I might be a companion or something of that sort," vaguely, "so that I may have somewhere to go when you leave here."

Lady Hannah did not answer at first. Cynthia looked at her imploringly; once more she was struck with the lack of response, with the absolute rigidity of the invalid's features, with the eyes hidden by their blue spectacles. It was like talking to a mask, she thought.

"If you have really made up your mind to take a situation," Lady Hannah said at length in her queer, whispering voice, "if you have decided not to go back to your husband, we must help you. I will tell my husband and see what can be arranged. Would you care to go into apartments in London until you decide upon something?

I could recommend some people I used to know who would make you comfortable."

Cynthia bit her lip—she felt desperate. It seemed to her that her cousin's lack of comprehension was wilful, that Lady Hannah wished her to understand that she accepted no responsibility with regard to her.

"I have no money," she burst out. "I must get something to do at once, Cousin Hannah. I cannot live on air."

Lady Hannah moved her head about in the old restless way.

"Are matters really as bad as that? Lord Letchingham ought to make you an allowance—you must have had settlements."

Cynthia threw back her head proudly.

"I would rather not take a penny from him!" she said passionately. "I would rather beg my bread from door to door. I—"

"That is all very well," Lady Hannah interposed impatiently, "but you know you are talking nonsense. No! If you are foolish enough to refuse to avail yourself of the provision that has been made for you, I suppose I must allow you a certain amount until you have got some work. I will speak to my husband about it. You can use my name as a reference, though I do not approve of the plan."

Cynthia clenched her hands together in the effort to keep back the words in which she longed to refuse the offer thus grudgingly made; but already she had learnt that the world is a very hard place for a penniless, friendless woman, that for such a one as herself to earn even her daily bread was a matter of no small difficulty; and, ungracious though her manner was, Lady Hannah's help was true kindness. It would at least give her a chance of surmounting her difficulties.

"Thank you, Cousin Hannah!" she said meekly at last. "It is very kind of you. I hope that I shall soon get a situation and that I shall not trouble you long."

The invalid made no response, but moved her head about as if in discomfort.

"Can I do anything for you, Cousin Hannah?" asked Cynthia, who was much affected by the evident suffering of the invalid. "May I raise you or move the pillows?"

"No, thank you; no, thank you! Keep away, please! I cannot bear to be touched. I think I hear voices"—as Cynthia, much hurt, moved back—"probably Henry is taking that man—Mr Squires—round. Just look out and tell me which way they are going."

Cynthia raised the blind, which was closely drawn to-day, and peeped out.

"They are standing outside on the lawn. I think they are taking measurements or something. Do you hope he will buy it, Cousin Hannah?"

"I do, indeed!" For once the thick tones sounded shrill in the invalid's excitement. "I am tired of being here. I want to get away. I hate Greylands now!"

Cynthia dropped the blind.

"I am not surprised you want a change," she said quietly. "You must find the time long here."

"Long—yes, it is terrible!" Lady Hannah spoke with emphasis. "I would never have come if I had known what it would be like. It—it is a hateful place!" her voice quavering with excitement.

Cynthia looked at her in some astonishment.

"You liked it at first—it was your own choice!" she said.

"Oh, perhaps it was! Don't worry me, Cynthia," irritably. "That is the worst of you, you will talk and ask questions. Sybil is content to sit still—she is much more restful."

"I am so sorry," Cynthia said penitently. "I see you so seldom that there seems so much to talk about, but I will be more careful in the future. I really think you are looking better to-day."

"You are a good girl, Cynthia, and I am a tiresome old woman," Lady Hannah said unexpectedly. "Yes, I feel sure I am better; I am beginning to feel some pain now, and that is a sign that the nerves are recovering their strength. I am anxious to try the baths and the treatment at Nauheim. As soon as I can stand the journey I shall go over. What are they doing outside now?"

Cynthia raised the blind again.

"They are going down the path into the fir plantation," she reported.

"Ah, my husband is going to show Mr Squires poor Spot's grave! He buried him just under those oak saplings that he has been transplanting, and I am anxious that his poor little bones should not be disturbed. I shall make a stipulation to that effect. Could you read the paper to me a while, Cynthia? It is a day old, but I have not heard it all yet."

Cynthia took up the paper obediently, and began one of the leading articles. The invalid interrupted her impatiently:

"Not that dry stuff! Turn to the Court news and the weddings. I want to hear about those."

Cynthia turned obediently to another part of the paper. In the subdued light it was no easy matter to make out the small print. She read on steadily for some time, and then laid the paper down to rest her eyes for a minute. Her cousin was lying still now; it seemed to Cynthia, looking at her, that the distortion of the face was much less apparent than usual, that the likeness to Sybil was stronger than she had ever seen it.

Her eyes wandered to the slim white hands that lay folded in pathetic immobility on the counterpane. Their utter unlikeness to the hands she had seen for one brief moment as she stood on the coachhouse roof struck her afresh, and for the hundredth time she wondered how the transformation could possibly be accounted for, and marvelled what could be her cousin's motive for feigning a greater degree of helplessness than was actually the case.

She had never wavered in her certainty that there had been no occupant of the bed when she first looked in, and neither Sybil's persuasions nor Farquhar's attempted explanations could make her doubt the evidence of her own eyes.

Lady Hannah was in a restless mood to-day, and seemed inclined to resent her silence.

"Go on, go on!" she commanded. "Read the dramatic notes and criticisms."

"I wonder where they are?" Cynthia remarked and turned the paper over. "It seems a long time since I was at the theatre," she went on conversationally. "The last time was at the St James's. Ah, here is a paragraph about the future arrangements at His Majesty's. It seems there is to be a revival of *The Tempest* and Marcus Hill is to play Ferdinand again. I wonder—" she stopped short.

"Go on!" Lady Hannah ordered. "Let me hear what it says. Who is to take Miranda?" Cynthia made no effort to obey her; she did not glance at the paper she still held; instead her eyes were fixed on those hands looking so white still against the Oriental bedspread; she caught her breath sharply. On one of the delicate, blue-veined wrists there was a long, jagged scratch, and as Cynthia gazed at it, with dilated eyes, she knew that she had made no mistake—she remembered where she had seen that scratch before.

Chapter Twenty

"GO ON, Cynthia! Why are you stopping?" The queer, thick tones were as harsh as ever; from behind the blue glasses a pair of eyes were watching the girl's face anxiously.

There was no response. Cynthia sat motionless, her gaze still centred on those tell-tale innocent-looking hands. As she watched, her breath began to come in short, panting gasps. At length she leaned over and very deliberately turned the left wrist towards her.

"What are you doing, Cynthia? Go farther away! You know I do not like to be touched." This time, underlying the irritation, there was distinctly a note of fear in the voice, and the crooked mouth began to twitch painfully.

Cynthia was ghastly white now; the colour had faded even from her lips. In contrast her eyes looked unnaturally big and dark. As she still gazed at the pale, mask-like face on the pillows her agitation and her anger grew, and with them a haunting, terrible dread, indefinable as yet even to herself. In that countenance, notwithstanding its contortion, its pallor, it seemed to her that a new and yet a familiar personality was becoming more apparent every moment.

The Cousin Hannah about whom she had speculated, and whose help and sympathy she had claimed, was gone, and in her place there was—what? A chimera! A trick!

The silence grew oppressive. Not a sound was heard but the ticking of the grandfather clock in the corner, the quickened breathing of the two women confronting one another.

At length Cynthia spoke; her throat was dry and parched, her lips felt cold and stiff, and she brought her words out with infinite difficulty.

"What—does—it—mean?" she asked, with a slow, painful pause between each word. "Why—did—you—do it?"

There was another silence. Then the woman on the bed opened her mouth. It was the same hoarse, unnatural voice:

"I don't understand! Cynthia, you are making me ill!"

Cynthia held up her hand.

"Not now, please, because I know—it is no use!"

"You know what?"

As she spoke the handle of the door turned. In her absorption Cynthia did not heed it, but pointed to the hands lying on the bed, to the red, inflamed mark on the wrist turned uppermost.

"That told me! I knew it was the same! Oh, I have been blind, blind"—raising her voice with sudden fire—"not to have guessed it before, not to have seen that you are not Cousin Hannah at all—that you are Sybil!"

"Ah!" It was a long-drawn sob, almost a cry. The white hand with its ugly scratch was raised and pointed behind Cynthia.

The girl turned quickly. Gillman stood in the doorway, an evil smile in his blue eyes. He glanced from the woman now cowering amid the pillows, her hands thrown over her face, guilt-stricken, to Cynthia, standing upright before him, her accusing, reproaching eyes fixed upon him.

"Why have you done this?" she demanded passionately. "Where is Cousin Hannah?"

He shrugged his shoulders.

"It seems to me that this is scarcely the tone to adopt to me, my dear Cynthia. I cannot guess to what you allude. My wife—" He glanced at the prostrate figure.

"Oh, what is the use of talking like that—what is the use of pretending?" Cynthia broke in hotly. "Don't you see that I know? Sybil"—she bent forward and caught the other woman's sleeve—"tell him that I—"

She was drawn away. Gillman's arms held her back, as though in a vice.

"I cannot allow this. You must leave the room. Cynthia."

As he released her in the passage the girl staggered back.

"How—how dare you?" she stammered indignantly.

Gillman held up his hand.

"Hush! I will not allow this," he said in a low stern voice.

Cynthia, half-cowed by his tone, opened her lips to remonstrate, but she shrank back appalled and silenced by the indescribable malice of his glance.

As she cowered away from him, catching at the wall for support, Gillman stepped back into the bedroom and closed the door behind him.

Utterly overwhelmed at the discovery of this duplicity and unable as yet to do more than recognize the stupendous fact that Sybil had been personating her cousin, while Gilman had certainly been a participator in, if not the instigator of, the fraud, Cynthia leaned, white and trembling, against the wall, feeling dazed and well-nigh stunned.

The puzzle that had troubled her so long, that had perplexed Farquhar, was partly elucidated now. The end of the clue to the mystery that had hung like a pall over Greylands from the day of her first coming was in her hands, but at present she could not realize all that her discovery implied.

At length she turned, and, catching feebly at the wall, gasping with terror and bewilderment, made her way to her own room. There she went over to the window, and, leaning against the frame, looked with blank, unseeing eyes into space.

She seemed unable even to think clearly; one phrase seemed to repeat itself over and over again with sledge-hammer force and iteration:

"Sybil is Cousin Hannah; Cousin Hannah is only Sybil!"

In vain she tried to fit in the various events that had puzzled her since her coming to Greylands with this new and astonishing knowledge; her mind could not as yet solve the puzzle or grasp in any way its true significance.

A glimpse of the pine-wood recalled Farquhar to her, but she shivered forlornly as she thought that she could not now go to him for help or counsel. Yet she told herself that it was imperative he should hear of this new development, that she must put her own feelings aside and write to him without delay.

How long she had stood there she never knew, but the shadows on the lawn below were growing longer when there was a low, hesitating tap at her door. It was opened cautiously, and she saw that Sybil stood outside—a very different-looking Sybil from the butterfly creature to whom Cynthia was accustomed. There was an indescribably crushed and dejected aspect about the girl's whole appearance. She was trembling, her hair was disordered, her eyes were swollen by weeping.

"May I come in?" she said timidly, casting an apprehensive glance behind her. "Oh, Cynthia," as she did not reply, "I must tell you—you must let me explain! Indeed—"

Her words faltered and died away in a sob as she met Cynthia's steady glance. Cynthia had not moved forward to speak to her; she had drawn herself up from the window-frame and stood, straight and tall, silhouetted against the window curtain, her eyes fixed upon Sybil's guilty face.

"That will be difficult, I think," she said with uncompromising directness.

"Yes, if you look at me like that," Sybil sobbed; then, before the other girl had realized her intention, she rushed across the room and flung herself down beside her, clasping her round the waist so that Cynthia could not move. "Indeed, indeed, you must listen!" she pleaded with a fresh burst of tears. "I shall die if you do not let me tell you!"

In spite of her anger Cynthia relented a little as she glanced at the pleading eyes, at the quivering lips. Some of her old affection for Sybil asserted itself. Sybil was quick to take advantage of the momentary softening in her face.

"It was all done in fun at first!" she sobbed. "I see now that you think I was mean and deceitful, but indeed, indeed, I did not mean any harm! When—when—Cousin Hannah came back I thought you would be amused!"

Cynthia tried in vain to free herself from the clinging hands.

"Why did you do it? I cannot understand! Where is Cousin Hannah? When did she go away?"

Sybil's tears were coming thick and fast now.

"I will tell you," she said, her voice choked by sobs. "Indeed, I will tell you everything if—if you will not look at me like that!" hiding her face against Cynthia's brown skirt.

Almost against her will, it seemed to Cynthia, her hand touched the ruffled golden head gently.

"Go on," she said gently.

"It was like this," Sybil began, her voice low and broken, her breath catching in a sob every now and then. "Cousin Hannah would come here—you know how determined she always was. Cousin Henry tried his best to persuade her to take a house nearer town, where she could have some society, but she said she did not wish to see anyone—she only wanted to be alone. Then, when they came here, her temper got worse. Cousin Henry thought, though she would not confess it, the loneliness tried her. She was always finding fault with him—and with everything else for that matter—and they could not keep any servants. She wrote to me to come for a long visit—and I suppose you too—but before we, either of us, arrived, she had a violent quarrel with Cousin Henry and went off suddenly without a word of explanation.

"Cousin Henry was terribly upset; he knew that all our relatives had always disliked the match, and he felt sure that they would blame him entirely. Hoping that she would perhaps come back in a day or two, he simply told Mrs Knowles that she was ill and keeping her room. Then you came just before he expected me, and he did not know what to do; finally, as you know, he gave you the same explanation he had given to Mrs Knowles. When I arrived it was a different matter; I had stayed with them before, I knew what Cousin Hannah was, and he told me everything."

As Cynthia listened her eyes had wandered back to the pine-woods, to the clouds that were massing on the horizon. She did not see that the golden head was raised cautiously, that the blue eyes shot a quick, suspicious glance at her unconscious face. She did not speak, and presently Sybil went on:

"Then, when he told me that he did not know what to do, that if you found she was away and that he had no idea where she was, you would tell the other relatives, and there would be such a bother, perhaps ending in a regular separation. I was so sorry for him. I always liked him better than Cousin Hannah, and I proposed that I should take her place for a week or two, until she came back. I thought it would only be for a short time, and I had always been thought so good at private theatricals and at making up. So that was how it was," she concluded vaguely.

Cynthia had turned now, and was looking at her with a growing perplexity and something like horror in her dark eyes.

"Do you mean," she said, her voice trembling, a strange inexplicable chill shaking her whole frame, "that you have been personating Cousin Hannah all the time—that I have never seen her at all?"

In spite of this morning's revelations she had not yet realized the full extent of the fraud practised upon her.

Sybil dried her eyes with a tiny, lace-trimmed handkerchief.

"It has been me all the time," she replied fretfully. "I thought you knew that. It was weeks before we heard from Cousin Hannah at all, but at length she wrote from Biarritz, and that is why Cousin Henry is selling the house. We are going to join her over there. I shall be glad when all this deception is over and I am really myself again. Half the time now I feel like Cousin Hannah, but I wish you had not found me out, Cynthia. Cousin Henry is so angry; he thinks she—Cousin Hannah—will not like it."

"Will she ever know?" It seemed to Cynthia that the question rose unbidden to her lips.

Sybil paused, handkerchief in hand, and raised her limpid, candid eyes.

"Why, certainly she will, Cynthia! Cousin Henry will tell her everything as soon as they meet, and that will be soon, for Mr Squires has agreed to take the house as it stands, furniture and everything, except the old family relics, which they would not like to part with, and so Cousin Henry says we will all go over to Biarritz one day next week. He thinks it will be better for you to go with us now. Cousin Hannah said in her letter of this morning that she should like you to come. When you did not know that she had not been here at all, we could not see how it was to be managed, but now everything will be easy. You will come, won't you?"

"I must think—I do not know!"

Something in Sybil's tone jarred upon Cynthia's susceptibilities. Though the explanation sounded fair and plausible, and though she had not yet had time to discover the flaws in it, she had an uneasy feeling that there was more to come, that even now, in spite of Sybil's apparent candour, she was being duped and cajoled.

"Oh, you must!" Sybil went on caressingly. "Then when you meet the real Cousin Hannah she will be able to help and advise you ever so much better than I can. I have been so sorry for you all this time, Cynthia, my poor dear, but I have never dared to tell you."

The pretty, childish manner was not quite what Cynthia wanted to-day; she drew herself decidedly from the clinging clasp.

"You are very kind," she said, the restraint in her manner becoming more marked, "but I think we will not talk of that. It is never pleasant to know that one has been deceived. I must think matters over well by myself before I come to any decision. The only thing I can see plainly is that I cannot stay—that I must get away from here at once."

In spite of her resistance Sybil twined her arms round her once more.

"No, no! I cannot part from you like this. Poor girl! You look so worried and I feel so guilty, for it is all my fault. I made Cousin Henry let me do it—you must not blame him. You must be faint; you have had nothing to eat for hours. Come down now; we are going to have a sort of meat tea."

Cynthia shuddered violently.

"Oh, I couldn't—indeed, I couldn't! No, Sybil, please do not ask me! I could not meet Mr Gillman now that I know—"

Sybil looked at her consideringly.

"Well, perhaps you will be better alone for the rest of the evening, and to-morrow you shall have a talk with Cousin Henry. I will bring you a cup of tea here."

Despite Cynthia's remonstrances she went downstairs and presently reappeared with a daintily- arranged tray. Cynthia turned from the food with loathing, but she drank the tea feverishly, and after a time Sybil persuaded her to eat a tiny sandwich. Then the girl begged to be left alone. The house seemed strangely still and silent, she thought; no echo of any sound reached her as she lay on her bed, white and shaken, trying to determine what must be her course of action in the circumstances. Upon one thing only was she decided at all hazards. At risk of exposing herself to his scorn, Farquhar must be informed of what had happened.

The scheme suggested by Sybil that she should go to Biarritz to meet Lady Hannah commended itself even less to her upon reflection than it had done at first, and after much troubled deliberation she made up her mind to return to London without delay and apply to Bolt & Barsly for assistance, informing them, if necessary, of the circumstances in which she had left Greylands. Though she had barely enough money to pay her fare, she had one or two good pieces of jewellery which she had inherited from her mother, and she had made up her mind that in this extremity she must part with them, cherished though they had hitherto been.

As soon as her resolution was taken she sprang off the bed and began to put her things together. She found on consulting a time-table that it was already too late to dream of getting the last train from Glastwick that night, but there was an express which stopped at Clastor at nine o'clock the next morning, and she determined that at all hazards she must catch that.

At length, having made what preparations she could, she opened her door and turned towards the staircase. Farther down the passage the door of the room which Cynthia had become accustomed to think of as Lady Hannah's stood ajar, and she glanced at it with shuddering aversion. As she went down the stairs she heard voices in the dining-room, and the sound of her own name caught her ear.

"I do not think Cynthia would—" It was Sybil who was speaking.

"I tell you thinking will not serve my purpose— there is too much at stake. I mean to make sure." The remark was Gillman's, and so curt and savage was the tone that Cynthia stopped involuntarily. "You have got to do your share, mind that!"

"No, no!" Sybil's voice had an accent of pain. "I cannot! I dare not! Sometimes I am frightened—"

"Pshaw!" Gillman ejaculated contemptuously. "You must get over that. It will not hurt the girl, and what need have you to concern yourself about her? You have not"—with a certain meaning emphasis—"always been so particular."

"Ah!" the exclamation was almost a sob. "Perhaps—perhaps that is why I do not want—this!"

There was a long pause; only the sound of the wind rustling through the pines broke the silence. It seemed to Cynthia, as her heart beat with great suffocating throbs and her breath came faster, that surely the pair in the dining-room must hear, that they would come out and discover her; but presently Gillman went on:

"There is nothing to be so squeamish about; it will do the girl no harm to be shut up for a day or two."

"Oh, no! If that is all—but I don't know—and I am afraid—" Sybil's speech ended in a burst of tears. "Oh, don't look at me like that! Indeed, indeed, I cannot bear it!"

Cynthia could not catch the purport of the whispered words that followed, but at length Gillman spoke in a louder key:

"That is my own good girl! I knew you would not fail me, Sybil!"

"Yes, I shall do as you want me to the end." There was a note of passion in the trembling tones.

"Hush! Hush!" Gillman's tone was very impatient. "Now do what I tell you. Go up to the girl's room and see what you can manage."

Cynthia started; she heard Sybil move to the door and then pause as if for a last word, and then in a moment the sudden realization of her own peril dawned upon her. It was perfectly evident that the discovery of Sybil's impersonation had upset Gillman's plans, and she now knew enough of his character to be certain that he would be utterly unscrupulous in his method of getting her out of his path.

A very real fear for her own safety took possession of her. Whatever scheme it might be that Gillman had proposed for ensuring her silence, she now knew that Sybil would interpose no obstacle in the way of its fulfilment. She could not look to her for help or protection. Her only hope lay in getting away from Greylands as quickly as possible, but she saw plainly that it would have to be accomplished without Gillman's knowledge. She knew too much to be allowed to carry her story to Lady Hannah's friends.

Fearing that Sybil should find out how much she had overheard, the girl turned and with tottering steps made her way back to the room she had left.

Then, as she waited, expecting every moment to hear Sybil's step upon the stairs, the recollection of the figure she had seen in her cousin's bed when she and Sybil were upon the penthouse roof recurred to her. She roused herself and tried to think clearly. That Sybil was no party to the impersonation on that occasion was certain; she asked herself who could have been in the bed—whether Lady Hannah had for once taken her rightful place, and whether, instead of being at Biarritz, as Sybil had explained, she was either kept in confinement or hiding of her own free will in the neighbourhood of Greylands.

Think as she would she could discover no solution to the problem that appeared either satisfactory or probable, and her thoughts would keep going back to that figure in the bed—to the large brown hand that had lain on the counterpane.

It seemed to her now that there had been in her mind the haunting consciousness that the hand was not utterly unknown to her, that somewhere, in different circumstances, she had seen it before.

Chapter Twenty-One

"You will remember, Gleeson, the gun-case is to be sent to the Court, and you are to stay as long as you like; and when you are tired lock the place up and let Bolt & Barsly have the key. That is all, I think!"

"I'll take care it is all done as you say, Sir Donald." Gleeson's comely, wrinkled face was puckered up; her eyes were dim with tears behind their spectacles. Her young master had been the apple of her eye in the old days when she had been Lady Hannah's maid. It sometimes seemed to her that he was even dearer to her now that they had gone through these weeks of anxiety with regard to her beloved mistress together. And he was going with his purpose all unaccomplished—the reconciliation with his aunt upon which he had set his heart apparently as far off as ever.

No wonder that Gleeson felt dull and miserable, and that all the morning she had been furtively bringing out her handkerchief to wipe away her tears.

Farquhar's face was unmistakably gloomy as he picked up the handbag that stood at the foot of the stairs.

"Good-bye, then, Glee!" he said, going back to his old boyish name for her; and then, moved by some sudden impulse, he stooped and touched the old woman's cheek with his lips. "Mind you don't stay a day longer than you like. You know there is always a home for you at the Court. I don't like your being here all alone."

"You are very kind, Sir Donald!" Gleeson responded, much touched, "I shall do very well. I have come to that time of life when it is pleasant to sit still and think over the days that have passed and the faces that we shall see no more; and it is borne in upon me sometimes that perhaps my lady is wanting me, and I feel happier like near her."

"You are a good woman!" Sir Donald paused a moment irreso-lutely; then he caught up his bag. "Good-bye, take care of yourself, Glee! And"— keeping his face resolutely from her as he went through the porch—"if that young lady who came here should want any help, you will do what you can for her, I know."

"Miss Hammond? Why, certainly I will, Sir Donald!" Gleeson's tone was full of comfortable assurance. "A sweet young thing like that, and the very image of my lady as she used to be!"

"That is all right, then." Sir Donald walked quickly down the garden-path, turning at the gate to wave a farewell.

Gleeson stood in the porch, shading her eyes with her hand as she watched his tall figure striding away into the distance.

"I misdoubt me there is something wrong with the lad," she muttered to herself. "I misdoubt me there is something wrong."

Long after Farquhar had become a mere speck on the horizon and finally disappeared from her vision, she still stood, her eyes mechanically turned towards Glastwick, her lips silently moving.

Farquhar, meanwhile, was rapidly nearing Glastwick. His thoughts, to judge by his expression, were none of the pleasantest, his eyes looked gloomy and absorbed, his lips were pressed tightly together. He was not one of those natures that take things lightly, and beyond all doubt his discovery of the deception that Cynthia had practised upon him had hit him hard.

There had been something about her unprotected position, about her isolation at Greylands that had appealed to him from the first. Her brown eyes, with their long upcurled lashes, and her pretty, plaintive smile had done the rest. He was surprised to find how strong was her hold upon him, how difficult, nay, how impossible it was to put her image out of his heart.

In vain he reminded himself of all her sins against him, of her marriage and her refusal to live with her husband; he found his thoughts dwelling on the little tendrils of hair that curled so prettily round her ears, on the soft delicious curve of her cheek.

The express was due in five minutes when he reached Glastwick; he had allowed himself no margin of time for accidents. As he took his ticket a trunk with "c.h." painted conspicuously upon it in white caught his eye. As he was looking at them the station-master strolled up.

"Good morning, sir!"

"Good morning, Mr King!" Farquhar responded with the pleasant smile that made him a general favourite. "You got my note in time to have the express stopped, I hope?"

"Oh, yes, sir! But as a matter of fact I had telegraphed up to Alnwick before it came. Mr Gillman he wrote last night; his niece is going up to town to-day. Leastways if she is in time. They are drawing it rather fine. Ah, there they are!" as a dog-cart dashed into the station yard.

Farquhar waited to recognize the slim, brown-clad figure by Gillman's side; then he turned and fled.

When the train came in he hurriedly ensconced himself in an empty first-class smoking carriage, and, keeping himself well in the shadow, carefully watched the platform. Though he was anxious above all things that Cynthia should not recognize him, and though he told himself that his greatest wish was that they might never meet again, yet he could not deny himself one last look at her face, but in spite of his efforts he was destined not to obtain it. At the last moment Gillman came quickly out of the booking-office and opened the door of the very next compartment to that in which he was sitting, and Farquhar, to his intense disappointment, saw that the girl behind him had swathed her head and hat in a thick veil. As she stood back while her escort opened the carriage-door Farquhar from his post could almost have touched her coat, she was so near him. There was a mark on one sleeve that had been made when they were walking in the wood and she had brushed against a tree-trunk. The sight of it recalled a thousand memories and associations. He would have given much for just one last glance, but the veil defied his efforts.

When the train started he told himself that that chapter of his life was closed for ever, but as he leaned back in his corner he found the knowledge that only the wooden partition separated him from Cynthia singularly disquieting. In vain he tried to turn his mind to other subjects—her pleading voice, her sweet, beseeching eyes, haunted him; her words, "Forgive me, Donald; indeed I did not know!" seemed to ring in his ears with a maddening iteration.

The first stop was at Derby, and, in spite of his resolution, Farquhar was at the window as the train began to slow down. It was possible that Cynthia might need some refreshment; at any rate the probabilities were that she would want a paper or periodical and he might be fortunate enough to get a glimpse of her. As they stopped, the door of the next compartment opened, and he caught sight of a slim brown figure. She was getting out, then? He drew back in his corner; his eyes as he watched were very bright and eager. Then he started forward with a smothered exclamation. The girl who stood on the platform wore a brown dress, certainly, but the veil had been discarded in the train, and as she stopped a moment before the window, instead of Cynthia's chestnut hair, he saw Sybil's gleaming golden tresses. Yet from where he sat he could see plainly the mark on the sleeve which he remembered; undoubtedly she was wearing Cynthia's gown, and the trunk at the station had been marked "c.h." As he wondered what could be the meaning of it she accosted a porter.

"I think there is a train to Clastor in a few minutes?"

"At 1.10, miss," the man responded. "That is in a quarter of an hour. It goes from platform Number Two. You will have to cross."

"Thank you!" She hurried down the platform. Farquhar got out and stood looking after her with an expression of absolute bewilderment. Clastor was a station a few miles from Glastwick on a different line. What could be the girl's motive, he wondered, in coming down to Derby, evidently only to hurry back again at her earliest opportunity? And why was she masquerading in Cynthia's dress? He could not help fancying that the veil had been assumed as a disguise, that both she and Gillman had intended her to be taken for Cynthia. Why? He could not see daylight in the matter at all. A porter touched his arm impatiently.

"Now, sir, time's up! Are you going on?"

Farquhar took a sudden resolution. He reached for his handbag.

"No," he said curtly. "Which is the platform for Clastor?"

"Number Two, sir!" The man banged the door, and the next moment the train was off.

Farquhar, walking down the platform, wondered whether he had done a silly thing. It was quite possible, he told himself, that the events that had puzzled him were capable of a perfectly innocent explanation. Very probably Cynthia had lent her dress and trunk to her cousin; it was quite possible that the other had forgotten something that rendered her return necessary, and it might be that she knew of some reason that made it easier to get to Greylands from Clastor than from Glastwick.

Reason as he would he could not rid himself of an uneasy sense that there was something wrong, that Cynthia was in some peril. When he reached the platform he saw that Sybil was walking briskly up and down; with a shamed feeling that he was in some sense a spy he betook himself to the waiting- room until the train came in; then, carefully keeping out of her sight, he made his way to a smoking compartment as far away from her as possible.

It was a slow train. Though Farquhar kept a careful look-out at the various stations he saw nothing of Sybil until they reached Clastor. There he waited until she had alighted and passed quickly through the booking-office. As he followed more quietly, he saw that Gillman was waiting outside in his dog-cart. Evidently Sybil was expected, and Farquhar asked himself again what could possibly be the reason of this extraordinary journey and how far Cynthia's connexion with it went.

As he stood in the road outside the little station and watched Gillman's trap bowling away in the distance, and reflected upon the weary miles that lay between him and the cottage on the moor, he was inclined to think that he had been a fool for his pains.

Gleeson was just bestirring herself to set her cup of tea, when the sound of the opening gate made her look round, and she saw Farquhar coming up the path. She lifted up her hands.

"Eh, Sir Donald, and here I have just been fretting myself to death thinking I might not see you for years, and you walk in at the gate your very self! You look tired, sir."

Farquhar threw himself down on the seat in the porch.

"So you would be if you had walked from Clastor, Glee!"

"You never have, Sir Donald!" The old woman looked at him. "Then you'll not say another word until you have rested. I'll bring you your tea here."

She bustled into the house to make her preparations, and presently reappeared with a dainty tray.

Farquhar did ample justice to her providing, and as he ate and drank he related the events that had brought him back.

"What do you make of it, Glee?" he asked.

Gleeson's face was very grave.

"I misdoubt me it means some harm to the poor lamb, Sir Donald. Mr Gillman would stand at nothing to serve his ends. When I think of her and my lady both in his power my heart aches sorely. What will you be going to do, Sir Donald?"

"I don't know. Now that I am here I do not seem to be any good," Farquhar said slowly; "but I could not go away and leave things in this uncertainty."

"Bless you, Sir Donald, no!" Gleeson agreed heartily. "You know I was always against your going. It does seem to me as her nearest of kin ought not to rest till my lady is out of that villain's hands."

"If she hugs her chains, if she will not let us take her away, what are we to do, Glee?"

"I can't say that I rightly see the way, Sir Donald, not yet; but I shan't believe as my lady wants to stay in that lonely place until I hear her say so with her own lips. If I was you, Sir Donald, I should walk up to Greylands in the morning and insist on seeing Miss Cynthia."

"Perhaps I had better." In spite of his resentment against her Farquhar's heart leapt at the prospect of meeting his cousin again.

Already the gloaming was setting in, and as he watched the shadows deepening on the moor his uneasiness grew, his conviction that some danger threatened Cynthia increased, and at length, feeling the impossibility of remaining inactive until morning, he determined to walk as far as Greylands, and, though it was too late to ask to see Cynthia, at least to give himself the satisfaction of feeling that he was at hand should she need any help or service.

It was dark when he reached the pine-wood; he could just see that there were lights in the upper windows at Greylands. After waiting some time he tried the gate and found that it was locked. Evidently it was useless to attempt to get inside, and it was difficult to see what use he could be outside the walls. Nevertheless he could not bring himself to go back, and after waiting some time longer he turned and walked slowly round the fence that encircled the pines. As he did so, he heard a noise within. Evidently some one—a man—was running about among the pines, brushing the undergrowth aside and plunging through it recklessly, uttering every now and then a sharp exclamation or a smothered imprecation; then a dog barked.

Wondering what it might mean, Farquhar paused. The sounds were not so audible now; the man, whoever he might be, was getting farther away. Farquhar still waited; at length he bethought himself of the little gate opposite the wood. It was possible he might find that open. It seemed to him that the mystery was deepening, and the necessity to assure himself of Cynthia's safety was becoming more imperative.

As he turned the corner at the end of the pine shrubbery, his thoughts intent on what was going on inside, he ran violently into a man coming from the opposite direction.

"What—I beg your pardon—" the stranger began. Then, with a start of amazement, "Sir Donald! I had no idea you were in this neighbourhood!"

"Mr Barsly!" Farquhar's tone was one of unmixed amazement. "Is there anything wrong?"

The lawyer coughed.

"A good deal, I am afraid, Sir Donald. In fact, matters that have come to my knowledge have been so unsatisfactory that I decided to come down myself, and—what was that?"

It was a slight noise, almost like a sob, sounding close to them, evidently just on the other side of the fence.

Both men were silent, but not the least movement was to be heard now, and Farquhar was beginning to think that it must have been merely some animal in pain, when across the stillness of the night there rang a woman's shriek, a long piercing cry of anguish.

Chapter Twenty-Two

"FIVE! Six! Seven! Eight!" Cynthia sat up in bed and listened. Eight o'clock!

She would have to get up without delay if she meant to catch her train. She threw back the bedclothes. Over-excited by the terrible discovery of the preceding day, she had been unable to sleep. Distracted by anxiety as to her cousin's fate, and by fears for her own safety, she had tossed restlessly about in her bed and had only towards morning dropped into an uneasy doze.

There was a knock at the door, and Sybil, looking bright and smiling, came in with her breakfast tray.

"I knew you would be a wreck this morning," she said, looking with pitying eyes at Cynthia's pale face and the deep purple shadows near her temples, "and I made up my mind you should have your breakfast in bed."

Cynthia looked at her, feeling heavy-eyed and barely awake. In the clear morning light, glancing at Sybil's smiling face, it seemed to her in that first moment that she must have dreamt that dreadful discovery in Lady Hannah's bedroom, that it could not have taken place; but as Sybil drew forward the little table and placed the tray upon it, she caught sight of the ugly inflamed scratch on her wrist, and shuddered from head to foot.

Sybil drew her brows together as she marked how Cynthia shrank from her, but her tone was playfully affectionate as she poured water into a basin and brought it to her bedside.

"There, when you have sponged your face and hands and had some breakfast you will feel better."

"You should not have troubled," Cynthia said slowly, as, feeling somewhat refreshed, she leant back among her pillows. "Indeed, I ought to have been up long ago, for I must get over to Glastwick as soon as I can. I want to catch the morning express."

Sybil looked disappointed.

"You have quite made up your mind not to go to Biarritz with us? I wish you would, Cynthia. How I shall miss you!"

The tone was perfectly natural. Looking at the clear, limpid eyes, at the pretty smiling mouth, Cynthia found it almost impossible to believe that Sybil had consented to become a party to the plot that would in any way injure her; but she could not doubt the evidence of her own ears, and she knew that it behoved her to be careful.

"You are very good," she said with apparent carelessness, "but I must try seriously to get a situation now. I have been idle quite long enough, and I do not think it would be wise to leave England."

"Must you really go this morning? Do make a good breakfast, Cynthia—you ate nothing yesterday."

Cynthia toyed with one of the daintily-rolled slices of bread and butter.

"I should like to get to London as soon as possible," she said.

"Well, they say we ought to speed the parting guest." Sybil poured out a cup of coffee and held out the silver jug of hot milk to Cynthia. "I will go and tell Cousin Henry he must be prepared to drive you to the station. I suppose it will do if you start in an hour's time."

"I suppose so," Cynthia answered, setting down her cup with a wry face. "There is rather a funny taste about the coffee this morning, Sybil, I think."

Sybil pouted.

"Funny taste, indeed! When I took ever so much trouble with it to get it exactly right, and my old French nurse taught me just how it ought to be done!"

Cynthia took another sip.

"It is generally very nice, but this morning it seems somehow different."

"It must be your mouth. I hope you haven't got indigestion, Cynthia? Have some cream?" Sybil caught up the jug and poured out a liberal supply. "I don't think it an improvement myself, but I know you like it. Isn't that better?"

"Yes, I think so," Cynthia agreed doubtfully. "I—I dare say my taste is wrong. I have scarcely slept at all."

"That is it, then. There is Cousin Henry in the garden. I will go and ask him about taking you to the station." Sybil hastened out of the room.

Left alone, Cynthia, telling herself that she would need all her strength for the journey that lay before her, did her best to make a hearty meal, but it seemed to her that there was a disagreeable taste about everything.

"It is all right," Sybil said, running back.

"Cousin Henry says that he is very sorry you are going, but he will drive you to the station. You naughty girl, Cynthia, you haven't eaten your egg."

"No, I can't. My head aches rather. Do you mind leaving me, Sybil? I have a good deal to do if I am to be ready."

Sybil did not look quite pleased.

"Oh, certainly, if you would rather I went away!" Then, relenting somewhat as she noted Cynthia's listless movements. "Yes, I will go. I know it is horrid to be bothered when one is dressing. Only I am so sorry to lose these last few minutes with you, but I shall come back presently!" And with a laughing nod she turned away.

Cynthia sprang out of bed and began to dress herself. Though she had allowed Sybil to ask Gillman about driving her to the station, she had no intention of waiting for him. She meant to leave her luggage to be sent after her, to get out of the house unobserved if possible, and to make her way through the pine-wood to the cottage on the moor. There, even if she should not find Farquhar at home, she would at least be able to consult with Gleeson as to what course to pursue in the circumstances.

As she brushed out her hair her thoughts became vague and confused, and an overwhelming desire for sleep assailed her. She looked at the great four-poster longingly. Surely she would have time to lie down for a minute or two; but as she crossed the room towards it her limbs felt heavy and nerveless, her head began to ache intolerably, black spots floated before her eyes; she clutched at the bedpost. She was going to be ill, she thought despairingly, and she was alone in the power of a man whom she believed to be utterly unscrupulous. Then, as she looked wildly round, she caught sight of her empty cup, and with the certainty of inspiration the truth flashed upon her.

"Drugged!" she said slowly as she fell forward. "I must have been drugged!"

She never knew how long she lay there in a heavy induced slumber. When next she opened her eyes the sun was high in the heavens, and for the first few minutes she was conscious of nothing but a feeling of deadly nausea, a dull sickly aching in her temples. Presently, however, the recollection of what had happened recurred to her, and, catching at the bed-curtains, she pulled herself up. The room was darkened and oppressively hot; some one had been in and closed the window and drawn down the blind. Cynthia's limbs were strangely weak and shaky as, catching at the furniture, she managed to get across the room and push the window up; the air revived her, the blood rushed back to her torpid brain, and she realized something of her danger and knew that her only chance lay in dissimulation. She tried her door; it was locked on the outside. She was a prisoner! As she crossed the room again she heard the sound of wheels in the drive, and she peered out. Sybil sat by Gillman's side in the dog-cart, which was driving towards the house.

To Cynthia's intense amazement she saw that Sybil was wearing her brown coat and skirt, the one in which she herself had intended to travel that day.

Marvelling what it could mean, Cynthia leaned forward. Sybil was laughing and talking to Gillman as if she had not a care in the world. She was carelessly folding up a motor veil. Cynthia could not see Gillman's expression, but he was looking down at the girl's bright, upturned face with an air of almost lover-like attention.

Cynthia's eyes grew dark with fear.

"Why is she wearing my dress?" she questioned herself. "With that motor veil on she might almost be taken for me. Did she mean to be?" The blood receded from her heart as she turned faint and sick.

Presently Cynthia heard the outer door open and close, and then Sybil ran lightly upstairs to her own room. A few minutes later the instinct of self-preservation made Cynthia fling herself on the bed just as the key was cautiously inserted in the lock.

Sybil opened the door softly.

"Cynthia, are you awake? Cynthia!"

Though every nerve was throbbing with nameless terror, though her pulses were beating like sledgehammers, Cynthia constrained herself to open her eyes slowly.

"Yes!" she said weakly. "Yes! Is it Sybil?"

"Yes." The girl came into the room. She was wearing her own blouse and skirt now, and there was no trace of hurry or travel about her dress or her elaborately-arranged hair. "What a long time you have been asleep, Cynthia! I have been in two or three times, and Cousin Henry got ready to take you to the station, but you were so sound asleep that we could not find it in our hearts to disturb you, so you will have to wait till to-morrow. How do you feel now?"

Cynthia passed her hand over her eyes.

Prepared as she ought to have been by her previous knowledge of Sybil's duplicity, she was yet utterly taken aback by this fresh evidence of her treachery, but she saw plainly that her only hope now lay in appearing to acquiesce in Gillman's plans and in keeping herself ready for the first opportunity that offered for making her escape from Greylands.

"I do not feel very well, thank you!" she said slowly. "My head aches worse than ever, but I dare say it will go off in a while if I get up."

"I hope so," Sybil was beginning; then, as the blind moved in the air, her glance wandered to the open window.

Her expression changed, a hard look came into her eyes, and for one second she compressed her lips tightly.

"I think it will be better for you to stay here," she said author-itatively. "You are certainly not strong enough to get up yet. I will bring your luncheon to you."

Cynthia realized that she had made an irrevocable mistake—that Sybil knew that she had been out of bed, that her suspicions were aroused, and that she herself was virtually a prisoner. A few minutes later the fact was brought home to her more fully, when Sybil, after having supplied her with an ample luncheon, calmly locked the door as she went out.

Parched and faint though she felt, Cynthia was too much afraid of being drugged again to touch the food; she took a long draught of water from her water-bottle and finished her dressing. As she caught sight of her face in the glass she could hardly believe that she was looking at her own reflection, so wan and heavy-eyed was it. Outside on the landing she could hear voices, Gillman's and Sybil's. She knocked loudly at her door and demanded to be let out, but call as she would there was no response.

At length, feeling the uselessness of appealing to her captors, she went to her window, but a glance told her that it was hopeless to think of escaping that way: there were no creepers on the old stone walls of Greylands, and there was a clear drop of twenty feet at least from the sill. She turned back and sat down on the edge of the bed.

The knowledge that she was in sore danger, that she was at the mercy of a man who would stop at nothing to gain his own ends, seemed in some sort to brace and steady her nerves. She turned her mind resolutely from the subject of Lady Hannah's fate. Terrible as were some of the misgivings that would present themselves to her when she recalled the various events, trifling perhaps in themselves and capable of an explanation when taken alone, but of terrible and sinister significance when reviewed together, she told herself with a shudder that she could not, dare not think of them now. The more she reflected upon her own situation the more desperate did it appear, but with the further knowledge of the difficulties in her way there came the determination to overcome them at all costs. The initial step was to get out of Greylands.

An idea flashed into her mind; she had heard of bedclothes being fastened together and of marvellous escapes from giddy heights being effected by their agency; it would surely be possible, even should the door be kept locked, for her to lower herself by them from the window. The sheets were strong and of a good size, and it would not be difficult to tie them together. She decided to make the attempt after dark, and thus minimize the danger of being seen by Gillman.

Already it was growing dark, and she began her few preparations. Making her little store of money and the jewellery she had with her into a parcel, she fastened it inside her dress. Then she began to put her rope together; it was not a hard task to make the knots firm, but when it was completed she glanced at it doubtfully; it did not look exactly the thing to trust to, she thought, and she very much doubted her own ability to get down by it. It seemed, however, to offer, at any rate, a chance of freedom, and she determined that no cowardice on her part should prevent her from availing herself of it. But she wanted something to which to fasten it, and she began to drag forward the heavy bed-stead. As she did so a sound caught her ear—a sound she had heard the night of her arrival—that of some one digging in the shrubbery. Despite all her resolution she quailed as she stood and listened.

What had Gillman been doing that first night? she asked herself with whitening cheeks. What was he doing now? As a certain sinister suggestion presented itself to her mind she shivered from head to foot. Clinging to the bedpost, she waited; the digging went on, now slowly, now almost with feverish haste. At length the sound stopped. Cynthia still waited motionless, hardly daring even to breathe. In the silence that followed there was a step in the passage outside, the key was turned stealthily.

Cynthia stood up, her limbs paralysed by fear, her eyes fixed as if spell-bound upon the door. It opened slowly, and Sybil put her head in.

"Cynthia!" She set down the lamp she carried and came swiftly across the room. "You must go! Do not stay one minute! Go—go at once!" catching at Cynthia with hot, dry fingers.

Still Cynthia did not stir; she stared back at the other as if fascinated. Sybil's whole aspect was changed; she looked like a creature over whom there had passed a terrible blight. There was no trace of colour in face or lips, the pretty delicate features were pinched and drawn, her eyes were darkened and dilated by terror.

"Don't—don't you understand?" she whispered hoarsely, catching her breath. "Go—be quick; I have left the front door open! You may get out if you do not lose one minute!" She tore Cynthia from her hold on the bedpost and forced her through the door.

"It—Oh, I know you do not trust me, but do not stop to argue! Go!"

The passion, the tragedy of her tone carried conviction. Cynthia moved quickly, silently down the stairs. At the bottom she paused, glancing irresolutely at the open door.

"You are coming too, Sybil?"

The other shook her head.

"No! Go! Do not think of me! My place"—holding up her head with a certain pathetic dignity—"is here!"

Chapter Twenty-Three

CYNTHIA heard the door close behind her and the bolts shot into their places with a feeling of absolute helplessness. The night was very dark, and there were tiny little scuds of rain in the wind as it beat upon her face. Stealing across the grass, she made her way to the fir shrubbery, and as she hurried down the path to the gate she heard the sound of a man's footsteps and the echo of a song.

Drawing back, she concealed herself behind a tree, but Gillman was not coming towards her. Apparently he had turned off, and was striding towards the brushwood; then, quite close to her as it seemed, she heard him digging. As if impelled by some force stronger than her own will, she moved stealthily forward.

The moon shone out for a minute from behind the heavy bank of clouds, and she saw that she was quite close to Gillman, who was standing in a deep hole. Only his head was visible, and that was fortunately turned away from her. Working quickly, he was throwing out spadefuls of earth; but as Cynthia still watched, fascinated by terror, he hoisted himself out, not without difficulty, and then, throwing a branch over the opening, strode off to the house. When his steps had died away in the distance Cynthia crept forward timidly and drew aside the covering. She saw a deep oblong hole. As she peered down into it the recollection of her mother's funeral came into her mind, and she seemed to see again the coffin on the bier, the yawning, open grave. For what, she asked herself, crouching on the brink, for whom—shaking from head to foot with a nameless terror—had this hole been dug? Suddenly from the house she heard a quick, sharp exclamation:

"Sybil! Sybil!"

A light was flashing in her room, and she knew that her flight was discovered.

The front door was thrown open, and Gillman was shouting:

"Nero! Nero!"

He had brought the dog to hunt her! Cynthia's flesh crept with the horror of it. She could see no hope of escape now; dark though it was, Nero would track her. Out there on the moor she would have no chance. A wild thought of a possible refuge occurred to her, and moving aside the branch as little as possible she sprang into the hole. It was deeper than she had thought, and she fell with a thud that, it seemed to her, must be audible everywhere.

Presently, overhead, Gillman's voice sounded loudly.

"Good dog! Find her, Nero! Find her!"

Cynthia shivered; the dog was making straight for her hiding-place. She breathed one short, silent prayer. Her mind went back for one moment to her dead mother, to the little home they had both loved; then she braced herself to meet the fate that was coming swiftly towards her.

Nero knew his work well; she heard him scenting among the pines; then he came straight as a dart for her hiding-place. She could hear him rustling, scratching the pine-needles, and a tiny piece of earth fell upon her face.

"Nero! Good dog! Go home!" she whispered. "Go home!"

Nero hesitated a moment, but Cynthia had fed him with cakes and odd bones, his doggish memory was faithful, and with a sharp bark he trotted off. Gillman was following; Cynthia heard his muttered imprecation as he fancied that the dog had lost the scent. Then there was a short, sharp yelp, and the hurrying footsteps crashed on.

Cynthia waited breathlessly. In a minute or two he would come back, she thought. He would find her, and then—she did not dare to let her mind go beyond that. She leaned against the wet earth. It seemed to her that a sudden stillness fell upon everything, that near her unseen forces were gathering themselves up in the silence that precedes the storm. Gillman's footsteps came round again, died away in the distance once more, and the silence grew intense. The minutes passed on slowly; it seemed to Cynthia that she had been standing there for hours, and she prayed for anything—anything to end the suspense.

Suddenly near at hand she caught the sound of voices; she held her breath, telling herself she must be mistaken. It could not be Farquhar she heard speaking? She tried to answer, to call out, but no words came, only a long, hoarse sob.

Almost simultaneously an awful shriek rang out from the house—a cry of horror and despair.

"Sybil!" Cynthia gasped as she tried frantically to raise herself.

At all hazards she must get out now; she must not leave Sybil to suffer in her stead. She could find no foothold at first by which to climb up, for the crumbling earth gave way as she clutched it, but she struggled wildly, desperately, with feet and hands, and at length stood panting and distraught under the pines once more.

Then she gazed round bewildered. Instead of the silence that had reigned a moment ago it seemed to her that there were voices everywhere. Lights were twinkling among the firs; dark forms sprang over the fence, and, crossing through the brushwood, ran against her. The spell that had held her silent was broken, and she cried aloud:

"Oh, help, help! He is killing her—Sybil!"

"Cynthia! Thank Heaven you are safe!"

It was Farquhar's voice, and as she swayed towards him he caught the half-fainting girl in his arms.

"My aunt, where is she?"

"I don't know!"

Then the sense of protection, of help, brought the blood rushing back to Cynthia's paralysed brain, and she caught feverishly at his arm.

"Come! Come! Didn't you hear her? She let me out! She saved me! Now—now he will kill her instead!"

"Aunt Hannah!"

Farquhar's tone was full of mystification. Side by side they were struggling through the underwood, and now sprang on to the path.

Cynthia shook her head.

"No! No! She is not there. I don't know where she is! It is Sybil!"

They had emerged on the grass in front of the house, and as they did so a man rushed out. People seemed to spring up out of the shrubbery on every side; he was surrounded, there was a struggle, the sound of a pistol-shot, and a man's voice said:

"Ah, that is no use! You don't try it again, my fine fellow!"

Then the struggling mass coalesced and came towards them, and Cynthia saw four policemen keeping guard over one man who was handcuffed in their midst.

Farquhar drew her quickly away.

"We must go to the house; I don't know what has happened."

The old kindness was back in his tone, and, notwithstanding her terror, Cynthia felt a quick throb of gratitude. His warm clasp, the touch of his hand, sent a thrill of warmth through her chilled frame.

As they neared the door Mr Barsly met them; they could not see his face, but his tone was very grave.

"I am rejoiced to hear of your safety, Lady Letchingham, but I shall never forgive myself for having been so culpably blind. We have a carriage outside; let me take you to it."

Cynthia put him aside.

"Sybil! Where is she? Let me go to her!"

"She has been injured—not, I think, fatally; but it is no place for you, Lady Letchingham." Mr Barsly was endeavouring to keep her back. "She—I think you must have guessed it by now—she is no relative of yours or of Lady Hannah's; her name is not Hammond at all. She is a girl who was on the stage for some time, and her connexion with Gillman and his introduction of her to his household are—er—anything but creditable to either of them. Sir Donald, I must beg of you to use your influence with Lady Letchingham to prevent her coming into the house."

"It would not be any use," Cynthia said steadily.

It seemed to her as she heard Mr Barsly's words that a veil had been torn from her eyes—that things that had mystified her all along were becoming clear. Of one great black cloud of dread she dared not even allow herself to think, but her whole heart was now filled with an intense pity for Sybil. Whoever the girl might be, however she might have sinned, Cynthia could not doubt that through her agency she herself had been saved from Gillman, and that the girl had paid the penalty for her compassion. The hall was in darkness, but the door into the dining-room stood wide open. Sybil had been placed on a couch, and Cynthia looked from its red chintz cushions to the white stricken face resting on them with a kind of stupid wonder. It was all so familiar and yet so terribly altered. She must be dreaming, she told herself.

Then as Sybil slowly turned her head and looked at her everything else was forgotten in a great rush of pity. Cynthia could not withstand that piteous appeal, and she hurried forward.

Sybil held out her hands.

"He—they have taken him away, Cynthia?"

Cynthia moved her head in assent.

"I—I think so; but I cannot understand—only I know he hurt you, Sybil."

The injured girl stirred restlessly.

"That does not matter," she said loyally. "He was right. I—I had deceived him, because I could not bear—If I die, Cynthia, you will tell him, some day, I loved him too much to let him do that. It was for his sake."

"I will tell him," Cynthia promised. "But you are not going to die, Sybil," though she felt a terrible misgiving as she saw the girl's ashen face, heard her terrible gasps as she drew her breath.

"I think I am—I hope I am," Sybil said painfully. "Stay with me a while, Cynthia. I have a fancy that I should like to have you near me—that I should like to hear you say you forgive me before I die."

"I have nothing to forgive," Cynthia said, bending over her. "You saved me, Sybil; but tell me—where is Cousin Hannah?"

With a little cry Sybil shrank away among the cushions.

"It—oh, I don't know—don't ask me, Cynthia! I am frightened, so frightened! She—she"—trying to still the terror in her voice—"she went away to Biarritz, you know."

Cynthia did not answer, but slipped her arm under the pillows and raised them to ease the terrible gasping breath, noting with a shudder the dark stain on the cushion, the matted golden hair.

Sybil seemed to find some comfort in her proximity, and very gradually her weak hand stole out to find Cynthia's, her eyes sought the other girl's.

In vain Farquhar remonstrated. Cynthia would not leave her post until at length a cheery little man bustled into the room, whom Mr Barsly addressed as Dr Campbell. He at once took command of the situation and relieved Cynthia.

"Now you must leave us for a time, my dear young lady," he said peremptorily. "This is the district nurse from Glastwick," as a business-like, capable-looking woman came in. "What is that you say?" as Cynthia began an almost inaudible remonstrance. "Dying? Not a bit of it, young lady! My patient has had a nasty knock on her head, I understand. She had a blow that sent her backwards—that is the worst of the damage. She has given herself an ugly cut near the temple"— his deft fingers parting the hair—"but dying—pooh! She will be as well as ever she was in her life in a month. Dear, dear! What is this?" as Cynthia, feeling the room was going round with her, swayed slightly.

"I don't know!" she said faintly. "I can't see anything—Donald!"

The darkness seemed to close in around her; the doctor's voice seemed to come from a long way off. She put up her hands, staggered blindly for a few steps, and would have fallen had not Farquhar stepped forward quickly and caught her in his arms.

The doctor looked at her.

"The best thing that could have happened—the very best!" he remarked with professional sang-froid. "We might have had some difficulty with her but for this. Now all we have to do is to pack her in the carriage outside and send her to Lady Duxworth's, and she will not know anything until she awakes to find herself comfortably in bed!"

Chapter Twenty-Four

"I WISH we knew what has become of Cousin Hannah!" Cynthia raised herself a little among her cushions.

Lady Duxworth sighed and said:

"I wish we did indeed!"

Cynthia was silent for a minute; her eyes wandered to the window; through it she could see a range of hills, on the other side of which she knew that Greylands lay.

"It seems so strange that she does not write to anyone—if—if she can," her face paling. "I wonder whether they have asked Mr Gillman, whether he has said any more about her."

Lady Duxworth shivered; her eyes filled with tears.

"I believe he asserts that she will come to Glastwick for the examination before the magistrates on Saturday, but—I don't know."

"Then he must have heard from her!" Cynthia said quickly.

"I don't think he has."

Cynthia stirred restlessly.

"If I could only go over and search her drawers I feel sure I could find some trace of where she is. It is getting on my nerves. You—you do not know what horrible thoughts come into my head sometimes as I lie here. If Dr Campbell would only let me get up—and it is absurd making me lie here, for I feel quite well—I would go to Greylands at once."

"Dear Cynthia, Dr Campbell must know best," Lady Duxworth said softly. Personally, she was inclined to think that, being aware how highly strung was Cynthia's nervous temperament, Dr. Campbell was stretching a point in order to keep from her the reports that were current everywhere concerning her cousin's fate, to prevent her from seeing Greylands as it was now.

By Mr Barsly's order detectives had been busy for the past three weeks—ever since Gillman's arrest—in ransacking every hole and corner of the house to try and find some clue to Lady Hannah's fate. They had taken up flooring and sounded every inch of the walls, so far without the slightest result; or finding any clue to the missing lady's whereabouts.

This week the search had extended to the garden and the plantation round the house, and Lady Duxworth knew that Cynthia could not but read a sinister significance in the excavations that were going on if she should be allowed to carry out her wish and pay a visit to Greylands. For the rest, the long strain that she had undergone, and the terrible events of that last evening at Greylands, which had culminated in the fainting attack during which she had been brought to the Towers, had left Cynthia weaker than she quite realized, and though she chafed at Dr Campbell's restrictions she was not in reality strong enough to disregard them.

Sir Donald Farquhar had been a constant inquirer at the Towers since the night Cynthia was brought there, but so far the cousins had not met. Lady Duxworth was, to a certain extent, in Farquhar's confidence, but she knew that of late his overwhelming anxiety with regard to his aunt's fate had superseded all other interests, and her great hope now was that she might persuade Cynthia to become reconciled to her husband, and thus to show Farquhar the utter futility of any hopes that he might be cherishing with regard to her.

Gillman was still a prisoner in the county gaol; he had made his appearance before the magistrates to answer the charge of forging his wife's name on several occasions, and had been sent up for trial, but the prosecuting barrister made no secret of his opinion that unless Lady Hannah was found before the assizes it would be extremely difficult to secure a conviction.

Sybil had been moved to a nursing home at Clastor, where she was slowly making progress towards recovery.

"I can't understand how it all came about," Cynthia went on after a pause. "How they found out, I mean, and how the policemen came to be there just in the nick of time."

Lady Duxworth was doing some exquisite ribbon embroidery in a frame. She hesitated a little, and did a few stitches before she spoke.

"I really think my son and Lord Arthur St Clare had a good deal to do with it," she said. "You remember, perhaps, that the day you lunched here Petre said he had met a Gillman abroad who was a pretty bad lot, and who was accompanied by a good-looking young wife. Well, it seems that Lord Arthur St Clare, to his amazement, recognized in the girl who passed as your cousin, Sybil Hammond, a young actress who had been extremely popular, and whose sudden retirement from the stage had occasioned much surprise. He taxed her with it, and she, finding subterfuge useless, finally admitted the fact, but declared that she had assumed the name for a time in order to support her mother when they were very poor, and that she really was Lady Hannah's cousin. He saw no reason to doubt her assertion at the time, but later on he heard Petre discussing the Gillman affair with me, and Petre, who had been thinking matters over, suddenly said that the girl who was with Gillman and who had passed as his wife was exactly like Delphine Meldrum.

"That made Lord Arthur think that there was something queer about the whole business. He told me that Sybil had acknowledged it to him, and by Lord Duxworth's advice we carried the whole affair to Mr Barsly. He, as you know, had been seriously uneasy for some time about the way your cousin was disposing of her property. He thought that even paralysis did not account for the difference visible in some of her signatures, and he submitted them to an expert, who unhesitatingly declared two of them to be in Gillman's handwriting. We can never be sufficiently thankful that they went down to make the arrest in time to save you, child."

Cynthia covered her eyes with her hand.

"I can never bear to think of that time."

Lady Duxworth's eyes were full of compassion as she glanced at the girl's white cheeks, hollowed now by illness and anxiety.

"It would be much better for you never to do so," she agreed; "but if that is impossible it is just as well to talk about it, I think. The things that are never said are the ones that hurt the most, but there is another subject I should like to ask you about, Cynthia."

Some prevision of what was coming tinged the girl's pale cheeks with colour. She did not reply, but she fidgeted about uneasily and drew the silken coverlet more closely round her.

Lady Duxworth watched her anxiously for a minute or two, then she said slowly:

"I think you have guessed what I mean, Cynthia. When are you going back to your husband?"

"Never!"

Cynthia's face was turned away now; Lady Duxworth could only see the great burnished knot of hair on the nape of her neck, and one of the little, shell-like ears.

"I am sorry to hear you say that," she said gravely. "I know you think I ought not to interfere, but you have no mother. I knew and liked your father in the old days; your cousin, Lady Hannah, was my dearest friend. I cannot see you make a shipwreck of your life without at least trying to give you one word of warning. Your husband stayed with us a little time ago; he was looking sadly altered—aged and saddened. Do you not think your place is at his side?"

Cynthia put out her hands imploringly.

"No, no!" she said indistinctly. "Indeed I couldn't! He—he is not a good man, Lady Duxworth."

There was a pause; Lady Duxworth's eyes looked puzzled and thoughtful. Lord Letchingham's reputation was well known to her. Not for worlds would she have urged on a marriage between him and Cynthia, but now that it was an accomplished fact it seemed to her that the only thing to be done was for the girl to make the best of the situation and return to him.

"He is your husband, Cynthia," she said, "and I cannot but think that it is too late to talk of what he may have been in the past. You must remember that we are none of us perfect."

"No, no! I know that!" Cynthia covered her face with her hands; her voice sounded muffled and thick. "But he—oh, I should like to tell you about it, if you do not mind, Lady Duxworth—if it will not bore you."

"I should be glad to hear." Lady Duxworth was not without her share of Eve's failing. The "*affaire Letchingham*" had been canvassed *ad nauseam* in the boudoirs of Mayfair, but she was much too tender-hearted a woman to be merely curious, and far deeper down there lay a very real affection for Farquhar, a sincere liking for Cynthia.

"I did not understand then," Cynthia began, speaking with apparent difficulty and hesitation. "I did not love him—I never even fancied I did—but I thought he was a nice, kind old man who would be very good to me. Then, after the ceremony was over, I found out that he had ruined our greatest friend's life. She wrote to me to warn me against him, to beg me not to marry him—and the letter was delayed. I opened it when I came back from church—so I went away. It was the only thing to do."

Lady Duxworth uttered a shocked sound.

"My poor child! I can understand how terrible it was for you; but still I feel it is my duty to say it to you, Cynthia, that that is over and done with; it is quite impossible that it has not been sincerely repented of, and we are not one another's judges. Besides, you have made certain definite vows, and it seems to me that Lord Letchingham ought to have an opportunity of explanation. Will you let me see him for you?"

"It would do no good." She turned, and, catching Lady Duxworth's hand, pressed her lips to it gratefully. "How good you are to me! But indeed that would not help matters. I taxed him with it, and he—he only laughed at me, and—oh, it was dreadful! I cannot bear to think of it!"

Lady Duxworth's face was very grave and pitiful.

"Poor child! I am more sorry than I can say, Cynthia. At any rate you must stay with us as long as you like. I wish I could help you more effectually; but one thing must be done, dear. You must take your proper name; it is not fair either to yourself or others that you should pass as an unmarried girl."

All Cynthia's pallor had vanished now; her cheeks had flushed a hot, guilty red.

"I know what you mean," she whispered faintly. "I—I am so sorry, Lady Duxworth, but indeed I did not understand. I will do just what you think best in the future."

"Poor child!" Lady Duxworth said tenderly, laying her hand caressingly for a moment on the bright bent head. "Then you will stay with us a while, and later on we will try to see what is best."

Cynthia made no reply save by pressing another kiss on the soft hand. So long did she lie silent that Lady Duxworth thought she had gone to sleep, and only glanced at her occasionally as she went on with her embroidery, her thoughts busy with the story she had just heard.

It was difficult to see any way out of the tangle in which the unfortunate girl had involved herself. Look at it as she would, the situation seemed to Lady Duxworth beset with difficulties, and it seemed impossible to tell which was the right course to be pursued. Presently her busy needle ceased to fly in and out of her canvas, and she had fallen into a reverie, when she heard the sound of a horse and cart being urged up the avenue at the utmost speed.

Cynthia sprang up.

"What is it?" she cried. "Lady Duxworth, it is Mr Barsly bringing news! I am sure of it!"

Lady Duxworth rose hurriedly; her face paled.

Was it possible that that search at Greylands, of which Cynthia knew nothing, had resulted in something which had given the clue to Lady Hannah's fate? She laid her hand on the girl's shoulder.

"Don't excite yourself, child; it is probably nothing of any importance. Mr Barsly generally comes over to consult with Lord Duxworth when he is in the neighbourhood. He is our solicitor, too, you know."

Cynthia's agitation did not subside; she still sat up, her breath quickened, her eyes watching the door with a look of eager, almost feverish expectancy. Presently there was a knock, the door opened, and Lord Duxworth himself stood on the outside.

"Can you spare me a minute, Félicité?" he inquired. "There is something we want to show you."

Lady Duxworth rose, and Cynthia threw herself forward and clutched eagerly at her skirts.

"Ask him to come in—tell him I must know too!" she cried. "See, I will be quiet. Indeed, I can bear anything but suspense."

Lady Duxworth hesitated; there was a curious look on her husband's face that warned her he had no good tidings to give them. She glanced at Cynthia's flushed cheeks and fever-bright eyes, and then beckoned to Lord Duxworth to enter. The girl was right—any certainty was better for her than suspense.

"I think you bring us news!" she said. "You can speak before Cynthia; she has promised to be very brave."

Lord Duxworth cleared his throat and looked reproachfully at his wife. His manifest unwillingness to speak heightened Cynthia's anxiety. At length he said slowly:

"Barsly would have it that you were the only person we could come to, Félicité. It is most unfortunate that Farquhar should have gone up to town to-night. Barsly thinks you may have seen this—that you may recognize it." He held out a small object in the palm of his hand.

Lady Duxworth went up to him quickly. Cynthia slipped back with a sigh of disappointment. After all, she had been mistaken, she thought. Lord Duxworth's errand could have no connexion with her cousin's fate.

Presently Lady Duxworth looked up.

"It is a miniature," she said unsteadily, with trembling lips. "Though the glass is broken and stained with earth, I think, no, I am sure, that it is a portrait of Herbert Densham—Cynthia's father—one he gave Hannah Hammond when they were first engaged. Where did you find it?" a dawning horror in her eyes.

"Where I fear there can be little doubt we have found Lady Hannah herself," Lord Duxworth replied. "In the belt of pines round the house, beneath the oak saplings that Gillman has been planting."

Lady Duxworth interrupted her husband with a little cry as she caught at the nearest table for support.

"You do not mean—then it is true—and he murdered her!"

"Some one laid her in the earth, poor thing, and there can be little doubt the same hand sent her there before her time," Lord Duxworth said. "It is a terrible affair. Poor thing!"

He sprang forward just as Cynthia's head fell back, a deadly pallor overspread her features and she fainted away.

When next she opened her eyes it seemed to her that the whole room was impregnated with a pungent odour of burnt feathers and brandy and water, while some one was holding a particularly evil-smelling bottle to her nostrils. She put up her hand to try to push it away as she began to cough feebly.

"That will do, Parkes. You can go now. I can manage quite well."

At the sound of Lady Duxworth's voice Cynthia awoke to a fuller measure of consciousness and looked round, bewildered. It seemed to her that a horrible black cloud hung over her. She had a vague feeling that something intolerably painful had happened; then as she met Lady Duxworth's eyes she remembered.

"It—it can't be true!" she said hoarsely. "It was some mistake!"

Lady Duxworth drew her to her motherly arms.

"It is a terrible thing. We can only be glad she did not suffer much. My husband says the doctor told him that as far as he could judge death must have been instantaneous."

Cynthia lay still for a minute; then she raised her white face.

"I—I cannot help thinking that it was done the day I got there—that if I had been earlier—"

"Don't think of it, child," Lady Duxworth counselled amid her thickly-falling tears. "Poor Hannah! I shall always remember her as she was when we were girls together—when she loved your father, Cynthia."

Cynthia's thoughts could not be turned.

"He did it—her own husband—and Sybil—"

"She knew nothing of what had become of Lady Hannah, I believe, when Gillman persuaded her to help him with his impersonation scheme, but one cannot help fancying that of late she must have suspected."

"How could she do it! How could she do it!" Cynthia moaned. "I was so fond of her at first, and in the end, you know, she saved my life!"

"Lord Duxworth says that so far as he can judge, and from what he can hear, she must have been a creature of infinite charm, but that her whole life has been warped by her love for Gillman. You know she was his wife, Cynthia?"

"No!" The girl sat up, her whole frame trembling. "Then Cousin Hannah—"

"He deceived her by a false marriage. Probably at that time he meant to get rid of Sybil. Later on he changed his mind, as we know, and it was poor Hannah who met her death. I cannot help thinking of the one to whom this will be a sore trouble—poor Donald Farquhar! She was like a mother to him for so many years, and I know he has blamed himself for the quarrel between them, and feared that the ensuing loneliness led up to that most unhappy marriage."

"Ah, yes! It will be terrible for him now!" Cynthia sighed pitifully, her hand trembling in Lady Duxworth's. "Poor Donald! And, oh, poor, poor Cousin Hannah!"

Chapter Twenty-Five

IT WAS sunset at Sermoneta; not a breath of air was there to stir the cypresses on the hills. Slowly the sun, a great red ball of fire, was sinking to rest, his last rays streaking the horizon with a reflected glory of glowing amber, of flame-like scarlet melting into crimson that dashed the blue waters of the lake with blood, turned the grey-green of the olives round its shores to a warm russet-brown.

To Luigi, the old postman, trudging bare-legged up the hill beside his faithful mule, with its burden of letters and parcels, it seemed that the distance to the Villa Perponchi was even longer than usual.

He was for ever climbing up there, too, he grumbled to a couple of peasants who sat by the wayside tossing contentedly for their small silver scudi, since the English milord came to the villa. Before it had been but once a week or so. Now it was every day, and twice a day. Apparently they had nothing to do—these mad English—but to sit scribbling their foolishness to one another all day long.

Meanwhile, in the open veranda of the Villa Perponchi, Lord Duxworth was impatiently pacing backwards and forwards, growling discontentedly to the occupants of the two hammocks slung at the farther end on the iniquities of foreign countries in general and of their postal arrangements in particular. That a man could not get his newspaper until it was a day and a half old apparently more than counterbalanced the beauties of Sermoneta in his eyes.

The appearance of Luigi with his mule created a pleasant diversion, and Lord Duxworth hurried across the grass to meet him. Lady Duxworth turned over in her hammock with a sigh of relief.

"Now we shall have a little peace; it is astonishing what a nuisance a man becomes if he does not get his newspaper regularly every morning."

Lord Duxworth's step was brisker as he came back, his face was glowing with satisfaction.

"Here's a letter from Barsly; it seems there is some fuss about Wilcher's lease. I'm not at all sure that I shall not have to run over for a day or two just to put matters straight, and leave you to look after Cynthia and Marion, eh, my lady? Here is your pile"—handing several letters to her—"and here, Cynthia, is one for you."

Cynthia raised herself a little to receive it.

"From Sybil!" she cried with a flush of excitement.

Lady Duxworth looked interested.

"Is it over, my dear?"

"I think so," Cynthia said as she began to read. "Yes, she entered upon her novitiate yesterday. Henceforth, she says, she will be known as Sister Dolores."

"A very suitable name, poor thing!" Lady Duxworth said, with a sigh.

Cynthia did not reply; she was absorbed in her letter.

During the six months that had elapsed since the tragedy at Greylands she had been slowly creeping back to convalescence; the tinge of pink in her cheeks, the brightness of her eyes spoke of renewed health and strength.

Very seldom now did she mention any of the actors in that terrible drama, but Lady Duxworth knew that immediately after Gillman had paid the penalty of his crime Sybil, whom it was difficult to think of as Delphine Meldrum, had entered a convent. The time of probation was now over, it appeared, and the novitiate, as to which there had been some doubt at the convent, had now been formally entered upon.

Lady Duxworth was inclined to think it the best thing that could possibly have happened; it put an end to a very awkward situation, for Cynthia, whose gratitude to Sybil she secretly considered to be somewhat excessive, had positively refused to give up her friendship for the girl.

So far the question of Cynthia's relations with her husband had remained in abeyance; Lord Letchingham had realized at the one brief interview which the doctors had permitted that the girl's health had been so shattered by the terrible experience she had undergone that a long period of rest and quiet would be necessary before the matter could be even discussed.

Lady Duxworth knew that his patience would not last much longer, and she was very anxious about the future of the girl, whom she had learnt to look upon as almost one of her own daughters. The passage of time had in nowise altered Cynthia's feelings towards her husband; her dread of him had, if possible, increased, and her shrinking from him when Lady Duxworth had persuaded her to: consent to the interview upon which he had insisted had been painful in the extreme.

She was independent of him now, for besides the house of Greylands, bestowed upon her by the deed of gift which Gillman had tried in vain to get revoked, Lady Hannah's latest will, drawn up by herself, had left an income of a thousand a year to her beloved cousin, Cynthia Frances Hannah, daughter of the late Herbert Densham. The rest of Lady Hannah's money went, as had been expected, to Farquhar, and her husband was not as much as mentioned among the list of legatees—a circumstance which proved that the poor woman before her death had become aware of something of the character of the man she had married.

Farquhar, after Gillman's trial, went to his estate in Scotland for a brief visit, and after setting his affairs in order betook himself to Central America on an expedition in search of big game. For the past three months they had heard nothing of him, and Lady Duxworth, knowing something of what had passed between him and Cynthia, and surmising more, was careful never to mention his name. Yet her thoughts were busy with him now as she went through her correspondence. An exclamation from her husband startled her.

"Bless my life! Poor old fellow! It is a bad job!"

"What is?" Lady Duxworth inquired, with some natural irritation. "Really, Duxworth, you forget that I do not know what you are talking about—I cannot read the paper from here."

Somewhat to her surprise Lord Duxworth rose.

"I'll bring it over to you, then you can read it for yourself. Here it is!" pointing to a paragraph and at the same time making a curious grimace, intended to be expressive of the utmost caution.

Lady Duxworth put up her eyeglass and regarded him with amazement.

"Really, Duxworth—"

"Read it! Read it!" he urged, glancing at Cynthia in a stealthy, sidelong fashion which at once attracted that young lady's curiosity.

She watched Lady Duxworth's face and noted how it changed.

"Oh yes, I see—it is very sad!"

"Dear Lady Duxworth, what is it?" Cynthia asked.

Lord Duxworth pushed the paper back.

"No, no! Keep it! I will look at it again presently. There is something here that must be answered." And gathering up his papers in his hand he hurriedly made his escape to the house.

In spite of her anxiety Cynthia could not forbear a smile.

"It must, indeed, be something important to make Lord Duxworth forgo his newspaper. Do tell me what it is!"

"It is important and it concerns one who is very near to you," Lady Duxworth said. "Your husband is dangerously ill."

"Lord Letchingham!" With a curiously stunned feeling Cynthia sat up in her hammock. Such an eventuality as her husband's illness had never entered into her calculations. "How—what do you mean?"

"It is not very clear," Lady Duxworth said helplessly. "Perhaps there is something before that we have missed."

Cynthia sprang down, and, standing beside her, read it over her shoulder:

> "We regret to hear that Lord Letchingham, whose seizure while speaking in the Upper Chamber last week occasioned such widespread regret, is still lying dangerously ill at his residence in Grosvenor Square. Last night Dr Broadbent and Sir Anthony McDowell were called in consultation and stated that his lordship's condition was extremely critical."

The hand that Cynthia laid on Lady Duxworth's shoulder tightened its clasp until it became absolutely painful; the girl's face looked white and strained.

"I—oh, what must I do? I must go to him!" she cried incoherently.

"Go to him now? My dear, there is no necessity," Lady Duxworth said after a pause. "He is sure to have every care—and you—what is it now, Duxworth?"

Lord Duxworth was emerging from the house, looking very red and uncomfortable.

"I have just heard from Laurie—his place is near Letchingham's, if you remember. He says Letchingham is in a bad way—a very bad way; he is completely paralysed."

"Oh, I must go to him at once!" Cynthia cried, clasping her hands. "He—oh, I think perhaps I have been wrong before! I do not seem to be able to see clearly; but at any rate I am his wife, and I must go to him!"

"Is Lady Letchingham at home?"

The pompous butler hesitated.

"If you will walk in, sir, I will inquire. What name, sir?"

"Sir Donald Farquhar."

In spite of his grandeur the butler looked impressed. The name of Sir Donald Farquhar was well known; his fame as an explorer of unusual daring had reached even the servants' hall at Letchingham Castle, and as a mark of respect to so distinguished a man, Jones himself preceded Sir Donald to the drawing-room.

Farquhar, as he followed, felt vaguely chilled; the mistress of this stately house must be strangely altered from the simple girl he had met on the moor. The imposing-looking butler, the magnificent room in which he was presently left, while Jones went to seek her ladyship, seemed to oppress him. He drew a long breath and straightened his shoulders as though throwing off a physical load as he recalled the scent of the pine-wood; there now, hot though it was here, the air would be stirring pleasantly amid the leaves, and under the great branches it would be cool.

A portrait of Cynthia was hanging on the opposite wall; he went across and gazed at it long and earnestly. It was by one of the most noted artists of the day, and the painter had contrived to catch some of Cynthia's elusive wild-rose charm; but there was a look of haunt-ing melancholy in the great brown eyes, a touch of pathos in the curve of the pretty soft lips that Farquhar had never seen in the Cyn-thia of Greylands. He sighed restlessly. Naturally she was altered, he told himself; he had been a fool to expect anything else. He knew little of her life during the four years that had elapsed since their last meeting; the papers, in recording Lord Letchingham's death nearly two years ago, had spoken of Lady Letchingham's constant care and devotion during the long illness that had preceded it, and from Lady Duxworth Farquhar had learned that husband and wife had been fully reconciled before the end, and that Letchingham had come to lean upon Cynthia for everything. Of her inner life, of her thoughts and feelings, Lady Duxworth could tell him nothing.

Farquhar himself was indefinably altered. He was darker, his tall form sparer than of old, the close-cropped brown hair was sprinkled with white, the bronzed rugged face was lined and worn, but the steadfast grey eyes, the firm kindly mouth, told alike of sorrow nobly borne, of trouble bravely lived down.

As he stood there, looking at the portrait, a slight sound close at hand made him turn quickly. Cynthia stood within the open window, one hand parting the curtains above her, the other hold-ing a great bunch of roses. She paused, startled, not able, coming straight from the sunlight outside, to recognize the man who con-fronted her in the scented dimness of the shaded room.

Farquhar went forward.

"Cynthia!"

At the sound of his voice a sudden gladness flashed into the brown eyes, the warm red lips smiled a welcome. Cynthia held out her hands; the roses spread themselves in a sweet shower on the skirt of her white gown, on the ground at her feet.

"Donald! You have come!"

The man bent low over the outstretched hands.

"Yes!" he assented. "Cynthia, I have been very patient, but now I have come for my reward. Will you give it to me?"

The girl's eyes drooped; the long upcurled lashes made dark shadows on her hot cheeks.

"I—perhaps—I do not know," she said vaguely. "I have hardly realized that it is really you yet!" striving uneasily to draw her hands away.

The man held them closely prisoned in his firm, warm clasp; the glad hope that sprang to light at his first sight of her sweet blushing confusion grew and strengthened. He stooped his dark head nearer hers.

"Have you no better welcome for me, Cynthia?"

She stirred restlessly and tried in vain to raise her eyes.

"I—I am glad to see you!"

The triumph in the man's eyes brought the hot blood to her cheeks; he drew her inside the room.

"I want more than that, Cynthia; I want to hear you say, 'I forgive you all those wild words at Greylands, Donald, and I love you, just a little!'"

Cynthia's lips looked mutinous. Farquhar watched her in silence for a few minutes; then he released her hands.

"I have come a long way to hear you say those words," he said slowly. "If you cannot, Heaven knows it is not for me to blame you. I was a fool to expect—to trust—"

Cynthia caught a fold of the curtain and plaited it carefully.

"No, no! It was not that!" she began incoherently. "I do forgive you, Donald—I mean there is nothing to forgive—it—it is the rest I can't say!"

When Farquhar spoke again his voice was hoarse and altered.

"I see!" he said heavily. "I have been a fool, but I understand now. Forgive me for troubling you."

Cynthia did not raise her eyes; she went on plaiting her curtain diligently, and a tiny smile crept round the corners of her mouth, "You asked me to say 'I love you a little, Donald.' I couldn't because—oh, don't you understand?"

"No! Tell me, Cynthia!" An almost incredulous joy transformed Farquhar's face. "What is it, sweetheart?"

"Because—oh, you know—because I love you a great deal!" Cynthia whispered tremulously. With a glad sound Farquhar drew her to his breast, and as her head rested on his shoulder his lips sought hers passionately, strayed with longing over her throat and eyes and hair.

For a time Cynthia rested, silent, quiescent; then she released herself with a certain gentle dignity.

"Donald!"

"My sweetheart!" Farquhar, keeping one arm round her waist, looked down at her with fond, possessive eyes.

"I just wanted to tell you," Cynthia faltered. "I had really forgotten until this moment—but I must tell you that I have only what Aunt Hannah left me. All this"—with a comprehensive gesture that included the great house, the grounds sloping down to the lake—"all this goes from me if I—"

"If you marry me," Farquhar finished calmly as he drew her head back to its resting-place and let her hide her crimson cheeks against his coat. "I know it does, darling, and I am thankful that it does. You will be all mine, then, Cynthia. These weary years of separation will seem like a terrible dream, and you will be my own, my sweetheart—my wife!"

THE END

www.ingramcontent.com/pod-product-compliance
Lightning Source LLC
Chambersburg PA
CBHW070906030525
26133CB00024B/419